MR. MONK IN
OUTER SPACE

MR. MONK IN OUTER SPACE

LEE GOLDBERG
BASED ON THE USA NETWORK
TELEVISION SERIES CREATED BY
ANDY BRECKMAN

THORNDIKE
CHIVERS

This Large Print edition is published by Thorndike Press, Waterville, Maine, USA and by BBC Audiobooks Ltd, Bath, England.

Thorndike Press, a part of Gale, Cengage Learning.

The text of this Large Print edition is unabridged.

Other aspects of the book may vary from the original edition.

Set in 16 pt. Plantin.

Printed on permanent paper.

LIBRARY OF CONGRESS CATALOGING-IN-PUBLICATION DATA

Goldberg, Lee, 1962–
    Mr. Monk in outer space / by Lee Goldberg ; based on the USA Network television series created by Andy Breckman.
    p. cm. — (Thorndike Press large print laugh lines)
    ISBN-13: 978-1-4104-0584-5 (hardcover : alk. paper)
    ISBN-10: 1-4104-0584-2 (hardcover : alk. paper)
    1. Monk, Adrian (Fictitious character) — Fiction. 2. Private investigators — Fiction. 3. Eccentrics and eccentricities — Fiction. 4. Psychics — Fiction. 5. Large type books. I. Breckman, Andy. II. Monk (Television program) III. Title. IV. Title: Mister Monk in outer space.
    PS3557.O3577M77 2008
    813'.54—dc22   2007049227

BRITISH LIBRARY CATALOGUING-IN-PUBLICATION DATA AVAILABLE

Published in 2008 in the U.S. by arrangement with NAL Signet, a member of Penguin Group (USA) Inc.

Published in 2008 in the U.K. by arrangement with NAL Signet, a division of Penguin Group (USA) Inc.

U.K. Hardcover: 978 1 405 64494 5 (Chivers Large Print)
U.K. Softcover: 978 1 405 64495 2 (Camden Large Print)

Printed in the United States of America
1 2 3 4 5 6 7 12 11 10 09 08

To Valerie and Madison,
the brightest stars in the galaxy

ACKNOWLEDGMENTS

This book was written in Los Angeles, New York, London, Hay-on-Wye, Berlin, Cologne, Munich, Lohr, and the skies in between. At times I felt like I was the one in outer space. I would like to thank my friend Andy Breckman for sharing Adrian Monk with me and Kristen Weber, Kerry Donovan, and Gina Maccoby for their unwavering enthusiasm, understanding, and support.

I look forward to hearing from you at www .leegoldberg.com.

CHAPTER ONE:
MR. MONK
AND THE GNARLED HANDS OF FATE

I almost killed someone the other day. It was a guy I'd been dating casually for a few weeks. During that time, we never went further than a passionate lip-lock, thank God, and that wasn't so great anyway. It was like sticking my tongue into a bottle of Listerine. (Note to men: Too much breath freshener is almost as bad as none at all.)

His name was Scooter, which should have been my first hint that this relationship wasn't going to work out. I thought the nickname was cute at first, that it was a reflection of his boyish charm. I didn't realize it was a reflection of his short attention span on matters that didn't center on him.

But that wasn't why I wanted to wring Scooter's neck. It had to do with the demise of our relationship. He dumped me because, and I quote, "You're too needy."

Me? Needy? It was ridiculous.

I always considered myself a strong, fiercely independent woman. I spent ninety percent of my time taking care of others. By "others" I mean my daughter, Julie, and my employer, Adrian Monk, the famous detective.

Julie, like any twelve-year-old, is a real handful, but she's nothing compared to Monk, who has such a strong obsessive-compulsive disorder that it generates a whole other universe parallel to our own.

For instance, Monk once found a cobweb in his apartment and ordered me to immediately evacuate everyone from the building and establish a quarantine until an emergency-response team from the Centers for Disease Control could arrive.

I'm not kidding. It's a true story.

That was a typical day for me, except that there were no murders involved. I'm not talking about my own homicidal urges, but *real* murders. Monk is a special consultant to the San Francisco Police Department and I help him with that, too, which is definitely above and beyond typical assistant work.

So how can Scooter call *me* needy?

I'm not needy. I'm the one needy people rely on for their needs.

I'm the rock.

But I have to tell you, being everybody's rock is hard work. And it's not like I don't have fears and unfulfilled dreams and problems of my own.

Ever since my husband, Mitch, was shot down over Kosovo, there has been no one to take care of me. I don't have a Natalie of my own. I'm not allowed to fall apart — there's nobody there to help me put myself back together again.

But I do stumble sometimes anyway and usually I hate myself for it.

Just a couple of days ago, in fact, I was hit out of nowhere by this awful crying jag. It happened in Monk's apartment, right in front of him. I was reading an article in the *San Francisco Chronicle* about the restoration of a Craftsman-style house in Mill Valley, the kind Mitch and I had dreamt of having, and I just lost it.

God, it was embarrassing.

Monk started spraying Lysol all around me. I wasn't sure if he was trying to help me or protect himself from whatever I was afflicted with.

I almost told him that Lysol couldn't shield him from what I suffered from. But I realized the truth was that Monk already knew that better than anybody. His wife, Trudy, was killed in a murder he'd been unable to solve. I think that's why he tries so hard to impose absolute order on the world. He does it to compensate for the order he can't impose on his own pain, loss, and longing.

Well, that's my guess anyway.

I didn't want Monk or my daughter to ever see me lose control of myself, to give in to my sadnesses and fears, because I had to be strong for them. I had to be their support, and if they couldn't count on me, I was afraid of what might happen to them.

So what could I do? Where could I go?

If I couldn't unload on somebody once in a while, especially after a glass or two of wine, then I was going to crack and —

Oh my God.

That's when it dawned on me, right there in my car on the way to Monk's place: All those dates with Scooter, what did I talk about?

Myself.

I talked about all of my problems, all of my needs, all of the difficulties in my life.

I unloaded.

I wasn't fun. I wasn't vivacious. I wasn't sexy.

I was needy.

Fine. I was needy. Shoot me and toss my

corpse into a ravine.

If Scooter had been there in the car with me that morning, I would have told him this: Sure, maybe sometimes I whined a little too much, but part of romance is finding someone who needs you as much as you need them.

I would have said that maybe if he'd shown me a little understanding and a little neediness of his own we might have discovered something truly magical and wonderful. We might have found that we needed each other. And needing someone — someone who also needs you — well, that can be pretty great.

Your loss, Scooter.

Yeah, that's what I should have said when he told me I was too needy.

But what I actually said was nothing at all. Clever, huh? I just turned my back on him, walked into my house, and slammed the door in his face.

Why is it you always think of the perfect thing to say long after the right moment to say it has passed?

Unfortunately for me, belatedly coming up with the perfect retort to Scooter didn't resolve the issue in my mind. I couldn't stop thinking about my so-called neediness. I began to look at my whole life from a different perspective and I didn't like what I saw.

The only people I met, outside of my daughter's teachers and her friends' parents, were cops, grieving relatives of victims, murder suspects, and killers. Not the best dating pool, which may be why I glommed on to Scooter, an insurance salesman I met at Starbucks on my way to Monk's house one morning.

It was worse for Monk. He basically met no one. I was his social life, which, by extension, made him largely mine, whether I liked it or not.

What I needed was more friends, more things happening in my life that didn't involve Adrian Monk or Julie.

As I parked my car outside of Monk's apartment building on Pine Street, I was determined to shake things up. I had been living in my own narrow world too long. I had to make a change.

And this was the perfect time to do it.

My daughter was away for a week on a school field trip to a camp near Sacramento, which meant I had a week to myself for the first time in years. So I planned to make the most of the free time. I figured if I was really lucky, nobody would get killed for a few days and I could even get a couple of days off.

I let myself into Monk's apartment. It was dark. All the shades were drawn and not a single light was on. I could hear whimpering.

"Mr. Monk?" I asked with trepidation.

The whimpering kicked up an octave.

I crept into the living room and found Monk sitting on the floor, resting his back against the wall and hugging his knees to his chest.

He looked devastated. I began to get scared.

"What's wrong?" I asked.

"Nothing," he said, his voice barely above a whisper.

I sat down beside him on the floor. The wall was cold against my back. "Then why are you sitting in the dark whimpering?"

He shrugged. "It's what I do when all my dreams are crushed and any hope I have for true happiness is strangled to death by the gnarled hands of fate."

"This happens to you so often that you have a standard reaction?"

"I have a standard reaction for everything," Monk said. "I made an indexed, color-coded list of them. Haven't you seen it?"

"I don't believe that particular list was part of my orientation packet."

15

"I wonder what other critical lists you've missed," Monk said. "I'll have to make a list."

"You're going to make a list of the lists," I said.

"See? My whole life is crumbling around me. I have nothing."

"I'm here, Mr. Monk. You have me." I put my hand on his knee and gave him a re-assuring squeeze. "What happened?"

"It's obvious."

"Not to me," I said.

"You're joking," he said.

"No, I'm not. I really have no idea what you're talking about."

Monk tipped his head towards the couch. "It's right in front of you."

I looked.

I saw the couch, centered in the middle of the wall.

I saw the four identically framed and sized photos of his wife, Trudy, on the wall, which I knew he carefully straightened and aligned each morning with a level and a ruler.

And I saw the coffee table, which was crooked in relation to the couch. It was the only item in the entire apartment that wasn't perfectly centered. But that wasn't the problem. It was intentional. Monk had explained to me that Trudy used to angle

16

the table that way so she could put her feet up on it and he could lay his head in her lap. He left the table crooked for her. Sometimes when I came to work in the morning, I'd find a pillow where Trudy once sat, the impression of Monk's head on it.

"I still don't see the problem," I said.

"Are you blind?" he said.

"It might help if I turned the lights on," I said, beginning to get irritated. "Or better yet, you could just tell me."

"The stain," he said.

I stared at him. "You're going through all this anguish over a stain?"

"It's a coffee stain and I can't clean it off the carpet."

I got up and opened the shades to let in some sunlight.

He winced. "Don't. The whole world will know my shame."

I looked down at the carpet, expecting to see some huge mess. But the carpet was spotless.

"Where's the stain?" I asked.

"Between the couch and the table," he said. "You can't miss it."

I went to the couch, sat down on the edge, and looked at the floor.

"I still don't see it," I said.

"Use the magnifying glass on the table."

"If I have to use a magnifying glass to see it, does it really matter?"

"What you can't see could kill you," he said.

"A coffee stain can't."

"No," he said, groaning. "It will merely destroy your will to live."

"So just slide the coffee table over a millimeter to cover it," I said. "I hide all kinds of stains under rugs and furniture."

"I'll still know the stain is there. I'll feel it. I'll hear it pulsating."

"It's a stain," I said. "It's not alive. It doesn't have a pulse."

"The only thing I can do is replace the entire carpet," Monk said. "Again."

"You've done this before?" I asked.

A hand grenade exploded in my house a couple years ago and I still didn't replace the carpet. I just bought a bigger rug and placed it over the scorch marks.

"Once," he said. There was a moment of silence. "Maybe twice."

"Twice?" I said.

"Three times," he said. "You need to give the carpet company a call. Their number is on the speed dial. They know the color and style. They keep a roll of the carpet on hand for me in case of major emergencies."

"So that's why you're so sad," I said.

"Because this is the third time you've spent thousands of dollars to recarpet your living room over a stain that's invisible to the naked eye."

"The fourth time," he said.

"Four times?" I said.

"Definitely no more than five."

I stared at him. "How is it that you can never afford to give me a raise but you can find the money to recarpet your house *five times?*"

He opened his mouth to speak, but I interrupted him, pointing my finger at his face.

"If you say 'six, no more than seven,' there are going to be bloodstains on the carpet and they won't be mine."

He closed his mouth.

I can tolerate most of his quirks, except the ones that cost me money. I make little enough as it is without him squandering my future raises on pointless expenditures. But I knew this carpet thing was a fight that I couldn't win.

"Call the carpet company yourself, Mr. Monk," I said. "I can't bear to do it."

He got up, went into the kitchen, and made the call. While he did, I took his seat on the floor. I felt as depressed as he was, but for entirely different reasons. I was looking at a future of poverty and despair because he couldn't live with a stain that a normal human being couldn't see even with an electron microscope.

Monk came back into the living room. "They can start tomorrow."

"Good," I said.

"The bad news is that I have to move out for two days while they do it."

"Where are you going to stay?" I asked.

Monk looked at me.

I looked back at him.

He tried to gaze at me imploringly, which made him appear as if he was suppressing a burp or trying to swallow a golf ball.

"Can't you go somewhere else?" I said.

I'd had Monk as a houseguest once before and it was not an experience I was eager to repeat, certainly not during one of the rare weeks when I had the house to myself. Monk would put a kibosh on any romance I might have. Even simple pleasures like eating ice cream out of the carton would be impossible with him around.

"It's just two nights," he said. "Maybe three."

"Three?"

"Four at most," Monk said.

I was about to give him all the reasons why this was a terrible idea, and why it wasn't going to happen, when my cell phone rang. It was Lieutenant Randy Disher.

"This is Lieutenant Randy Disher, SFPD," he said.

He always said that, even though he knew I would instantly recognize his voice even if my caller ID didn't inform me who was calling. He just liked hearing himself say it. I think he even identified himself that way when he called his mother. He probably flashed his badge when they met face-to-face.

There was only one reason Randy Disher ever called me.

"Where's the corpse?" I asked with a weary sigh.

He told me.

CHAPTER TWO:
Mr. Monk and the Glimpse of Hell

Unless you live in a cave, or are Adrian Monk, you've not only seen a Burgerville restaurant, you've probably eaten in them a couple of hundred times. It's as inevitable as life, death, and high cholesterol.

As unhealthy and unimaginative as Burgerville food is, you can't deny that the fanciful, hamburger-shaped restaurants have become an inextricable part of American popular culture.

I'd always imagined that their national headquarters would be the world's biggest hamburger, perhaps surrounded by a complex of buildings shaped like fries, a shake, and a soft drink. So I was deeply disappointed to discover that Burgerville's corporate offices were housed in an unremarkable five-story building hidden in the shadows of the more distinctive skyscrapers that surrounded it in the financial district.

I came through the revolving door and

found Captain Leland Stottlemeyer in the wood-paneled lobby, leaning against the donut-shaped reception desk and talking to the fat uniformed guard sitting in the center. The two of them were smiling and appeared relaxed as they talked, so I brilliantly deduced that this wasn't the first time they'd met.

It was nice to see Stottlemeyer smile for a change. A pained expression seemed to be a required part of his professional demeanor, though in the months leading up to and following his divorce, he'd carried the same look around off duty as well. Only in the last couple of weeks had he begun to loosen up a little as the stress in his personal life eased and he settled into being single.

Stottlemeyer was in his late forties and had a bushy mustache that got bushier as his hairline receded. If his hairline continued its retreat, in a few years his mustache would be so thick that he'd have to breathe exclusively through his mouth.

The captain turned to me and jerked a thumb towards the guard, who looked to be about his age and easily twice his weight. I figured the guard was probably making the most of his employee discount at Burgerville restaurants.

"Natalie, I'd like you to meet Archie

23

Applebaum," Stottlemeyer said. "He's a security guard here, but back in the day he used to walk a beat in the Tenderloin."

"Leland and I went through the academy together," Archie said, offering me his pudgy hand. I shook it. "He rose up the ranks and me, well, I got sidelined by a bad back."

"Once a cop, always a cop," Stottlemeyer said. "You've demonstrated that by the way you secured the crime scene before we got here."

"I just used common sense," Archie said.

"Your average rent-a-cop would have hopelessly messed things up," Stottlemeyer said. "But you're the real deal."

"Except nowadays I wear a plastic badge, like something you'd buy for your kid. I'm surprised they don't give me a cap gun, too."

"Your badge may not be silver, but I bet your pay and your pension plan are a lot better than mine."

"I'd trade it all to be back on the beat," Archie said.

"I hear you." Stottlemeyer turned to me. "Where's Monk?"

"I had to parallel park," I said by way of explanation.

He groaned knowingly. The captain was the only person, with the exception of

Monk's previous assistant, Sharona Fleming, who truly understood my daily misery.

Archie shifted his gaze between Stottlemeyer and me, trying to read the situation.

"What am I missing?" the guard asked us.

"You remember a cop named Adrian Monk?" Stottlemeyer asked.

"Wasn't he the guy who ticketed a hundred people outside a movie theater for not lining up according to their height?"

"That's him," Stottlemeyer said. "He's the best detective I've ever known. But right now, he's outside measuring the space between Natalie's car and the ones around hers."

"What for?" Archie asked.

"He wants to make sure my car is perfectly centered," I said. "Then he's going to check the other cars on both sides of the street."

"If they aren't all equally spaced, he's going to demand that we find the drivers and have them align their cars properly," Stottlemeyer said. "Or if we can't find the drivers, he'll want me to have the cars towed."

"You're kidding," Archie said.

"God, I wish I was," Stottlemeyer said.

"So what are you going to do?" Archie asked.

"Shoot him or shoot myself," Stottlemeyer said. "I haven't decided yet."

Stottlemeyer went outside and I followed him.

We found Monk crouched between my Jeep Cherokee and the Volkswagen parked in front of it. He rose up when he saw us and examined his tape measure.

"You're going to have to move your car forward half an inch, Natalie," he said. "But you did a much better job than the scofflaws parked on this street. There isn't a single car that isn't a good four inches out of alignment."

"There isn't a law anywhere in the penal code requiring people to center their cars when they parallel park," Stottlemeyer said.

"It's a natural law," Monk said. "Like gravity."

"I'm afraid that's outside my jurisdiction," Stottlemeyer said.

"You are a law enforcement officer, are you not?" Monk asked.

"Yes," Stottlemeyer said.

"Then you have a sworn duty to uphold the law," Monk said. "You can't just pick and choose the ones you want to enforce. That's the first step towards anarchy."

"I thought mixed nuts were the first step," I said.

"There are many first steps," Monk said.

Stottlemeyer sighed, defeated.

"You're right. I'll have an officer get right on it." Stottlemeyer waved a uniformed cop over to us. "In the meantime, you're needed on the fifth floor."

"I'd prefer the fourth floor." Monk rolled his shoulders. "Or the sixth."

"The body is on the fifth floor," Stottlemeyer said.

"You could move the body," Monk said.

"No, I couldn't," Stottlemeyer said as the officer approached. "That would disturb the crime scene."

"But the crime scene will disturb me," Monk said.

"You wouldn't be human if it didn't." Stottlemeyer turned to the officer and gestured towards the cars on the street. "Officer, these vehicles are violating the natural laws of the universe. Act accordingly."

The officer looked puzzled.

Stottlemeyer turned his back to the poor man and led Monk and me to the building.

The captain and I went through the revolving door, but when we got into the lobby, we both stopped. We realized at the same moment that Monk hadn't followed us. We turned and saw him standing outside, staring at the revolving door, looking perplexed.

"It's a revolving door, Monk," Stottle-meyer said. "You just push it and it spins."

"I can't," Monk said.

There was a standard glass door beside the revolving one. I pointed at it.

"You can go through the other door, Mr. Monk."

"It's locked," Archie said from his seat at the reception desk. "You need to swipe a key card through the reader beside the handle to open it."

"So do it," I said.

"He can't," Stottlemeyer said. "That's how the killer got in. We need to take both of the key card readers in to the lab for forensic examination. We can't risk losing evidence by swiping another card through them."

"Is there any other way in?" I asked.

"There's a loading bay in the back," Archie said. "If you don't mind the trash in the alley."

I wouldn't, but Monk would. I looked at Monk.

"Just run through, Mr. Monk," I said. "It will be over before you know it."

"I'll know it," Monk said.

I studied the door. Stottlemeyer joined me.

"What's his problem with this?" he asked me.

I shrugged. "You got me, Captain. I see a circle divided into quarters. Everything is even. He should be okay with it. It must be the coffee stain."

"I don't see a coffee stain," he said.

"It's at his apartment," I said. "But you can't see the stain there, either."

A vein was beginning to throb on Stottlemeyer's forehead. I call it the Monk vein, because it shows up on people's foreheads when they are enduring his unique form of escalating mental duress.

Stottlemeyer shouted at Monk: "What's your damn problem with the revolving door?"

"If I step in there," Monk said, "it will be three-quarters empty."

"I'll go in with you," I said.

"That won't do any good," Monk said. "Two quarters will be unoccupied. That's just so wrong."

"Captain Stottlemeyer and the police officer can step in as the door turns and then all four quarters will be filled."

Monk shook his head. "But when I come out, you three will be in a revolving door with one unoccupied quarter. I couldn't leave you like that."

"That won't bother us," Stottlemeyer said.

"It will bother me," Monk said.

"You could live with it," Stottlemeyer said.

"I'm pretty sure that I couldn't," Monk said. "It would haunt me until my dying day."

"This will be that day if you don't come through that damn door," Stottlemeyer said.

"You're not helping, Captain," I told him and then turned back to Monk. "What if the security guard steps in at the same moment you are stepping out?"

Monk mulled that over for a moment. "That could work. But the timing is going to be crucial."

Stottlemeyer glanced at Archie. "Do you mind?"

The guard got up from his station and waddled over. "Is it always this hard to get him into a building?"

Stottlemeyer sighed. "Every day is a new challenge, Archie."

Monk took out a stopwatch, waved the officer over, and then explained how the timing would work. I won't bore you with the mathematics involved, mainly because I've forgotten them. But it involved synchronizing our watches and moving at a uniform rate of speed.

On Monk's signal, I entered the revolving

door at the same instant that he did. We turned the revolving door and, at the appropriate moment, Stottlemeyer entered one quarter and the officer entered another. Monk exited his quarter as Archie stepped into it, and for an instant it looked like they might both get stuck in there together. But Monk managed to squeeze out at the last possible second, leaving all four quarters occupied.

He spilled out into the lobby and leaned against the security desk for support, breathing hard, his back to the revolving door as Stottlemeyer, Archie, and I came in after him. The officer went back outside to enforce the laws of nature.

Monk caught his breath and turned to us.

"If there's an entrance to hell," he said, "I guarantee it has a revolving door."

I'm pretty sure he's right about that.

CHAPTER THREE:
MR. MONK
AND THE BODY

We took the stairs to the fifth floor and emerged into the corridor, which was crowded with crime scene photographers and forensic technicians who were going in and out of one of the offices.

"We're on the fifth floor," Monk said.

"Yes, Monk, I know that," Stottlemeyer said.

"It feels awkward," Monk said and glanced at me. "Don't you feel awkward?"

"No more than usual," I said.

I'd been to a lot of crime scenes since I'd met Monk, but I still felt like I didn't belong there. I wasn't a cop, for one thing. I had no purpose except to assist Monk, which usually meant doing what I could to limit distractions and keep him focused on the case at hand.

"I think we'd both feel more comfortable on the fourth floor," Monk said. "Or the sixth. I'm sure the victim would, too."

Stottlemeyer grabbed Monk by the arm and led us into the outer office across from the stairwell.

"The victim is Brandon Lorber and he was CEO of Burgerville," the captain said. "He was working late last night. The killer came in the front door using a key card while the security guard was doing his rounds. Archie didn't know there'd been an intruder or that anything had happened until he found the body."

The walls were covered with framed photos of a man I presumed to be Brandon Lorber standing in front of various Burgerville restaurants in dozens of cities, though I wouldn't have known the shots were taken in different places if the locations hadn't been engraved on each picture frame.

"The guard didn't hear the gunshots?" Monk asked.

Stottlemeyer shook his head. "The killer must have used a silencer."

From the pictures, I could see that Lorber was one of those men whose gray hair made him look distinguished, intelligent, and rich rather than old. He was in his fifties and wore the years well, at least until he got killed.

"What about the video surveillance cameras?" Monk asked. "You must have the killer on tape."

"We do," Stottlemeyer said. "But he was wearing an overcoat and a cap pulled down low over the face. He also turned his body in such a way that we couldn't get a clear view. He knew where every single camera was from the lobby to the fifth floor."

"We're dealing with a professional killer who was efficient and well prepared," Monk said.

"A dispassionate professional who knows how to cover his tracks isn't going to leave the kind of traces that your garden-variety killer will," Stottlemeyer said. "He's probably gotten away with murder many times before. I don't want him to get away with this one. That's why I called you, Monk."

We went past the secretary's desk into Lorber's inner office, which reeked of cigar smoke. On the plus side, the odor was so strong it nearly masked the smell that came from Lorber's dead body in the chair behind the large oak desk.

Monk started to cough, which attracted the attention of Randy Disher, who was standing beside the desk, jotting down notes.

"What took you so long?" Disher asked.

"Look who I am with and use your imagination," Stottlemeyer said. "The possibilities are endless."

Disher scrunched up his face as he thought about it. "Was it the broken parking meter?"

"There's a broken parking meter?" Monk turned to go, but Stottlemeyer grabbed him by the arm and pushed him back into the room.

"Randy was joking," Stottlemeyer said, looking hard at Disher. "Weren't you?"

"I was joking," Disher said.

Monk faked a laugh. It sounded like his cough. "Right. Good one."

Since Monk had no sense of humor and was self-conscious about it, he wasn't going to question Disher's lie. Instead, he began surveying the crime scene, if only to hide his embarrassment at not getting the joke.

"Any new developments while I was gone?" Stottlemeyer asked Disher.

"I've got it all figured out except whodunit," Disher said.

"You do?" Stottlemeyer asked skeptically.

I glanced at Monk, who'd already begun wandering around the room, doing his Zen thing, holding his hands out in front of him like a director framing a shot.

"The body tells the story," Disher said. "You'll notice he's been shot twice in the chest and once in the head."

"Yeah," Stottlemeyer said. "I noticed."

"But did you see that he's also got a through-and-through gunshot wound to his right hand?" Disher asked.

I peered over the table and saw Lorber's right arm dangling over the edge of the chair, a bullet hole through the middle of his palm.

"Yep, I saw that, too," Stottlemeyer said.

Looking at a wound like that used to make me sick. I still felt uncomfortable, but I was slowly becoming more analytical and less emotional in my reactions to the bodies of people who'd met a violent end. I guess it was an inevitable psychological adjustment, considering how many corpses I ended up seeing in a typical month.

I glanced at Monk, who was studying a cigar box that had fallen off the table near Lorber's feet, spilling its contents on the floor.

There was a big bowl of individually wrapped coffee candies on the desk. Between the cigars and the candy, it seemed to me that Lorber was a guy with an oral fixation. I wondered if he'd been breast-fed as a child.

"It's the deadly triangle," Disher said.

"Excuse me?" Stottlemeyer said.

"The two shots to the chest and the coup

de grâce to the head," Disher said. "It's the deadly triangle a hit man uses to assure that he's made his kill."

"So why did he shoot Lorber in the hand?" I asked.

"That wasn't his target," Disher said. "Lorber looked up, saw the killer standing in front of him with a gun, and held up his hands in a halting motion, as if to say 'stop, please don't kill me.' The killer shot *through* his hand to his heart."

Disher held up his hands in front of him to demonstrate. It made sense to me. Even Stottlemeyer was nodding with approval.

"Good thinking, Randy." Stottlemeyer looked over at Monk, who was squinting at the top desk drawer, which was open slightly. "What's your take?"

"There's one big problem with your theory," Monk said to Disher. "Brandon Lorber wasn't murdered."

"There are bullet holes in his chest and head," Stottlemeyer said.

"The deadly triangle," Disher said again.

"Yes," Monk said. "I can see that."

"Then how can you say that it isn't a murder?" Stottlemeyer asked.

"Because it's not," Monk said. "He died of natural causes."

"I'm not a detective, Mr. Monk," I said,

"but I don't think there's anything natural about getting shot three times."

"That's not what killed him," Monk said.

"Nobody could survive getting shot between the eyes and right in the heart," Stottlemeyer said. "Those are definitely fatal wounds."

"If he was alive when he was shot," Monk said. "But Lorber was already dead. He died of a heart attack."

We all stared at Monk. We do this a lot.

"How do you know that?" Stottlemeyer said.

"His shirt is wrinkled," Monk said.

"So is mine," Stottlemeyer said. "And I'm not having a heart attack."

"I'm feeling some palpitations," Monk said, looking at the wrinkled shirt.

"If you can convince me you're right about this," Stottlemeyer said, "I'll get my shirt ironed."

Monk took a pen from his pocket and used it to point at Lorber's chest.

"Lorber was right-handed," he said. "When he felt the stabbing pain, he instinctively grabbed his chest with his right hand, wrinkling his shirt."

Stottlemeyer, Disher, and I all leaned over the desk to look at Lorber's shirt. It was wrinkled at the chest, which I didn't notice before. I was paying attention to the bullet wounds. I think Stottlemeyer and Disher were, too.

"He flailed around in desperation," Monk explained. "He knocked his box of cigars off the table with his left hand as he tried to reach the top desk drawer, where he kept his nitroglycerin tablets, but he didn't make it."

Disher opened the drawer with his gloved hand and, sure enough, there was a prescription bottle full of tablets inside.

"It was almost worth the trouble of getting you in the building for this," Stottlemeyer said to Monk. "So you figure that the shock of seeing a guy with a silenced gun aimed at him gave Lorber a heart attack."

"It would give me one," I said.

Monk shook his head. "He had the heart attack before that."

"How can you be sure?" Disher asked.

"There isn't enough blood here," Monk said. "If his heart was still pumping when he was shot, there would be a lot more of it. I'm certain the medical examiner will confirm my observation."

"Of course you are," Stottlemeyer said.

"What about the bullet wound in the hand?" Disher said. "Doesn't that prove he was pleading for his life with the killer?"

"If you look more closely," Monk said, "you'll see that the exit wound is in the palm, not the back of the hand, which indicates he was still clutching his chest when he was shot. If he'd been holding his hand up, the entrance wound would be in his palm."

Stottlemeyer took a piece of coffee candy from the bowl, unwrapped it, and popped it in his mouth while he considered what Monk told him. I cringed.

"So this isn't a murder," Stottlemeyer said.

"No, it isn't," Monk said.

"It certainly looks like a murder to me," Disher said. He ate a piece of candy and shoved a couple more in his pocket for later. I cringed again.

"But it's not," Monk said.

I stared at Stottlemeyer and Disher. "How could you put those candies in your mouth?"

Stottlemeyer shrugged. "Well, I guess it's because we like coffee candy, Natalie."

"But a man died in here." I tipped my head towards the corpse behind the desk for emphasis. "He's sitting right there."

"Yes, I can see that," Stottlemeyer said. "So what?"

I couldn't believe they couldn't see the

problem.

"There's deadness all over it," I said.

"Deadness," Stottlemeyer said. "I can't say that worries me. How about you, Randy?"

"Nope," he said.

"Okay, fine," I said. "How do you know the candy isn't poisoned? Maybe that's what killed Lorber."

"If he'd eaten a candy before his death, there would be a wrapper somewhere," Monk said. "There isn't one."

I looked at him. "I thought you, of all people, would agree with me on this."

"Deadness?" Monk said. "C'mon, Natalie. That's just silly."

As opposed to, say, running your doorknobs through the dishwasher once a week. But I didn't bring that up. I had better ammunition.

"Then how come you aren't having some candy?"

"It causes tooth decay," Monk said, examining a piece of candy and putting it back as if it had scalded his fingers. "Decay and I are mortal enemies."

"I'm surprised, Monk. Everything decays. It's a natural law," Stottlemeyer said. "Like gravity."

Stottlemeyer grinned, pleased with himself. Monk gave him a cold look.

"Why would someone shoot a man who was already dead?" Disher asked.

"I don't know and I don't care," Stottlemeyer said. "If the medical examiner can establish that Lorber was already dead when he was shot, then there's no crime here."

"Yes, there is," Monk said. "Someone has desecrated a corpse."

"What I meant, Monk, is that it's not a homicide and therefore it's not a crime that I'm responsible for investigating."

"So who is?" Disher said.

Stottlemeyer shrugged. "I don't know, Randy. The Desecration Squad, I suppose."

"Do we have a Desecration Squad?"

Stottlemeyer looked at Disher for a long moment. "Yes, we do."

"We do?"

"In fact, you're in charge of it," Stottlemeyer said.

"I am?"

"You are now," Stottlemeyer said.

"My own squad," Disher said, beaming. "Do I get a raise?"

"The honor is its own reward, don't you think?"

"Can we call it a special unit instead of a squad?" Disher asked.

"Call it whatever you want. Just get the

medical examiner to rush the autopsy on Lorber so I can clear this case off my desk," Stottlemeyer said, then turned to us. "We're not going to need your services on this one, Monk. You can go home and work on that carpet stain."

"It's a hopeless cause," Monk said with a groan.

"I'm sorry to hear that," Stottlemeyer said.

Not as sorry as I was.

"Now you can go get the wrinkles ironed out of your shirt," Monk said.

"I will," Stottlemeyer said. "The first chance I get."

"This is it," Monk said.

"I can't just drop everything to get my shirt ironed," Stottlemeyer said. "I've got a job to do."

"But this is a personal emergency," Monk said. "And we had an agreement."

"Yes, we did." Stottlemeyer sighed and glanced at Disher. "You'll have to wrap things up here without me, Randy. I've got to go get my shirt pressed."

"You'll thank me later," Monk said.

"Don't count on that," Stottlemeyer said as he walked out of the room.

CHAPTER FOUR:
MR. MONK
GOES HOME

The carpet wouldn't be installed for two more days, but Monk couldn't live in the same apartment as that coffee stain. And yet he had no problem moving into my place, where he knew that countless stains were hidden under furniture and rugs.

It's a contradiction, but don't expect me to explain it. I have a working knowledge of many of the Rules of the Monk Universe, but not all of them. If I tried to learn them all, I'm afraid I would go insane.

The last time Monk stayed at my house in the Noe Valley neighborhood of San Francisco, he called a moving company and had them bring all his furniture, clothes, and even the food in his refrigerator. So I considered myself lucky when I got him out of his apartment with only eight suitcases, a case of Sierra Springs water, and all of his dishware.

On the way to my place, I laid down the

law. I told him he couldn't rearrange my furniture, my artwork, or anything else. I told him he couldn't go through my cupboards, my drawers, or my closets. I told him he couldn't try to change my personal habits, no matter how repulsive, objectionable, or dangerous he might think they were. My home was my space to do as I pleased, regardless of how it made him feel.

But I did cut him a little slack. I gave him permission to do all the housecleaning, dishwashing, and laundry that he wanted.

That made him happy and, to be honest, he'd be doing me a favor. I hadn't done much housecleaning. The fact is, after a day spent with Monk, I'd usually had as much cleaning and disinfecting as I could take, even if I wasn't the one who was doing it. I actually took pleasure in my slovenliness after being with him. It became a form of relaxation and maybe even a little rebellion.

I'm afraid Julie followed my poor example. Her room looked like a hurricane had swept through it. I was afraid of what I might find in there, but I probably wasn't as frightened as Monk was going to be when he saw it.

At least the guest room was the way Monk had left it the last time he stayed with us. I guess I'd known on some level that he would be back someday.

We walked into the living room, each of us carrying two of his matching suitcases. We were halfway down the hall to the guest room when he froze, cocking his head to one side.

"What's that?" he asked.

"What's what?"

"That noise," he said.

I listened. I heard a little rumble.

"Oh, that's just the wheel," I said.

"What wheel?" he asked.

"Hammy's wheel," I said. "She's on that all day."

"Who's Hammy?"

"Julie's hamster," I said, ignoring the handmade DO NO ENTER, NO TRESSPASS-ING, and HAZARDOUS WASTE signs and opening Julie's bedroom door. "I'm taking care of Hammy while Julie's away at camp."

The three-level cage was on a piece of newspaper near Julie's bed. The hamster was running on her wheel, moving so fast she was almost a blur.

So was Monk.

When I turned around, his suitcases were there but he was gone.

Monk's older brother, Ambrose, still lived in the Victorian-style two-story home where they'd grown up, in the quaint little town of

Tewksbury, just over the Golden Gate Bridge in Marin County. In fact, Ambrose never left. He suffered from agoraphobia.

Ambrose was socially awkward, which is to be expected from a guy who had little or no interaction with people. But he was extremely well-read on hundreds of obscure topics and he'd taught himself to speak six languages, including Mandarin, skills he put to use writing technical manuals, encyclopedias, and textbooks.

As far as I know, Ambrose had left the house only twice in thirty years, once when the place was on fire and again when he needed emergency medical care because he thought he'd been fatally poisoned.

Monk had something to do with both of those incidents, which, as it happened, were tied to murder investigations. Those are long stories, so I won't bore you with them now, but in light of those experiences, it was only natural that Ambrose showed some trepidation when he opened his front door and saw the two of us standing there.

He grabbed the doorframe as if he was afraid we might drag him out into the front yard.

Ambrose wore an argyle sweater vest, a long-sleeved flannel shirt buttoned at the cuffs, corduroy slacks, and a pair of Hush

Puppies so shiny they made Dorothy's ruby slippers seem dull by comparison. Like Monk's, his shirt was buttoned at the collar.

"Hello, Adrian," Ambrose said hesitantly. He did just about everything hesitantly. "Hello, Natalie."

"It's good to see you, Ambrose," I said.

"It's an unexpected pleasure to see you, Natalie." Ambrose looked at Monk. "Who died?"

"Nobody," Monk said. "I'm visiting."

"You never visit. You only come if I call, and I didn't call. So if someone didn't die, why are you here?"

"Does a man need a reason to visit his ancestral home?" Monk asked.

Ambrose looked past Monk and smiled at me. "Not when he's accompanied by such a beautiful woman."

I blushed. Ambrose had a little crush on me. I don't think it was due to either my sparkling personality or my ravishing beauty. The truth is, he'd had a thing for Sharona, too. We were the only two women who'd come to see him in years.

But I was flattered anyway. His feelings were genuine, and feelings, especially genuine ones, are hard to find in a man these days. At least for me.

In the year or so since I'd met Ambrose, I'd spent a few evenings with him, playing checkers and eating popcorn. He was a sweet guy. But I was careful not to see him too often because I didn't want him to get the wrong idea about us.

He motioned us inside. We came in and he immediately closed the door behind us and latched the dead bolt.

I was surprised to see that the living room was still stuffed with file cabinets full of mail and thirty-five years' worth of newspapers stacked nearly to the ceiling.

Ambrose had been saving it all for their father, who went out for Chinese food in 1972 and didn't return until a few months ago, when he unexpectedly called Monk for a favor. Their father, who had become a trucker, was in jail on an outstanding warrant for unpaid parking tickets or something minor like that. He needed Monk to get him out of jail or he'd lose his job for not making his delivery on time.

Monk didn't talk to me much about the reunion, but I knew they'd come to some kind of understanding and that their father had stopped to see Ambrose on his way out of town.

"Why do you still have all of this junk?" Monk said, straightening one of the piles of newspapers.

"I'm saving it for Dad," Ambrose said.

"But Dad came back," Monk said. "You can stop saving it now."

"He told me to hang on to it until he has a chance to pick it up."

"He's never going to pick it up," Monk said.

"You were the one who said he'd never come back," Ambrose said. "And you were wrong. He came back."

"Only because he needed something from me," Monk said.

"He needs this from me," Ambrose said. "He'll be back for it all."

"He was blowing you off," Monk said.

"Are you saying he doesn't need me?" Ambrose yelled, startling me. "Do you think you're the only one he needs?"

"He doesn't need either one of us," Monk said. "Not until he does."

"You're not making any sense, Adrian."

"Dad isn't someone you can count on, especially when it comes to considering the feelings of others. Look at how he's inconvenienced you."

"It's no problem for me. I have been doing it for years."

"That's my point," Monk said.

Ambrose ignored him and smiled at me.

"Would you like a glass of water?"

"No thank you," I said.

"How about an Eskimo Pie?" Ambrose asked. "They are quite delicious."

"I wish I could," I said, "but I am watching my weight."

"That must be how you stay so slim and shapely."

I think there may have been a contradiction in there, but I smiled anyway.

He picked up a stack of books from the coffee table. They were tied with a red ribbon. He presented them to me.

"I've been saving these for you," he said.

"You save everything," Monk muttered.

"These are copies of my latest books," Ambrose said.

I glanced at the spines. There was an owner's manual for the Linknet WMA24Z7 Wireless Router, the installation guide for a low-voltage outdoor lighting system, and instructions in Swedish and English for putting together an elaborate bookcase. I'm sure he wrote both versions.

"Thank you," I said. "I look forward to reading them."

"They're inscribed," he said proudly.

I opened the cover of the Linknet manual. He'd written: *To Natalie, May all of your connections, wireless and otherwise, enjoy unin-*

terrupted throughput.

"You're very sweet, Ambrose," I said and kissed him on the cheek. "Nobody has ever inscribed an owner's manual for me before."

"I have it in Spanish, if you're interested," he said. "I wrote that one, too."

Monk cleared his throat. Ambrose looked at him as if he'd forgotten that he was there.

"Why are you here?" Ambrose said.

"I need to stay for a couple of days," Monk said. "It's an emergency."

"What kind of emergency?"

"A coffee stain emergency," Monk said.

Ambrose nodded gravely. "Why didn't you say so to start with?"

"I didn't want to shock you," Monk said.

Ambrose put his arm around Monk, who immediately went rigid. "If you can't come to me for support when you're in trouble, what kind of brother would I be?"

"I made the stain," Monk said.

Ambrose patted him reassuringly on the back. "It's okay, Adrian."

"You don't understand," Monk said. "It's not the first time."

"I know," Ambrose said.

"I'm so ashamed." Monk leaned his forehead against his brother's shoulder.

I slipped away discreetly and went outside to get the luggage.

CHAPTER FIVE:
MR. MONK
AND THE FREE DAY

I left Monk at Ambrose's house and headed out into the big wide world to enjoy my first totally free day in ages.

I drove back into the city and made a detour to Fisherman's Wharf, an area I usually avoid because of the crush of tourists. But there's a Boudin Bakery on the waterfront and they make the best sourdough bread on earth. The lure of a hot loaf of bread to bring home for dinner was too strong for me to ignore.

I spent twenty minutes looking for a parking spot and then stood in line for bread, watching the tourists take pictures of themselves in front of the Fisherman's Wharf sign to prove to everybody back home that they'd actually been there. I wasn't sure why they bothered. I didn't think there was anything worth visiting, much less remembering, on the wharf besides the bakery.

The wharf hadn't been a real shipping or

industrial spot in decades. It had degenerated into a brazen tourist trap, a storefront shopping center with a seaside motif and a carnival midway feel. It was all schlocky souvenir shops, dreary fast-food franchises, and tacky seafood restaurants that put more effort into covering their walls with fishing nets and seafaring knickknacks than making decent food. The wharf had very little left that was authentic or charming, and even less as time went on. That sad state of affairs seemed to be true of just about everything these days, including a lot of people that I knew.

It was a nice, clear day with a crisp, salty breeze blowing off the water, so rather than go back to the car, I wandered up to Victoria Park, which is right below Ghirardelli Square and has a great view of the bay.

The park is also the turn-around point for the cable cars. The tourists line up there in droves waiting for a ride, so there are plenty of street performers, caricature artists, and sidewalk vendors hoping their captive audience would rather spend money on crap than do nothing.

I sat on a bench and looked out at the nineteenth-century schooners permanently docked at the Hyde Street Pier, the sailboats skipping over the whitecaps, and the ferry on its way to Alcatraz. It was nice, and I zoned out for a while.

Before I knew it, I'd absently finished off the entire loaf of bread. So much for watching my weight.

I got up and browsed the jewelry that the vendors were selling on card tables and apple crates. I bought a necklace and some earrings for Julie so she'd know I'd been thinking about her while she was away. I wondered if she missed me. She was probably glad to be on her own for a change, just like I was. I never got the chance to sit in the park, eat bread, and mock tourists. I was having a grand time.

I walked over to Ghirardelli Square, a shopping center in what once was a famous San Francisco chocolate factory. The chocolate is made in San Leandro now, but Ghirardelli doesn't make a big deal about that. Nobody ever left their heart in San Leandro.

There's a bookstore in the square devoted to art and architecture books. I browsed through a big book on tiki and Hawaiian style and remembered my trip to Kauai with Monk. I recalled it with far more amusement and affection than I'd felt at the time, but the past is like that sometimes. You remember what you want to remember.

I wondered how Monk was getting along with Ambrose. Were they having fun? Were they fighting? Or were they off in separate corners of the big house, barely acknowledging one another's presence?

I was tempted to drive over and see for myself. I shook off the thought and called Firefighter Joe, my friend-with-benefits, to inquire if he was free for dinner. Unfortunately for me, Joe was at the firehouse, two days into a four-day shift.

So I tried Dr. Polanski, a dashing dermatologist and recovered leper whom I met on one of Monk's cases. I struck out with him, too. He was at a leper convention in Miami. Lucky him.

I started to call Scooter, but I came to my senses halfway through keying in his phone number.

What the hell was wrong with me?

I glanced at my watch. Two hours of my first afternoon of freedom had passed and I already didn't know what to do with myself.

And that's when I realized that I'd sat down to make my calls on a chair in front of one of those caricature artists. The guy was older, maybe in his fifties, and looked like he'd eaten something so sour it had permanently puckered his sun-beaten face. His would be an easy face to caricature, even for me, and I can't draw.

The artist was already busy immortalizing me in charcoal by the time I realized I was sitting there, so it was too late to apologize and walk away. I was stuck, in more ways than one.

What had happened to making a change in my life? To taking some chances? To making new friends? San Francisco was full of nightclubs, galleries, and cultural events. *So what was I doing sitting here?*

I wondered if Julie and Monk were as lost without me as I apparently was without them. I doubted it. It made me wonder who really needed whom. Maybe Scooter was right about me.

The artist finished my caricature, slipped it into a cardboard frame shaped like a cable car, and proudly presented it to me like it was a priceless heirloom.

I gave it a glance. I suppose the drawing could have been me. It also could have been Barbara Bush, Nicole Kidman, Eddie Murphy, or any of the tourists waiting for the cable car. The face was characterless and unmemorable.

Maybe that's how I really looked to him. It was certainly how I felt. Perhaps it was my soul and not my face that he'd captured.

I wondered if I looked different when I

was with Monk or Julie. I'd have to come back sometime and see Mr. Puckerface when I was with one of them.

I gave him ten bucks, walked back to Boudin Bakery for another loaf of bread, and then drove home.

I did laundry, paid some bills, and for dinner I made myself a tuna fish sandwich and had a glass of white wine that cost almost as much as my caricature.

Do I know how to live or what?

I refilled the wineglass and took it with me for a nice long bubble bath, where I settled in with Ambrose's installation guide for low-voltage outdoor lighting.

It wasn't thrilling bubble-bath reading material, but I was impressed by his imagination. You wouldn't know from the writing that he'd never actually seen a low-voltage lighting system in someone's yard, much less installed one himself. His descriptions were clear, colorful, and written with authority. The inscription wasn't bad either: *To Natalie, You're a high-voltage system as far as I am concerned.*

Considering that I was spending my first free night in ages sitting in tepid bathwater, sipping cheap wine, and reading an instruction manual, it was reassuring to know I could set off sparks somewhere.

■ ■ ■ ■

I was at Ambrose's front door at nine a.m. sharp, ready for work. You might even say I was eager.

"Good morning," I said. "How was your night?"

"We watched *Jeopardy!* and then I made linguine for dinner," Ambrose said. "Adrian measured the noodles."

"Didn't that drive you nuts?"

"Yes, it did," Ambrose said. "But what could I do? It makes him happy."

"I know exactly how you feel."

I was impressed. Ambrose was a guy who struggled with his own crippling psychological problems, but they hadn't blinded him to his brother's unique needs nor made him any less compassionate about them. I looked at Ambrose in an entirely new light.

"It was an excruciating experience," Ambrose said, stepping aside to let me in.

"I can imagine, believe me," I said. "I live with it every day."

"I much prefer to measure the noodles myself."

I was about to laugh, but choked it back when I saw the look on his face. He wasn't joking.

"You measure your noodles?"

"It's not like there's anyone else around to do it for me," Ambrose said. "I'm not used to trusting someone else with that responsibility anymore, even though it was Adrian's job when we were kids."

I couldn't imagine what it was like growing up in that house, but I was beginning to understand why their father had fled, not that I approved of his doing it, of course.

"You're a good brother, Ambrose," I said. "Where's Mr. Monk? Is he in the kitchen, counting the Wheat Chex in his bowl?"

"He did that hours ago," he said. "Adrian is hanging out in his room."

I went upstairs and found the door to Monk's room wide open. He was lying on top of his tiny single bed, grinning to himself over a book of Marmaduke cartoons. They were his favorites.

"Found a good one, Mr. Monk?"

"They're all good, but this one is a classic." He turned the book so I could see the panel.

Marmaduke, the enormous dog, was licking the roof off a car. Behind the dog, a child stood on a street corner holding a sign that read CAR WASH $5.

"Isn't it hilarious?" Monk said. "I can't stop laughing."

60

"You aren't laughing," I said.

"Yes, I am. Look at me."

"Trust me, you aren't. You just have a big grin on your face."

"That's laughter," he said.

"No, that's a grin. Laughter is different. There are sounds."

"I must be laughing inside."

"That's probably it," I said.

"Uproariously," he said.

"If you say so."

I looked around the room. It was sparsely decorated. There was a 49ers banner, a hand-drawn map of the fire exits, the periodic table, and a family photo of Monk, Ambrose, and their parents, all standing rigidly, arms at their sides, about two feet apart from one another. They were like statuary. It was scary.

He had a shoe-shining machine, something you don't usually see in a kid's room — or anybody's room, for that matter. There was also a floor mat for wiping your feet. He had two matching umbrellas in a stand, a rock-shining kit on his desk, and a complete collection of *Encyclopedia Brown* mysteries on his bookshelf.

I was heading over to look at the books when I noticed that his closet door was ajar. The edge of a woman's smile caught my eye. I opened the door and was stunned to see a Farrah Fawcett poster taped to the other side.

"You like Farrah Fawcett?" I asked him.

"I'm not familiar with that company," he said. "Keebler faucets are the best. They have great knobs."

"I'm talking about her." I tapped the poster with my knuckle. "Farrah."

"Oh yeah," Monk said. "She was a baby."

"You mean a babe," I said.

Monk nodded. "She really knows how to rock."

He obviously had no idea who she was. My guess was that he had the poster in his room only because all the other boys had one. They all thought she was hot and Monk wanted to fit in. I found it sweet and also achingly sad.

I decided not to embarrass him by pressing the point.

"How does it feel to be back home and sleeping in your old room again, Mr. Monk?"

He put his book down and looked at me. "Strange. I used to sit in this bed and dream about what life would be like when I grew up. And now here I am."

"Did things turn out the way you imagined they would?"

"Not exactly," Monk said. "I thought I'd be an inspector with the California State department of weights and measures. I used to go down to the gas station on the corner and check the pumps for accuracy, just for fun. Those were some wild, wild times."

"It sounds like it," I said. "What changed your mind?"

"They wouldn't take me. They said I was overzealous. How can you be too exacting for the department of weights and measures?"

"It's mind-boggling," I said.

"So I became a police officer instead. It's not that different from weights and measures. I maintain the proper balance of things."

"You certainly do."

"Last night, I measured the linguine for Ambrose," Monk said, lowering his voice. "He's never really gotten the hang of it. Even if he could leave the house, he clearly lacks the basic survival skills necessary to exist in the outside world."

"Like measuring noodles," I said.

"It's so sad," he said.

Yes, it was, for both of them.

What kind of mother makes her kids confirm that all the noodles on their plates are the same length? Mrs. Monk must have been crazy. But I know that they loved her anyway.

Thinking about what childhood must have been like for Monk and Ambrose made me want to cry and to take back every bad thing I ever said about my own parents. They'd never asked me to measure my noodles.

My cell phone rang. I glanced at the caller ID and knew without answering the phone that some unfortunate person in San Francisco wasn't going to be celebrating any more birthdays.

CHAPTER SIX:
MR. MONK AND THE FINAL FRONTIER

The San Francisco Airporter Motor Inn was a decaying example of early-1960s architecture.

The name of the hotel was written in peeling plywood script across a lava rock facade. The entire front of the building was slightly angled to evoke a tail fin and a sense of motion. Instead, it looked like the place was about to tip over — if it wasn't flattened first by one of the incoming planes that were flying in so low their landing gear nearly scraped the roof.

The hotel was not only in the airport's flight path but it was also right off the 101 Freeway, and I was pretty sure that the only person enjoying a quiet stay was the dead guy that we'd come to see.

So I couldn't figure out why the parking lot was full of cars and the NO VACANCY sign was lit up in the lobby window. I'd rather sleep in my car than stay in a place like this.

There was a taxi parked close to the loading dock at the rear of the hotel's "convention center," a converted factory warehouse attached to the main building by a long breezeway. The right rear passenger door of the car was open, and just beside it was the body.

Crime scene techs were taking pictures of everything and scouring the immediate area for forensic evidence. Two bored guys from the morgue stood beside a gurney with an empty body bag, waiting for the okay to take the corpse away.

Disher was interviewing the taxi driver, an Asian man who talked rapidly in Chinese and gestured even faster. The lieutenant had his pen in hand, ready to write something down in his notebook the instant he understood any of what the taxi driver was saying.

Stottlemeyer stood by the body, his hands in his pockets, and chewed on a toothpick, watching us as we approached.

"Thanks for coming down."

At least I think that's what he said. The words were drowned out by the sound of a landing airplane.

I saw some movement out of the corner of my eye. The taxi driver was pantomiming a man popping up and shooting a gun. It was very vivid. The taxi driver would have been great to have as a partner in a game of charades. At least now Disher had something to put in his notebook.

Monk circled the body, examining it from various angles. I did too, for lack of something better to do. After a moment or two, I looked up and saw Stottlemeyer studying me. He waited to speak until the plane passed over us.

"So what do you think happened here?"

I felt a shiver of anxiety. It was seventh-grade French class all over again. I used to sit in the back of the room and pray that the teacher, Gino Barsuglia, wouldn't call on me.

"I'm really not qualified to offer an opinion," I said.

"I wouldn't say that. You're sharp, you've been to a lot of crime scenes, and you've been hanging around cops for a while now. I bet you know more about this job than you think you do."

Maybe he was right. Judging by the taxi driver's dramatization of the shooting, the location of the taxi, and the position of the body, it seemed obvious to me what had happened, so I gave it a try.

"Okay. It looks to me like the taxi pulled

up and the minute the victim got out of the car, someone jumped out from behind the Dumpster there and shot him."

I walked over to where I thought the shooter had stood and I turned to look at the scene from his perspective.

I was facing the car head-on.

"If the killer was standing here," I said, "the taxi driver must have had a real good look at him."

I saw a security camera mounted over the loading bay, another one above the door to the convention center, and one more on a tall light in the parking lot.

"And if those cameras were working, you should have no problem getting a good look at him yourself, considering that the shooting happened in broad daylight and the killer was standing out here in the open."

Stottlemeyer nodded. "Not bad."

"You gave me an easy one. This wasn't exactly the work of a criminal mastermind," I said. "It's just a straightforward shooting."

"It certainly seems that way," Stottlemeyer said and turned to Monk, who was leaning inside the backseat of the taxi. "Unless there's anything else you'd like to add."

"There's fresh gum under the seat." Monk stood up straight and pointed accusingly at the corpse. "And I'm certain that he was responsible."

"That's good to know," Stottlemeyer said. "That'll be one less question keeping me up at night."

Disher joined us, shoving his notebook into his inside jacket pocket. "The taxi driver picked Stipe up at the Belmont Hotel in Union Square and brought him straight here. He confirms what we know and what the other witnesses told us. Well, at least I think he does. My Chinese is a little rusty."

"You speak Chinese?" Stottlemeyer asked.

"No," Disher said. "That's why it's rusty. From lack of use."

"There were other witnesses?" I asked.

"A few people in the parking lot saw it and so did some others from the windows of their hotel rooms," Disher said. "We would have had even more witnesses if the gunshot hadn't been muffled by an airplane coming in for a landing."

"If you've got all those witnesses and the shooting on tape," I said, "what do you need Mr. Monk for?"

"We don't know who did it or why," Stottlemeyer said. "Or where to find him."

"Isn't that true at the outset of most murder investigations? I thought you only brought Mr. Monk in for the really tough ones."

"This one is a little more complicated than it seems, Natalie," Stottlemeyer said.

"Much more." Monk scowled at the corpse. "This man had a lot of enemies who wanted him dead. It could take us the rest of our lives to find them all."

"Why do you say that?" Stottlemeyer asked.

"Because he was a nasty, foul, disgusting human being," Monk said. "And nasty, foul, disgusting human beings make enemies."

"You don't know anything about him yet."

"He chewed gum," Monk said, as if that said it all.

"Lots of people chew gum, Monk. That doesn't make them bad people."

"This man stuck a glob of cud soaked in his putrid bodily fluids under the seat of a taxi. If he hadn't been killed here today, this taxi would have driven off, picked up another fare, and some innocent, unsuspecting, clean-living person would have sat on that seat. God only knows what might have happened then."

"I'll grant you that he wasn't very considerate. But that's not what makes this case a challenge."

Monk glared at the corpse. "I hope you burn in hell."

He said some other things, perhaps even

profane things, but they were drowned out by a plane passing overhead. It was so low that I instinctively ducked to avoid being decapitated by the landing gear or crushed by the collapse of the building. Once the plane passed, I spoke up.

"It's not like the guy drowned in midair or was attacked by an alligator or was found in a room locked from the inside. I don't see what's so complicated about this."

"That's funny," Stottlemeyer said, "because five minutes ago you didn't think you were qualified to offer an opinion."

I shrugged. "You have no one to blame but yourself."

"You'll understand the complexity of the situation after you've seen the surveillance tape," Stottlemeyer said. "I've got it queued up and waiting in the manager's office."

The captain motioned to the guys from the morgue to take away the body, then led Monk, Disher, and me across the parking lot to the lobby.

"By the way, Monk, I got the medical examiner's report on Lorber this morning," Stottlemeyer said. "You were right. He was dead for at least ten minutes before he was shot. It's not my problem or yours anymore."

"It's a case for the Special Desecration

Unit," Disher said. "Or SDU, as it's known in law enforcement circles."

"What 'law enforcement circles'?" Stottlemeyer asked.

"This one. You and me," Disher said, making a circle with his finger. "And Monk and Natalie."

"I'm not in law enforcement," I said.

"But you are in the circle," Disher said, twirling his finger again. "So you know. Everyone in the circle knows."

"The SDU has another case," Monk said.

"We do?" Disher said excitedly.

"The desecration of that taxi." Monk pointed at the car and then at the body bag being wheeled away on a gurney. "By that man."

"He's dead," Disher said. "There's not much more we can do to punish him."

"Justice must be served, Lieutenant," Monk said. "He needs to be held accountable, even if it's in name only."

"What *is* his name, by the way?" I asked.

"Conrad Stipe," Stottlemeyer replied.

The name sounded familiar to me. "Why do I know that name?"

"You'll see," Stottlemeyer said and opened the door to the lobby.

He took us into a cramped, windowless room behind the front desk, where there was a bank of eight VCRs and several monitors.

"Detectives from Vice and Narcotics have raided this place a few times over the years," Disher said. "So the management put cameras in plain sight everywhere to try to discourage solicitation and drug dealing."

What a charming place to stay.

Monk rolled his shoulders. "So why did the killer shoot him here? Why not somewhere else, where he wouldn't be on camera?"

"Because he wanted to be seen," Stottlemeyer said.

Disher hit PLAY on the VCR. The display on the monitor was separated into quarters, each one showing a different angle on the loading dock as the taxi drove up.

Stipe got out of the car. A man stepped out from behind the Dumpster, shot him once in the forehead, and then ran into the convention center.

It was sudden, violent, and shocking, and it happened just the way I'd said it did.

Well, almost.

The killer didn't look anything like I'd imagined. I'd pictured a tattooed gang member. But the actual shooter was wearing a bright orange shirt with a silver starburst insignia on the chest, black pants, and black boots.

The killer also had pointy ears, vertebrae visible under his forehead, and an elephant's trunk in the center of his face that dangled down to his chin.

I recognized him immediately.

"Oh my God," I said. "It's Mr. Snork."

CHAPTER SEVEN:
MR. MONK
AND THE FAN

Monk studied the freeze-frame image of the elephant-nosed killer. "You know that freak?"

"Of course I do," I said.

"Is he an old boyfriend?"

"No," I said. "Don't you recognize him?"

"I don't associate with freaks," Monk said.

"That's Mr. Snork, security chief of the starship *Discovery*," I said. "Well, not him exactly, but someone dressed up to look like him."

And that's when I realized why the victim's name was familiar to me.

"Wasn't Conrad Stipe the creator of *Beyond Earth*?"

Stottlemeyer nodded.

"It's one thing to shoot somebody. But this was more than that," I said. "Stipe was gunned down by a guy dressed up as one of the TV characters he created. Someone is sending a message."

75

"Now you're beginning to grasp the situation," Stottlemeyer said.

"How hard could it be to find a freak like that?" Monk said, pointing at the screen. "He ran into the convention center. With all those witnesses around, somebody must have seen him. It's not like he's going to blend in."

Stottlemeyer glanced at Disher. "Show Monk the feed from the floor of the convention center."

Disher hit some buttons and the image on the monitor was replaced by four views of a very large banquet hall that was full of hundreds of people. They were crowded into long, narrow aisles, browsing the dozens of vendors selling T-shirts, books, videos, models, and posters.

Most of the people were dressed in different-colored versions of the outfit the killer was wearing, with the same starburst insignia on the chest. And easily a third of those people also had pointed ears and elephant trunks. Another third had an alien mix of fangs, fur, tails, claws, scales, multi-colored skin, and an assortment of extra appendages.

Monk leaned forward and stared at the screen in disbelief.

"Arrest them all," Monk said.

"On what charge?" Stottlemeyer asked him.

"Are you kidding?" Monk said. "They're obviously high on LSD. They're tripping out, man. Go ask Alice."

"Who's Alice?" Disher asked.

"It was a book, Randy," Stottlemeyer said.

"It was a lyric in a Jefferson Airplane song," I said.

"It was a warning, my friends, and you'd best heed it," Monk said. "Say no to drugs or you'll rip out your own eyeballs."

"I don't remember Alice ripping out her eyeballs," I said.

"It was the subtext," Monk said.

"I don't see any evidence of drug use here," Stottlemeyer said.

"Look at them, Captain. They are drug-crazed hippies. What other explanation could there be?"

"It's a *Beyond Earth* convention, Mr. Monk," I said. "They're all dressed up like aliens from the TV show."

"What TV show?" Monk said.

"The one Conrad Stipe wrote and produced back in the seventies," Stottlemeyer said. "It has a cult following."

"Ah, so they're a cult," Monk said, nodding knowingly. "Now it all makes sense. We'd better arrest them now before they sacrifice a virgin."

"There's a virgin?" Disher said. "Where?"

"They're probably all virgins," I said.

"I'd like to make an arrest, Monk," Stottle-meyer said. "I'd like it to be the killer. But how are we going to pick him out of that crowd? There's got to be a hundred Mr. Snorks in there. It would be like picking a needle out of a box of needles."

"I could pick a needle out of a box of needles," Monk said.

"I know. That's what I'm counting on," the captain said, "because when the killer ran into the convention center, he immediately got lost in the crowd. Nobody would have given him a second look. If anyone can spot him in there, it's you."

"Can't you test everyone attending the convention for gunshot residue on their hands and clothing?" I asked.

"First I'd have to find a judge insane enough to give me a warrant. But even if I could, for all we know the killer changed out of his getup and slipped away before we got here."

"Oh," I said, and then I had another idea. "Couldn't you trace him by checking the places that sell Snork noses, pointed ears, and Confederation uniforms?"

"There must be fifty vendors in the dealers' room of the convention alone who sell the stuff, as well as countless merchants on the Internet," Stottlemeyer said. "That's not even counting the people who create their own makeup and costumes. And I doubt most of those people keep detailed sales records on every single purchase. We don't even know when the shooter bought the stuff. Was it today? Last week? Twenty years ago?"

"Oh," I said.

"As you can see, Natalie, this is demanding work best left to professionals," Disher said. "We have the experience, resources, and old-fashioned know-how to get the job done."

Disher looked at me, then at Monk, then back to the captain.

"In most cases. I'd say between half and two thirds of the time," Disher said. "More or less."

Stottlemeyer sighed wearily and looked at me. "Now do you see my problem?"

I did. And I could also see that it was about to become my problem, too.

Morris Hibler, the organizer of the convention, would have been a reasonably attractive man if not for the purple *Beyond Earth* uniform, the pointed ears, and the elephant trunk dangling from his nose.

Stottlemeyer, Monk, and I were talking with him in his Airporter Motor Inn suite, where he was drinking a can of 7-Up and awaiting the results of the diphenylamine swab tests for gunpowder residue that he'd graciously allowed a CSI technician to perform on his hands and clothing. Disher was still outside, taking witness statements.

"Conrad Stipe's murder is a tragedy of interstellar proportions for fandom," Hibler said. "The fact that it was committed by a Confederation officer is unthinkable."

"A Confederation officer?" Stottlemeyer asked.

"The *Discovery* is a Piller-class Confederation starship," Hibler said. "Every member of the crew has sworn an oath to respect all life in whatever form it takes. This heinous act is a gross violation of the Cosmic Commandments of Interplanetary Relations. It just sickens me."

"You should have another 7-Up," Monk said. "You'll feel better."

"No thanks," Hibler said. "I'm still working on this one."

"What was Stipe doing here?" Stottlemeyer asked.

"He was our guest of honor, of course. He was going to inaugurate the con, do a

Q&A with the stars, and screen some of the classic episodes."

"Do you have any idea what he was doing at the Belmont Hotel this morning?" Stottlemeyer asked.

Hibler nodded his head. "He was staying there. Stipe demanded four-star accommodations. We couldn't afford to rent convention space there and they wouldn't have us even if we could. They're sci-fi bigots. They don't want our kind on their premises."

"Who knew when he was going to be showing up here?"

"Just about everyone," Hibler said, taking another sip of his drink. "He does six or seven of these cons a year."

Monk rolled his shoulders and tipped his head towards the 7-Up. "You're required to drink those in pairs."

"No, you're not," Hibler said.

"Yes, you are. They're like socks," Monk said. "Only carbonated."

I'm sure that made sense to Monk in some way, but not to any of the rest of us. I pressed on.

"The show has been off the air for thirty years," I said. "You'd think Stipe would have gotten sick of answering the same questions over and over."

"Do you think the pope gets tired of discussing the Bible?" Hibler said.

"You're comparing *Beyond Earth* to the Bible?" Stottlemeyer said.

"What I'm saying is that it's like the Bible," Hibler said. "The more you delve into it, the deeper your understanding and appreciation becomes for the history, the values, and the enduring life lessons that it teaches."

"If you read the front of the can," Monk said, "you'd know you're supposed to have two at once. It's like the Bible, too. Only on a can. You need to follow it religiously."

"All it says is '7-Up,' " Hibler said.

"The dash means 'and,' as in 'and up to fourteen,' " Monk said. "It means you're supposed to go up to another can."

"No, it doesn't." Hibler shook his head, which made his elephant trunk swing.

"It's common sense," Monk said.

Stottlemeyer began to rub his forehead. The whole room shook as a plane passed over us.

"You're being ridiculous," Hibler yelled.

"Me? *Me?*" Monk yelled back. "Have you taken a look at yourself lately?"

Some more things were said back and forth between the two men that were, mercifully, drowned out by the plane. When the roar was over, Stottlemeyer spoke up first, silencing them both.

"Enough about the drinks, Monk. We're conducting a homicide investigation here," he said. "Let's stay focused on the facts."

"The fact is that the rest of us live in the real world," Monk said. "Where a man has been murdered, rational human beings don't wear pointy ears, and *seven plus seven equals fourteen!*"

"I'm not wearing pointed ears," Hibler said. "These *are* my ears."

We stared at him. That was a conversation stopper.

"They are?" I asked.

"I had them surgically enhanced," Hibler said.

"Why?" I asked.

"The erotic power," he said. "Surely you feel it."

I was feeling something, but it wasn't attraction. Quite the opposite, actually.

"What about the elephant trunk?" Monk asked. "Is that part of you, too?"

"Only in the emotional and spiritual sense. It's a prosthetic," Hibler said. "Made from the original mold they used on the show. But I follow Snork's example in life."

Stottlemeyer cleared his throat. "It must have cost you a lot of money to put Stipe up at the Belmont. Why bother inviting him at all? Surely you've heard everything he has to say."

"A Beyondcon doesn't have any credibility unless you've got Stipe and at least two of the original cast members attending," Hibler said. "We have four of the six. Only Captain Stryker and Starella aren't here."

"And they are?" Stottlemeyer said.

Hibler looked at Stottlemeyer in disbelief, as if he'd just been asked who the first president of the United States was.

"The commander of the *Discovery* and his concubine psychic from Umgluck."

Stottlemeyer rubbed his forehead again. Monk started rummaging around for something in the minibar. There was an awkward silence. I could feel the interview spiraling away from us.

When the captain spoke again, it was in a controlled voice, the kind he usually reserved for dealing with Monk.

"I meant in real life," he said evenly.

Hibler stared at him. Stottlemeyer stared back.

"Kyle Bethany and Minerva Klane," Hibler said. "What planet have you been living on for the last thirty years?"

"Earth." Monk yanked the 7-Up can out of Hibler's hands, startling him. "You should try it sometime."

"What are you doing?" Hibler said.

"Enforcing law and order." Monk handed Hibler a bottle from the minibar.

"What's this for?" Hibler said.

"It's a V8," Monk said.

"I can see that," he said. "Why did you give it to me?"

"This way you only have to hold one drink," Monk said.

"But I don't like vegetable juice," Hibler said. "I like 7-Up."

"It's for your own good," Monk said. "It's a very tasty, even beverage. You'll thank me later."

I was still thinking about Kyle Bethany. I had a big crush on him when I was a kid. I didn't like science fiction very much, but I could always count on two things in a *Beyond Earth* episode: that Captain Stryker's shirt would get torn off somehow and that he'd end up in a romantic clinch with a female alien. And if there were no female aliens around, there was always Starella, the space shrink with the cosmic halter top that seemed to defy gravity.

Bethany was a romantic hero, always jumping into danger and making passionate, chest-heaving speeches about freedom, democracy, and humanity. I don't remember the speeches, but I haven't forgotten the chest-heaving.

After *Beyond Earth* was canceled, Bethany did some guest shots on shows like *The Love Boat* and *Jake and the Fatman,* but he basically disappeared and I shifted my unrequited romantic longing to Rick Springfield.

Minerva Klane was on *The Young and the Restless* until she became one of the Old and the Incontinent. I saw her picture not long ago in the *National Enquirer* while I was waiting in the checkout line at Safeway. She'd had so much work done to her face that she looked like someone wearing a Minerva Klane mask.

"Why didn't Bethany and Klane show up?" I asked. "It's not like they're busy working."

"They're part of the Galactic Uprising."

"You've lost me," Stottlemeyer said.

"They're leading the Fen in the rebellion against the reimagining of the *Beyond Earth*–verse."

"I'm still lost," Stottlemeyer said.

"The UBS Network is producing new episodes of *Beyond Earth.*"

"Isn't that what you've been fighting for ever since the show was canceled in the seventies?" I asked.

"Yes and no," Hibler said. "They're bringing it back with a new cast, new writers, and what they're calling a grittier take on the storytelling. A lot of the fans feel betrayed."

"How did Stipe feel about it?" Monk asked. Now that Hibler was holding a V8, Monk could focus on the case.

"That's one of the questions we wanted to ask him," Hibler said. "The suits at the network brought in a new executive producer, the guy who did the *Eat Your Flesh* movies. But they couldn't have done it without Stipe's approval."

No wonder the fans were upset. I'd seen a few minutes of *Eat Your Flesh III* on Cinemax. It made snuff films look like Disney cartoons. The *Eat Your Flesh* films were incredibly bloody and inexplicably successful horror movies about a sadist who kidnaps nubile women and hunky guys and puts them in grisly situations where they have to chew off their own arm or eat someone else in order to survive. If you ask me, films like that are worse than pornography.

But they made money. Lots of it.

"The fans in this Galactic Uprising —" Stottlemeyer said.

"The Fen," Hibler interrupted.

"Yeah, whatever," Stottlemeyer continued.

87

"How upset would you say they are?"

"They want to prosecute Stipe for crimes against fandom," Hibler said. "They are out for blood."

"You think they'd go that far?" I asked.

"*Beyond Earth* is their culture and their religion," Hibler said. "Go back through history and look at what people have done to protect what they've believed in from being destroyed. Remember the Crusades? The Spanish Inquisition? New Coke?"

That's when the crime scene investigator returned. He was in his twenties and looked, judging by his pockmarked cheeks, like he'd spent half of those years picking at zits on his face.

"The swabs came back negative, Captain. No GSR. He's clean."

Stottlemeyer nodded. "Okay, Mr. Hibler, that wraps things up for now. All that's left is for Lieutenant Disher here to take your statement."

"And blood and urine samples," Monk said.

"What for?" the CSI asked.

"Drugs," Monk said.

"We aren't looking for evidence of drug use, Monk," Stottlemeyer said.

"We don't have to," Monk said, looking Hibler in the eye. "It's right in front of our faces. If we're lucky, it's not too late to rescue the virgin."

"Lots of men my age still live at home with their parents," Hibler said indignantly. "That doesn't make us virgins!"

"I can vouch for that," the CSI said.

"Thanks. That's good to know." Stottlemeyer took Monk by the arm and pulled him out of the room. "We're leaving now, Monk."

"I'm very sexually active," Hibler yelled after us. "With other people!"

CHAPTER EIGHT:
MR. MONK AND THE BAD BREAKFAST

"I understand that the behavior of these *Beyond Earth* fans offends your sensibilities," Stottlemeyer said to Monk in the hallway. "But if you can't see past that, you're no good to me or this investigation. I need you to control yourself."

"What about them?" Monk gestured to two women who were walking past us.

Both of the women were dressed like Starella and had four breasts, two of which I presumed were falsies. I didn't want to contemplate the alternative.

"They don't work for me," Stottlemeyer said. "You do."

"I'll do my best," Monk said. "But it's going to be an ordeal."

"It usually is," Stottlemeyer said. "I'm going to the Belmont with Randy. I'd like you to stay here and see if you can spot anything that doesn't fit."

Monk glanced at the two women again.

They each had a tail.

"It's all wrong."

"You've got to learn about the show and the world of these fans," Stottlemeyer instructed Monk. "You don't know what's normal in this particular world yet."

"There's nothing normal about them."

"Not to you or me, but I guarantee you that they've got their own rules," Stottlemeyer said. "Once you know what those rules of behavior are, you'll immediately see what's amiss and the murderer is as good as caught. That's your gift."

"And my curse," Monk said. "I'd like a copy of the security camera footage of the shooting."

"Sure thing," Stottlemeyer said. "We'll meet up later at the Belmont or at headquarters and compare notes."

He gave us two "all-purpose passes" to the convention and walked away.

I really admired the way the captain had handled Monk this time and made a mental note to copy the technique myself. Stottlemeyer gave Monk a clear mission, a structure for dealing with the madness around him. If Monk focused on the underlying framework of everyone's behavior, he might not be so distracted by the behaviors themselves. It was a brilliant strategy.

In fact, Monk seemed calmer and more centered already.

"Let's go visit the convention," he said, taking a deep breath. "Have your wipes at the ready."

"They always are," I told him.

We headed for the convention center, stopping first at the registration desk to pick up a program book. According to the schedule, there were three parallel tracks of panel discussions every hour throughout the day.

The panel topics included "Earthies vs. Earthers: Charting the Evolution of *Beyond Earth* Fandom," "The Galactic Economic Impact of the Cosmic Commandments of Interplanetary Relations," "Theories on the Creation of the Holocaust Satellite," "How to Write Compelling *Beyond Earth* Fanfiction," "Interspecies Sexuality and Captain Stryker," and "When Will Trekkers Give Earthers the Respect We Deserve?"

It might have been fun to listen in on a few of those panel discussions, but when we got to the convention center, there was a sign announcing that the entire program for the day had been canceled out of respect for Conrad Stipe.

The lobby outside the main hall was crowded with costumed attendees sharing their grief and seeking consolation. They were hugging each other, sobbing, and looking generally shell-shocked.

Monk had the same look, only for entirely different reasons.

"What is wrong with these people?" he said.

"The creator of the show they love was just killed, Mr. Monk. Surely you understand grief."

"Yes, of course I do," Monk said. "What I don't understand is their devotion to a TV show."

"*Beyond Earth* wasn't a typical series," I said. "Stipe created an entire universe of his own and then told stories within it. If you wanted to watch the show, you had to learn all about his universe and how it worked. You couldn't watch it as casually as your basic cop show. I guess some people got into it a lot more than others."

I thought about Hibler and his ears and cringed.

"How do you know so much about *Beyond Earth*?" Monk asked.

"I participate in this thing we call American popular culture."

"I wouldn't tell too many people that you're a member," Monk said, lowering his voice. "If word gets out, it could come back to haunt you."

"Everyone in America and in most of the civilized world is steeped in it," I said. "Except you."

"What if you ever decide to run for public office? The press will dig up your involvement. Your name isn't on any of their membership lists, is it?"

"There isn't a list, Mr. Monk."

"There's always a list," he said.

I decided to drop the subject before I got one of Stottlemeyer's Monkaches.

"Do you want to know about the show or don't you?" I asked.

"I guess I don't have much of a choice if I want to solve this murder."

"Okay, so it goes like this," I said. "When Earth's first starship *Discovery* broke the boundary of our galaxy, it passed an alien satellite that had been sitting there for millions of years and triggered its automated program."

"That's the show?"

"I'm just getting started," I said.

"Oh God," he said.

"The satellite fired a missile that destroyed Earth, then it generated a wormhole and sent a signal of some kind through it. An instant before the wormhole collapsed, the *Discovery* flew into it and was hurled light-years into the unexplored reaches of deep

94

space. So with Earth destroyed, the multi-ethnic crew of the *Discovery,* the planet's best and brightest, are all that remains of humanity."

"That's a terrible show."

"I'm still at the beginning," I said.

"There's more?"

I explained that the crew soon discovers that they aren't the only ones in this terrible plight. They join up with the survivors of other worlds that met the same fate. They band together and create the Confederation of Planets. Their shared goals are to find the evil alien race responsible for this galactic genocide and prevent it from happening to any other worlds, to find new planets on which to reestablish their races, and to promote peace and understanding throughout space.

There were about a dozen characters on the show, but I told Monk about only the major ones.

The big three were the adventurous Captain Stryker, of course, and the sexy and mysterious Starella, and the brilliant Mr. Snork. But there were others also: teenage stowaway Bobby Muir, and the intellectual scientist slug-creature Glorp, and pioneering surgeon Dr. Kate Willens, and, finally, the unspeakably evil Sharplings, the aliens with inside-out bodies who ate souls for snacks.

"How could their bodies be inside out?" Monk said to me.

"Their organs were on the outside of their bodies instead of inside."

"Then what was inside?"

"Their outsides," I said.

"That makes no sense," Monk said.

"But it was scary," I said. "Whenever the Sharplings came on, I had to watch the show from outside the room."

"How could you be scared by something that makes no sense?"

"You're scared of phone booths," I said.

"But that makes sense. They're death traps," Monk said. "That's why you don't see them anymore."

"You don't see them anymore because now we have cell phones. Phone booths aren't scary at all. But aliens with intestines hanging from their bodies who can suck your soul out through your eyeballs are terrifying."

In fact, as I said it, someone dressed as a Sharpling walked past and I almost grabbed Monk for protection. I knew it was just someone in a suit, but it still gave me the shivers.

"Phone booths exist," Monk said. "Sharplings don't. They have no basis in reality."

Neither did Monk, but I didn't say that.

"Not all shows can be as good as the Weather Channel," I said.

"I can't believe that a show with inside-out characters was a success."

Okay, he had me there.

"Actually, it wasn't," I said. "*Beyond Earth* was canceled after only two seasons. But it came back ten years later as a cartoon, with the original actors doing the voices."

"Did anyone watch that?"

I shook my head.

"So why are they bringing the show back now?"

"Maybe because there are so many people who are still passionate about it, thirty years after it was canceled. There aren't a lot of TV shows that inspire that kind of devotion."

"You say that like it's a positive thing," Monk said.

We walked into the convention hall, where I saw that Stipe's murder wasn't stopping the fans from shopping. The place was mobbed and the dealers seemed to be doing a brisk business in *Beyond Earth* merchandise.

Perhaps the fans were working through their grief by buying mementos from the show. I know that my mother often deals with stress by shopping. When I eloped with Mitch, she immediately ran out and spent three grand on clothes.

I stopped at the table of a dealer who was selling *Beyond Earth* lunch boxes, board games, and action figures, most of which appeared to be in their original packaging.

There were even unopened packs of *Beyond Earth* bubblegum, the ones with trading cards featuring pictures of the cast and scenes from the show. The price tag showed the packs were $350 each. I figured the decimal had to be in the wrong place.

I reached out to examine the price tag more closely when the woman behind the table lightly slapped my hand and gave me a stern look.

She was my age and twice as wide, wearing a Confederation uniform that was too tight to hold her girth.

"Don't touch. These are antiques," she said. "They can only be handled with gloves. Moisture from your fingertips could harm the packaging."

"I'm sorry," I said. "I didn't know."

"Didn't you get the 'FAQs for Newbies' at the registration desk?"

"No, I'm afraid not."

"It's required reading," she said. "It also

has recommendations for newbies on how to begin building a collection. *Beyond Earth* plates are a fun and inexpensive way to start."

"Why couldn't I start with *Beyond Earth* toys?" I gestured to some plastic spaceships that were still in their original wrapping.

"That's like starting your art collection with a Picasso. You really have to be an expert to appreciate their value and understand how to care for them," she said. "These are very rare, museum-quality pieces."

I couldn't imagine what museum would be interested in them.

"They arc? What makes them so rare?"

"The only way you could get one of these was by purchasing a Burgerville kid's meal in February 1978. These have been kept in pristine condition in a dust-free, temperature-controlled room ever since."

"I used to treat my toys the same way," Monk said.

He was on the far side of the table, looking at some *Beyond Earth* cereal boxes.

"It was more fun than a barrel of monkeys," he said. "If there aren't actually any monkeys in the barrel, and never were any monkeys in the barrel, because monkeys make a mess and they are very unsanitary.

In fact, it's the most fun of all when the barrel is untouched and the monkeys are on another continent."

I gave him a look. "So you're saying that keeping your toys hermetically sealed was as much fun as an empty barrel."

"Those were good times."

I turned back to the *Beyond Earth* kid's meal toys.

"It's a shame they were never opened," I said to the woman. "I think it's cruel to give a toy to a child but not let them play with it."

"I didn't want to," she said. "I never played with any of my *Beyond Earth* toys."

"Why not?"

"I didn't want to break them," she said.

"But toys are meant to be played with and broken," I said.

"That's just crazy talk," Monk said to me.

"It's fun, Mr. Monk. It's part of growing up. It's called childhood."

The dealer held up one of the toys in her gloved hand. "You wouldn't say that if this was a Ming vase."

"But it's not," I said.

"It is to me," she said.

That was when she was distracted by a movement at the other end of the table. And then she let out an anguished wail, an expression of pain and fury that seemed to claw its way out from the depths of her soul. In fact, it sounded just like the cries people made when they were being devoured by the Sharplings.

She was staring in horror at Monk, who was standing in front of a trash can at the far end of the table.

"What have you done?" she yelled at him.

"I just cleaned up a few things," Monk said. Then he motioned to me. "Wipe. Wipe."

I gave him two.

The woman's wail drew dozens of people, who gathered around the garbage can to see what the fuss was about. I joined them and we all peered inside.

On top of a bunch of hot dogs, melted ice cream, and other sticky garbage were four unopened cartons of *Beyond Earth* breakfast cereal. The front of each box showed a smiling Captain Stryker about to joyfully eat a spoonful of glittering, sugar-coated cereal shaped like stars. Mr. Snork stood at his side, enthusiastically snorting up cereal with his trunk.

At least that's what the boxes looked like before they were tossed in the trash on top of catsup, chocolate, whipped cream, and soft drinks.

The saleswoman's lip trembled with rage, her eyes filled with tears.

"Those were authentic boxes of *Beyond Earth* cereal," she said. "They survived three earthquakes, a flood, two marriages, three moves, and six cats. They have never been opened."

"It's a good thing they weren't," Monk said. "That cereal expired thirty years ago."

"Do you know how much those boxes were worth? I could have gotten a thousand dollars for the set." Her whole body shook with fury. "Now they're ruined. No one will ever buy them."

"*You* were selling them?" Monk was dismayed. "You should be ashamed of yourself. What if someone had eaten that cereal? It would have killed them faster than rat poison."

"You want to know what kills fast? I'll show you." She grabbed a curved knife off her table. "An Umgluckian ceremonial dagger!"

She leapt up on the table and threw herself at Monk, but I grabbed her by the ankle in midflight and sent her toppling into the trash can instead.

"Time to go," I said, leading Monk away.

Monk looked back at her. "You'll thank me later."

CHAPTER NINE:
MR. MONK AND THE GALACTIC UPRISING

"I think she did it," Monk said as I hustled him into the crowd and across the convention floor as fast as I could. "I think she killed Stipe."

"Just because she grabbed a knife and tried to kill you?"

I could still hear her wailing. Her cries seemed to echo through the entire place.

"She was trying to poison people with thirty-year-old cereal," he said. "She almost had me fooled with that story about keeping her toys in pristine condition."

"I'm not a world-famous detective, but I think she was heavier than the shooter we saw in the surveillance video."

"But she definitely has violent tendencies," Monk said. "She's a danger to society."

"Only if you trash the cereal boxes that she's been saving for decades."

"What kind of person saves a box of cereal

for that long?"

"What kind of person feels uncontrollably compelled to throw it out?"

"A Good Samaritan," Monk replied. "I was acting in the public interest. Those expired boxes of deadly cereal were within reach of children."

"Do you see any children?"

"I see people acting like children," Monk said. "That's just as dangerous."

I led Monk towards the back door, which, incidentally, was the one the killer had most likely used to escape into the convention center after shooting Stipe. It was the only way to leave the building without encountering that woman and her ceremonial dagger again.

We passed table after table selling Snork noses and Confederation uniforms, underscoring for me Stottlemeyer's point that it would be close to impossible to trace the killer through the purchase of his costume.

We went down the aisle of autographing booths, where *Beyond Earth* celebrities signed autographs and took photos with conventioneers for a fee.

There was a woman, easily in her seventies, surrounded with photos of herself from an appearance as Yeoman Curtis, who was reduced to a cube of foam and crushed in episode 17. There were a dozen middle-aged men in Confederation uniforms lined up to pay $20 to have their picture taken with her.

In the next booth were a turnip-shaped man with a bad comb-over and a midget. They were signing autographs and answering questions for three conventioneers. I recognized the actors as Bill Wheatley and Ricardo Sanchez, who played teenage stowaway Bobby Muir and Glorp, the interstellar slug.

"Ricky and I stayed in touch after the show, and a couple of years ago we got together to perform in a dinner theater production of *The Odd Couple,*" Wheatley was saying. "But in our *Beyond Earth* personas, so to speak."

"Being the slug," Sanchez said, "obviously I played Oscar Madison."

"All the dialogue was the same, because Neil Simon is a genius, and you don't mess with perfection," Wheatley said. "But we have a history, you know, and we tapped that in our performances. And I wore my Confederation uniform."

"And I wore my makeup," Sanchez said.

"It was a riff on popular culture, very self-referential and culturally hip."

The midget sighed. "It could have gone to Broadway if only we'd found a producer with some vision and some guts."

Monk and I moved on.

In the next booth was Willis Goldkin, the writer of the "Nagging Nanobots" episode, which I vaguely remembered. It was about these little robot mosquitoes that attacked the *Discovery* crew and took over their minds.

Goldkin had a stack of xeroxed autographed scripts in front of him that he was selling for $15 each. There were no takers.

There were more *Beyond Earth* guest stars and production personnel along the aisle selling their wares and their memories, but I avoided them. It was too depressing and pathetic.

Instead, I turned my attention to a dealer who was selling books, comic books, novelizations, and magazines about *Beyond Earth* as well as the DVDs and videos of the original series and the Saturday-morning cartoon.

I was tempted to buy Monk a DVD, just so he could see the show, but the boxed set was fifty dollars and I wasn't sure the SFPD would consider the purchase a legitimate expense.

The last booth — the one closest to the exit — was devoted to the Galactic Uprising. A couple dressed up like Mr. Snork and

Starella were standing behind the table handing out leaflets to conventioneers as they passed by.

Behind the couple was an enormous poster depicting the starship *Discovery* and the original cast, covered with bold type that demanded that the UBS Network immediately halt production on the show and bring back the "true classic" with the "beloved original actors."

The poster touted that the campaign was endorsed by "superstars" Kyle Bethany and Minerva Klane, as well as "famed writer" Willis Goldkin, which made me wonder why he wasn't sitting with his comrades in the rebellion rather than by himself two booths away.

I took one of the leaflets from the woman and stuck it in my purse.

"If you go to our Web site, you can download the JPEG of the poster and e-mail or text-message it to everyone in your address book, put it on your site, your blog, your MySpace page, your Facebook profile, and your Yahoo group," she said. "It's the individual responsibility of every single member of fandom to stand up and be counted in this epic struggle."

Mr. Snork spit and growled and coughed up something.

"My name is Natalie Teeger and I work for this man, Adrian Monk." I tipped my head to Monk, who was involved in his own epic struggle to avoid looking at the woman's four breasts. "He's a consultant to the San Francisco Police Department. Can you tell me who is in charge of the uprising? We'd like to talk with him."

Mr. Snork hacked and grunted and gurgled.

"Ernie is," she said, referring to the guy in the Snork makeup. "He's the one who first heard about what Stipe was going to do and he's been fighting the fight ever since. His dedication to fandom is unbelievable. Never say die!"

She looked at him with unabashed admiration.

"And you are?" Monk asked.

"His girlfriend, Aimee Gilberman," she said. "Before I met Ernie, I knew nothing about *Beyond Earth.* But now that I do, for the first time in my life I know what it really means to love."

"Aimee, I have a very, very dumb question for you, so please be patient with me," I said. "Aside from the fact that the producers aren't using the original cast, what's your problem with the new version of *Beyond Earth*?"

Ernie coughed and barked and made some choking sounds while waving his arms around.

The woman nodded in agreement with Mr. Snork and turned to me.

"They are changing everything," she said. "They are turning the characters, and I quote, into 'deeply flawed individuals.' Captain Stryker wasn't deeply flawed. He represented the very best of what it means to be human. They all did, even the aliens. But worst of all, they are turning Mr. Snork into a woman. Can you imagine that?"

"I assume you know by now that Conrad Stipe was murdered right outside that door." Monk motioned to the nearby exit. "Did you hear or see anything unusual this morning? By that I mean, above and beyond the twisted behavior that's occurring all around us at this very moment."

Ernie grunted and gagged and heaved and gestured wildly with his hands.

"Does anyone here know the Heimlich maneuver?" Monk said. "This man is choking."

Ernie stood up and gurgled and growled and coughed some more.

"He's not choking," Aimee said. "He's speaking in Dratch."

"Dratch?" Monk said. "What is that?"

She looked at Monk like he was a complete imbecile.

"Mr. Snork is a Dratch," Willis Goldkin said, stepping out from his booth and approaching us. "Ernie here is speaking the language of their home-world. You can blame me for it."

"You put him up to this?" Monk said.

Goldkin shook his head. "I wrote the episode where the crew visited a settlement of Dratch refugees. We were running a couple of minutes short, so I stuck in a pointless scene where Mr. Snork talked to his people in his native tongues."

"Tongues?" Monk said.

"The Dratch have three tongues," Aimee said. "One for catching insects, one for grooming themselves, and one for love. They speak with all three — hence the unique sound. It takes incredible skill for a human to speak it, but Ernie has achieved it."

"It was gibberish that I wrote in a drunken stupor. I was too wasted to write a real scene with actual dialogue," Goldkin said. "We recorded it twice and laid it over the original track to create the unusual sound. If you'd told me back then that thirty years later some linguist would analyze those lines, write his thesis on it, and extrapolate that into an entire language, I would probably still be a drunk today."

"Ernie has vowed to only speak in Dratch until either they do *Beyond Earth* right or cancel the current abomination," Aimee said. "He's doing it to show his solidarity with the character of Mr. Snork and the ideals that he represents."

Ernie gesticulated wildly, made some guttural sounds, and spit on the floor. Monk recoiled.

"What's Ernie saying?" Monk asked.

"If you want to understand him, and the values of *Beyond Earth,* learn Dratch," Aimee said. "If everyone would do that, if we all just made the effort to learn how other people think, the world would be a much more peaceful and accepting place to live."

"So by refusing to translate for us, you're making a statement," I said to her. "You want us to try to understand him and, by doing so, see the necessity of working hard to understand our fellow man."

Aimee nodded proudly. "We're living the values and the message of every episode of the original *Beyond Earth.*"

This prompted Ernie to gurgle and gag and bark like a sea otter.

Monk turned to Goldkin. "Do you know what he's saying?"

"Hell no," Goldkin said and reached for an enormous book on the dealer's table. "But if you want to, you're going to need this."

Monk looked at the book and gasped. It was as if he'd stained his carpet all over again.

"What is it?" I asked.

I assumed the sticker price was an odd number, or the price tag was crooked, or the symmetry of the cover was out of whack.

He held the book up so I could see it.

The title of the book was *The Dratch Dictionary: Words, Phrases, and Grammar of the Most Evolved Language in the Universe.*

The author was Ambrose Monk.

"Sweet Mother of God," Monk said. "My brother is one of *them*."

CHAPTER TEN:
Mr. Monk
Is Thrown
for a Loupe

Monk had had enough. He left the building.

I stuck around for a few more minutes and looked through some of the other nonfiction books on the dealer's table. There were a lot of them, with titles like *The Official "Beyond Earth" Episode Guide, The "Beyond Earth" Compendium,* and even *The Ultimate Book of "Beyond Earth" Facts.*

Ambrose had written them all.

The good news was this meant that Monk wouldn't have to return to the convention to learn more about the show. All he had to do was go home. When I told Monk that during the drive to the Belmont Hotel, it didn't make him feel any better.

"I always knew my brother was mentally ill," Monk said, "but I had no idea that he was a freak."

"He's not a freak, Mr. Monk."

"Did you see what he wrote?" Monk exclaimed.

"What's the difference between writing a book like *Beyond Earth* and an owner's manual for a blender?"

"You don't see people dressing up like blenders and speaking puree, do you?" Monk said. "It's a good thing my brother never leaves the house — he'd be locked up."

Monk glanced over his shoulder.

"What are you looking for?" I asked.

"I'm making sure we aren't being followed."

"Why would anyone want to follow us?"

"Because they're freaks, and freaks do freakish things," Monk said. "I don't want any of them knowing where I'm going."

"One of them might show up at your door and offer you a bowl of thirty-year-old cereal."

"Exactly," Monk said and shivered.

He kept to himself the rest of the drive.

The Belmont Hotel was right in the heart of Union Square and was one of the oldest, grandest, and stodgiest places to stay in the city. It was a five-star hotel with a six-star attitude. So they probably weren't too happy to have vehicles from the police department, the crime scene unit, and the morgue parked in front of their lobby.

Obviously, someone else had been killed. I wondered why nobody had called Monk.

I parked with the rest of the official vehicles and we went inside to find Stottlemeyer. It wasn't hard. We just asked the concierge where we could find the corpse.

Luckily for me and for Monk, the body was in a room on the sixth floor, an even-numbered room, with only a dozen flights of stairs for us to climb. It could have been worse for Monk. The dead body could have been on the nineteenth floor. It wouldn't have been so bad for me; I would have taken the elevator.

The sixth floor was cordoned off by police officers, but Disher was in the hallway, interviewing a maid at her cart, so he stepped away from her and cleared us to go through.

"What's going on?" I asked.

"We were just beginning to interview some of the convention's special guests who are staying here when the hotel manager came rushing over to us," Disher said. "A maid found a guy bludgeoned to death in one of the rooms. So we dropped what we were doing, secured the scene, and began an investigation."

"Two Belmont guests killed in one day," I said. "That can't be good for business."

"Stipe wasn't killed here," Monk said, "so technically his death doesn't count in the official tally."

"There's an official tally?" I said.

"There is now," Monk said. "I'm the official and I've just tallied. Why didn't anybody call us?"

"I guess it never occurred to anybody that we needed an official tally," Disher said.

"I meant why didn't anybody call us to aid in the investigation?"

"Because this is a simple case and you were occupied on the Stipe thing."

"But this is a murder," Monk said.

"So is that," Disher said.

"But this is a *real* murder."

"Stipe's murder looked real to me," I said.

"Do you see anybody here with an elephant nose?" Monk said to me before turning to Disher. "Let's trade."

"No," Disher said.

"I bet the captain will say yes."

Monk shouldered past Disher and marched into the hotel room.

"I bet he won't," Disher called after him.

I turned to Disher. "How's the Lorber case going?"

"The Special Desecration Unit has made some progress in between the Stipe shooting and this murder."

116

"I know it's not a murder, but I'm really curious why someone would bother shooting a dead person. Would you mind telling me about it later?"

"Sure, of course." Disher smiled, clearly pleased that someone was taking an interest in what he and the Special Desecration Unit were doing. "I'd be glad to."

"It's a date," I said, then immediately regretted my choice of words. "Not a date date, but an understanding that we'll meet at some future time in a purely nonromantic way."

"Right," Disher said. "I knew that."

I followed Monk into the hotel room before I could embarrass myself any further.

Stottlemeyer was at the far end of the narrow room, standing by the window and looking down at one of the two beds, where a very hairy dead man in his underwear lay tangled in the blood-spattered sheets.

A half-empty bottle of wine and two glasses were on the table. Monk was examining one of the glasses.

"There's lipstick on the rim of this glass," Monk said.

"Yes, Monk, I know that," Stottlemeyer said with a weary sigh.

"Who is the victim?" Monk asked.

"The front desk says his name is John

Bozadjian and that he checked in yesterday afternoon."

"Did he pay with a credit card?"

"Yes, he did."

"So where is it?" Monk asked.

"I would say it's probably in his wallet," Stottlemeyer replied.

"His wallet is missing," Monk said. "Isn't it?"

"Yes, it is."

"And he isn't wearing a watch or any jewelry," Monk said. "But he's got tan lines on his wrists and around the base of his ring fingers that suggest that he had some."

"Believe it or not, I noticed that too," Stottlemeyer said. "You know how I became captain of Homicide? I'll tell you how. By solving a lot of homicides. On my own."

Monk cocked his head and looked at the victim. Then he cocked his entire upper body and looked again. I didn't see how that changed his perspective, but I didn't understand most of what Monk did.

"It looks like a robbery," Monk said.

"Unfortunately, I see cases like this all the time," Stottlemeyer said. "An out-of-towner picks up a hooker for a night of whoopee and she rolls him for his cash and jewelry. Usually, it ends there and we never hear about it. Most guys are too embarrassed, or too married, to report it."

"So if the prostitute knew that the odds were her victim wasn't going to report the theft anyway," I asked, "what was the point of killing him?"

"The hooker probably only meant to hit him hard enough to put him out for a while. But clobbering someone on the head is a crapshoot. If you do it too lightly, they could hit you back. Do it too hard and you could put them down for good."

"Picking up a prostitute and bringing her back to your room is such a huge risk to your health and safety in so many ways," I said. "What are men thinking?"

Stottlemeyer gave me a look. "What do you think they are thinking?"

"Men are idiots," I said.

"Men are men," Stottlemeyer said.

"What are you going to do now?"

Monk squeezed past Stottlemeyer to examine the clothes on the other bed.

Stottlemeyer sighed. "We'll question the hotel doormen, concierges, and busboys — they're usually the guys who put the clients in touch with the ladies in exchange for a commission. They'll give us a name. We'll round up all the hookers in the area and question them. And we'll talk with the escort services. Meanwhile, we'll keep our eye on the pawnbrokers and fences who'd be most likely to move the stolen merchandise."

"It sounds like a lot of work," I said.

"That's how it gets done most of the time," Stottlemeyer said, watching Monk, who took out his pen and began to examine the clothes with it. "How did things go at the convention?"

"We met some interesting people and learned a lot about the show."

"What did you learn about Stipe's murder?"

"You'd have to ask Mr. Monk about that," I said.

Stottlemeyer looked at Monk, who was using his pen to lift up one of the sleeves of the victim's discarded shirt.

"Well?" Stottlemeyer said.

"When did the maid discover the body?" Monk said.

"After lunch. She came in to clean the room and there he was," Stottlemeyer said. "I was asking you about your investigation of the Stipe murder."

"So she hadn't cleaned the room since yesterday."

"Yes, Monk, that would be the logical assumption."

"Actually, sir, she didn't clean the room

yesterday," Disher said, stepping in. "Emilia, the maid who ordinarily handles this floor, called in sick today with a stomach flu. Paola — that's the maid who found the body — usually cleans on the seventh floor. Paola took a double shift to cover for Emilia today."

"Thank you, Randy," Stottlemeyer said, then turned back to Monk. "The ME is waiting to take the body."

Monk nodded and stepped between Stottlemeyer and me to examine the clothes in the closet. I peered behind Monk to look at the captain.

"Which other *Beyond Earth* people are staying here besides Stipe?"

The captain peered behind Monk to answer me.

"Kingston Mills, the executive producer of the new show, and Judson Beck, the star. But the really interesting thing is that Stipe's ex-wife Arianna showed up here last night with her divorce lawyer, Howard Egger."

"Why did she do that?"

"I don't know," Stottlemeyer said. "We were going to ask her about it when this came up. In fact, we were just about done with this crime scene when you arrived."

Monk leaned back from the closet.

"The victim has antacids, a jeweler's loupe, sixty-five cents in change, and three bits of lint in the left front pocket of his overcoat."

"That's fascinating," Stottlemeyer said.

Monk held his hand out to me. "Do you have any lint?"

"I don't know," I said.

"We need another piece of lint and I'm lintless," Monk said. "I'm always lintless."

Stottlemeyer narrowed his eyes at Monk. "You want to put another piece of lint in Bozadjian's coat pocket?"

"And one penny," Monk said.

"That's bizarre even for you."

"It's the right thing to do," Monk said.

"Monk," Stottlemeyer said, "you can't."

"I'm respecting the dead."

"You're contaminating the crime scene. You can't add stuff to the victim's personal belongings."

"I know that." Monk took an evidence bag out of his pocket. "We'll put our lint and our penny in here so it's with the other stuff, but separate."

"What does it matter if he's got three pieces of lint and sixty-five cents? He's dead."

"So that means we stop caring? What about this man's family? What would they think if they knew we showed such callous disregard for him?"

Stottlemeyer took a deep breath, let it out slowly, then jammed his hand in his pocket. He pulled his hand out, sorted through his loose change, and dropped a penny in the evidence Baggie.

"Happy now?"

"You don't have any lint?"

Stottlemeyer looked down at his open palm. "Isn't that lint?"

"That's a crumb," Monk said.

Disher dug around in his pockets. "I have lint."

He opened his hand and showed it to Monk, who took a pair of tweezers from his breast pocket, carefully picked up the lint, and dropped it into the Baggie.

Monk placed the Baggie in Bozadjian's coat, patted it gently, and smiled at us.

"There," he said. "That's better. Can't you feel it?"

"I feel cracks forming in my skull," Stottlemeyer said. "Are we done here?"

"Not quite." Monk went into the bathroom and looked into a large toiletry bag that was on the counter near the sink.

We watched as Monk took out a separate vinyl case from the toiletry bag and unzipped it to reveal several tiny syringes, some vials, and a red box that was marked NEEDLE CLIPPER/BIOHAZARD-OUS WASTE and had a pinhole at one end.

"Bozadjian was using drugs," Monk said.

"That's insulin, Monk," Stottlemeyer said. "He was a diabetic. The hooker probably took his MedicAlert bracelet with the rest of his stuff."

Monk cocked his head at the spare bed, crouched in front of one of the corners, and untucked the blanket.

Stottlemeyer groaned. "Now what are you doing?"

Monk motioned to the top sheet, which was folded around the corner and tucked under the mattress.

"Admiring the way this sheet is tucked in," Monk said, motioning to the top sheet, which was folded around the corner in a half-triangle formation. "It's like Emilia gift-wrapped the mattress. She should get a raise."

"I don't really give a damn. I'd like to get out of here and the ME is ready to take the body."

"Just one more thing," Monk said and left the room. We all followed him.

"No, Monk, no more things. It's time to go," Stottlemeyer said.

Monk approached the maid. "Can you

show me the last room you cleaned?"

Paola looked at Disher, who looked at Stottlemeyer, who looked at me.

"The sooner Monk grades her cleaning, the sooner we can get out of here," I said.

Stottlemeyer nodded at Paola, giving his consent. She unlocked the door to the room across the hall and stood to one side while Monk went in.

He crouched at the foot of one of the beds and untucked the blanket. The top sheet was tucked in a way that made the corners of the bed seem square, with tight, sharp creases in the fold.

"Excellent work," Monk said to Paola. "You were taught to make beds by your father, who was in the Salvadoran military."

She nodded shyly.

"You learned well," Monk said. "You could bounce a peso off that bed."

"We don't have pesos in El Salvador," Paola said. "We have colóns."

"Yes, but a colón wouldn't bounce on this bed," Monk said. "A peso would."

"Good to know." Stottlemeyer turned to Disher. "Tell Dr. Hetzer he can take Mr. Bozadjian to the morgue now."

"That's not Mr. Bozadjian," Monk said.

Stottlemeyer gave him a look. "Do you know John Bozadjian?"

"No," Monk said.

"Then how do you know that's not him?"

"Simple. Because that man didn't stay in that room," Monk said. "And that room is registered to John Bozadjian."

"Isn't that the victim's stuff in the closets and the bathroom?" Disher said.

"Yes, those are definitely his clothes and toiletries."

"So what makes you think he's not John Bozadjian and that he wasn't staying in that room?"

"It's obvious," Monk said.

Stottlemeyer rubbed his temples. "I hate it when he says that."

"Why?" I asked.

"Because it's never obvious until he explains what the hell he's talking about, and then I feel like a damn fool for not seeing it myself."

Monk went back into the victim's room. "This man was killed for his jewelry."

"That's exactly what I said happened here." Stottlemeyer looked at me. "You heard me, right?"

I nodded. "That's definitely what the captain said, Mr. Monk."

"I'm not talking about his watches and rings," Monk said. "I'm talking about the diamonds."

126

"What diamonds?" Disher asked.

"The ones that this man was selling and that he was killed for," Monk said. "He was never with a prostitute and he was never in this room."

"He's in this room now," Stottlemeyer said. "He's right in front of you."

"I meant he was never in this room when he was alive," Monk said. "And everything we see in front of us proves it."

Stottlemeyer, Disher, and I looked around the room for a long, quiet moment.

"I don't see it," Disher said and glanced at me. "Do you see it?"

I shook my head and looked at the captain. He looked at Monk.

"Don't just stand there, Monk," Stottlemeyer said. "Tell us what happened."

He did.

CHAPTER ELEVEN:
MR. MONK SETS THE WORLD RIGHT

Monk spent much of his life in a state of despair. That despair appeared to be caused by many things, but I believe that essentially it all came down to one thing.

Disorder.

It was all around him and nothing he did seemed to change it.

Except when it came to murder.

The only time Monk conquered that despair, and all felt right in his world, was the moment when he solved a murder and told us how he did it.

It was during his summation, his explanation of how the homicide was committed and who did it, that he restored order, that he set right what was in disarray.

In that moment, Monk was a different man.

He was strong, confident, and secure.

Because he was right. And therefore, for a painfully short time, so was the world.

It made me feel good to see him at peace, and yet it also saddened me because I knew how short-lived it would be.

That brief moment was now.

" 'John Bozadjian' is a fake name that the killer used to rent this room, presumably because that was the name on the stolen credit cards he used to pay for it," Monk said. "The victim was staying on the seventh floor in the room where he was killed. The victim's room is now occupied by the killer, who, if he hasn't checked out already, will be wearing the victim's MedicAlert bracelet on his left wrist."

"The seventh floor?" Stottlemeyer said. "Isn't that where this maid usually works?"

"She's the one who moved the body down here in her linen cart after the murder and helped stage the scene," Monk said.

Paola let out a little gasp and took a few steps back into the hallway, looking around as if she might run. But with officers at both ends of the hall, there really wasn't anywhere for her to go.

"Well, if I didn't know you were right before, I do now just from the expression on her face," Stottlemeyer said, turning to Paola. "Do you want to tell us what happened, or are you going to make him do it?"

Paola chewed on her lower lip but said nothing. I knew Monk was relieved, for all the reasons I just shared with you.

He didn't want to be robbed of his moment. I think Stottlemeyer knew it, too, and was having some fun of his own.

"Sorry, Monk. I'm afraid you're going to have to do all the heavy lifting."

"The victim was a diamond dealer," Monk said.

"You got that from the loupe in his pocket," Disher said.

Monk shook his head. "It simply confirmed what I already knew from looking at the right-hand sleeves of his shirts and jackets."

He took out his pen, went to the spare bed, and lifted up the right sleeve of the victim's shirt.

"If you look closely, you can see abrasions and scratches on the cuffs. That's because he always had his merchandise case chained to his right wrist."

Now that he mentioned it, I could see the marks. I wouldn't have, though, if he hadn't pointed them out to me. But now they were glaringly obvious. I was beginning to understand how Stottlemeyer felt.

"The killer murdered the diamond dealer and assumed his identity."

"Why bother?" I asked. "Why not just run off with the diamonds and be done with it?"

"Because he wouldn't be done with it," Stottlemeyer said. "He'd still have to fence the stolen merchandise, which means taking a big risk and cutting someone else in on the score."

"The killer's plan was brilliantly simple," Monk said. "He was going to sell the diamonds to the legitimate buyers and take the money that would have gone to the dealer."

"What if the buyers had already met Bozadjian face-to-face?" Disher said.

"They hadn't, and the killer knew it, or he never would have done this," Monk said with a trace of impatience in his voice.

Disher picked up on it and looked stung. "Okay, let's say you're right. Where's the proof?"

"There's so much evidence to choose from."

"Like what?" Disher asked.

"Like those wineglasses," Monk said. "The victim was a diabetic. He wouldn't have had alcohol."

"I know diabetics who drink," Stottlemeyer said.

"Do you know any diabetics who can live without insulin?"

"He has insulin," Stottlemeyer said.

131

"But he couldn't have taken it," Monk said, leading us to the bathroom and showing us the victim's kit. "Here are the syringes, the insulin vials, and the needle clip. Ordinarily, he injects himself, then clips off the needle into this hazardous waste container, then throws out the syringe. He's been here since yesterday, the room hasn't been cleaned since he checked in, and yet there are no syringes in the trash. If he'd taken his insulin, there would be."

"He could have taken his shot somewhere else," Disher said.

"Doubtful," Monk said. "But even if he had, it wouldn't have done him any good. The insulin is supposed to be kept refrigerated or on ice. These vials aren't. Why aren't they in the minibar? And where is the ice pack that goes in his kit? I'll tell you."

"Of course you will," Stottlemeyer said.

"It's still in the minibar upstairs. The killer took the vials out of the minibar when he removed the victim's things, but it didn't occur to him to look in the freezer for the ice pack also. That was his crucial mistake."

"The insulin thing suggests that he was moved," Stottlemeyer said, "but it doesn't prove it."

"You're right," Monk said. "It doesn't. The bed proves it."

"The bed is from upstairs?" Disher said.

"Of course not. That would be ridiculous," Stottlemeyer said, but he hesitated, then turned to Monk. "Wouldn't it?"

"The bed wasn't moved," Monk said.

Stottlemeyer looked relieved. I think that for a moment there he was afraid Monk was going to contradict him and show that the bed had, indeed, been moved in some fiendishly clever way.

"Paola said she walked in to clean this room and found the body," Monk said. "So how could she have made the victim's bed?"

Monk pulled up the blanket so we could see how the top sheet was folded under the mattress of the bed the body was on.

"The top sheet on the corner of this bed is tucked using the Salvadoran fold," he continued. "The top sheet on the other bed is folded around the mattress corners using the classic gift-wrap method. That proves that this bed was made after Emilia, the usual maid, cleaned the room yesterday. Paola brought the body down from upstairs in her linen cart. She remade the bed before placing the body in it to remove any possible forensic evidence the killer might have left when *he* slept in the bed last night."

We all looked at Paola, who chewed on her lip some more. Things weren't going well for her and she knew it. So did we.

"You've convinced me, but we aren't going to be able to make a case on how she folds sheets," Stottlemeyer said. "The DA would laugh me out of his office."

"Use the wineglasses," Monk said. "The lipstick on the rim is hers. It's as good as a fingerprint. The DNA aside, her upper lip is chapped, which is why she chews on it. The lipstick impression is an exact match."

Stottlemeyer nodded. "Read this woman her rights, Lieutenant, and arrest her."

While Disher did that, I asked Monk the one question I still had.

"How did Paola know that Emilia would be sick today?"

"She poisoned her, of course," Monk said.

"I told Roger it would never work," Paola said, shaking her head. "But he said it was foolproof, that we'd be long gone before anyone realized what had happened."

"You probably would have been, too, if it wasn't for Monk," Stottlemeyer said.

I had to give the captain credit. He never tried to minimize Monk's brilliance for his own benefit. He always made sure that Monk knew his work was appreciated and that he got full credit for it, even if it was at Stottlemeyer's or the SFPD's expense.

Stottlemeyer had his faults, but failing to

cknowledge the accomplishments of others to relieve his own insecurities wasn't one of them.

"So, Paola, are you going to tell us where to find Roger?" Stottlemeyer asked. "Or are you going to take the murder rap for him while he enjoys piña coladas on a beach somewhere with his new girlfriend?"

"He's in room 717," she said without an instant's hesitation.

Stottlemeyer glanced at Monk. "You want to come along for the arrest?"

Monk shook his head. "Seven-seventeen is a very odd number, and that can't be good."

Stottlemeyer glanced at the corpse. "It certainly wasn't for him."

CHAPTER TWELVE:
MR. MONK SORTS OUT THE NUTS

Solving a murder put Monk in a much better state of mind. He'd set the world right and, in doing so, seemed to center himself, too.

He was eager to talk with anyone who'd been involved with Conrad Stipe — as long as they were in the Belmont and not back at the convention.

So we headed downstairs to the bar, where Stottlemeyer had left Kingston Mills, the new executive producer, and Judson Beck, the actor playing Captain Stryker.

I think part of the reason Monk was so motivated to stick around and work on the case was to avoid going home and dealing with the fact that Ambrose might be an Earthie. Or an Earther. Or whatever the *Beyond Earth* fans were calling themselves these days (I missed the panel discussion on that topic at the convention so I didn't know which term was politically correct in the "*Beyond Earth*–verse").

I was eager to get to the bar, too, but for an entirely different reason. I was starving.

We were in the stairwell, two flights from the lobby, when Monk stopped on the landing, something occurring to him.

"I forgot to trade cases with the captain," Monk said.

"Yes, you did."

"I should have made the deal with him *before* I solved the Bozadjian case. If I'd done that, we'd be on our way home by now and solving the Stipe case would no longer be my job."

"You got caught up in the moment," I said. "You were on a roll."

"I wish my whole life rolled."

"Don't we all," I said and passed him, continuing down the stairs. I was too hungry to stand around in a stairwell. "Besides, even if you did trade, you wouldn't have been able to walk away from the Stipe investigation."

"Yes, I would."

"Not as long as the case remained unsolved. You wouldn't have been able to stop thinking about it."

"I would have gladly endured the mental anguish," Monk said. "It would be easier than having to be around those crazy people."

"People like Ambrose?" I said, opening the door to the lobby and, metaphorically speaking, a whole lot more.

Monk ignored the question, as I knew he would, and walked past me to the bar, which was off to one side of the lobby.

It was a very masculine space, all dark woods and leather and bookcases filled with leather-bound literary classics, which were glued into place in case, God forbid, someone was gripped by the mad desire to actually read one of them.

I had no idea what Kingston Mills or Judson Beck looked like. But I knew that Beck was an actor, and probably something of a celebrity, so I looked for two men sitting alone and other people stealing furtive glances at them.

Using that strategy, I spotted the men in about ten seconds. They were sitting at a table in the back, where they could be seen by everyone in the room and, at the same time, could see everyone who came in. There were several empty glasses on the table and two bowls of mixed nuts.

Mills wore an untucked aloha shirt in a futile attempt to hide his big belly, which spilled over his khaki slacks. His shirt was so colorful that it seemed illuminated in the dim light of the bar.

Beck was in form-fitting Abercrombie & Fitch clothes that were stylishly pre-faded, pre-torn, and pre-stained and showed off all of his muscular build. He seemed acutely aware of everyone who was looking at him, which included himself, since he kept admiring his reflection in the mirror behind the bar.

I marched up to the two men with as much authority as I could muster, Monk trailing me.

"Mr. Mills, Mr. Beck, I'm Natalie Teeger and this is Adrian Monk, a special consultant to the police. Captain Stottlemeyer sent us down to talk to you."

"You're the famous Adrian Monk?" Kingston Mills stood up and offered his hand to Monk, who shook it. "Somebody pitched me a series about you."

"A series?" Monk motioned to me for a wipe. I gave him one.

"A weekly detective show for TV." Mills grinned and gestured at Monk cleaning his hands. "You really do that?"

"What?" Monk gave me the used wipe, which I put into a Baggie and shoved in my purse.

"Clean yourself with a disinfectant wipe every time you shake hands with somebody."

"Doesn't everyone?"

Mills chuckled and glanced at Judson Beck. "I thought it was just a gimmick the writer came up with for his pitch. The writer even rearranged the papers on my desk and put the magazines on my coffee table into chronological order."

"I hope you thanked him," Monk said.

"It was a good pitch," Mills said, "but I said the series would never work."

"Why not?" I asked as we sat down with them at the table.

"Who wants to watch a clean freak every week? It would be too damn irritating. So we worked on it over lunch and came up with something a lot better — a detective who is a sex addict. Can you see it?"

Monk's eyes widened in horror. "Oh God, I *can.*"

"And his assistant is a stripper. We're going to Showtime with it next week," Mills said. "It fits right in with their shows about the dope-dealing mother, the Vancouver lesbians, the bigamist, and the cop who is a serial killer."

"What are you calling it?" Beck asked.

"Murdergasm."

"Cool," Beck said. "If *Beyond Earth* tanks, think of me for that part."

"I think of you for every part, Jud. You're

that versatile and unique."

Monk looked at me with a pained expression. "I can *still* see it."

"Think of something else," I said, then turned to Mills. "We're more interested in *Beyond Earth* and who might have had a motive to kill Conrad Stipe."

"Who?" Beck asked.

"The creator of the show you're starring in," I said.

"Oh, you mean the old guy," Beck said.

"Jud didn't have much interaction with him," Mills explained to me. "Stipe was really on the creative periphery of the show."

"But he created it," I said.

"Yes, but I *reimagined* it," Mills said.

Monk grabbed my arm. "Help me. It won't go away."

"Look." I pointed to the two bowls on the table. "Mixed nuts. And pretzels, too."

It worked. Monk immediately forgot about the sex addict detective and focused instead on this urgent public health crisis.

"What were they thinking?" Monk reached into his jacket for rubber gloves and prepared to deal with the problem. "You might want to push your chairs away from the table. This could get ugly."

I turned to Mills. "So what was Stipe's role on the show?"

"We were contractually obligated to give Stipe a consulting producing credit, but it was meaningless. He wasn't actually part of the day-to-day production," Mills said. "We only kept him around for publicity purposes and to draw the niche viewers."

"Niche viewers?" I asked.

Monk laid out napkins on the table, emptied the bowls onto them, and began sorting the nuts and pretzels.

"The original fans," Mills said, watching Monk. "We're only using them as a publicity hook. It gets us press. But it's just a launching pad for a larger promotional offensive. Our goal is to expand the franchise to a much broader, mainstream audience of intelligent, educated, free-spending consumers who have heard of the original show but probably never saw it."

"Don't you think the fans know what you're doing and resent being used?"

"They're morons who dress up in Halloween costumes and speak a fictional language from a crap TV show," Mills said. "Who cares what they think?"

I waved the waitress over. I ordered a hamburger and fries for myself and six empty bowls for Monk to use for sorting and sent her away before he could lecture her on the dangers of mixing nuts and baked goods.

"If you have such disdain for Stipe, the fans, and the original series, why are you bothering with *Beyond Earth* at all?"

"Because it's a pre-sold franchise," he said. "A brand."

"But it was a failure," I said.

"That doesn't matter," Mills said. "It existed before and people know that."

"Why not just come up with something new?"

"New is old school. It's too risky for the networks and for the audiences. People are much more comfortable with the familiar," Mills said. "Reimagination is the *new* New."

"It's more authentic," Beck said.

I glanced at Monk, who was carefully organizing the almonds, peanuts, cashews, and pretzels into individual piles.

I knew better than to assume from his silence and preoccupation with his task that he wasn't absorbing every word. But it irritated me anyway, since I was doing all the talking and I had no idea what to ask that was relevant besides "Did you kill him?"

So I just asked whatever interested me, hoping they'd say something that would help Monk later.

"How could it be more authentic?" I said. "It's a remake."

"A reimagination," Mills corrected me.

"What's the difference?"

"We're not remaking what was, we're going back and making *Beyond Earth* the show that it should have been," Mills said. "It's a new beginning. A fresh imagining of a pre-imagined concept. We're making it real."

"It's a show with inside-out aliens," I said. "That's not real."

"We're giving it an internal, unflinchingly honest reality consistent with the reality we experience every day," Mills said.

"Authenticity," Beck said, nodding sagely.

"The premise of the show is that humanity was destroyed and now all that's left of mankind are these people trapped in a spaceship," Mills said. "They should be miserably depressed, filthy, and barely scratching out an existence. But when you watch the original show, everything is bright and colorful and everybody is happy-go-lucky. That's not being true to the internal reality of the fictional universe."

"It's inauthentic," Beck said.

"Our show is more visceral," Mills said. "You can smell the sweat."

Monk looked up, disgusted. "Why would you want to smell sweat?"

"It's the scent of authenticity," Beck said.

"I wouldn't want to smell that either,"

Monk said and started brushing the piles of nuts into individual bowls. I told you he was listening.

"The characters are more psychologically complex now," Beck said. "Take my character, Captain Stryker. The only way he can deal with his inner turmoil, the conflict between his despair and his need to be a strong leader for mankind, is to mate with every female alien he can, no matter what they look like. They just have to be the female of their species."

"So, basically, he's a pervert," I said.

"But that's okay," Mills said. "He's a noble pervert that the audience can relate to."

"Because he's authentic," Beck said.

"Not many actors have the chops to pull off an edgy character like this and make him sympathetic and heroic," Mills said, putting his arm around Beck. "But Jud has chops to spare."

"How did Stipe feel about his series being reimagined into a crew of noble perverts?"

"All he cared about was getting a check," Mills replied. "He hasn't had a career since *Beyond Earth* was canceled. He saw this as an opportunity to make some money and maybe get back in the game. If *Beyond Earth* is a hit, everybody wins."

"Except the original fans," I said.

"They are only a small fraction of the audience that we're aiming for," Mills said.

"But it's more than a show to them," I said. "You're messing with their lives. Weren't you worried they might get really pissed off?"

"Not really," Mills said.

"Did Stipe get any threats?"

"Not that I know of."

"Are you getting any?" I asked.

"Just some hate mail and petitions from the Galactic Uprising," Mills said. "But I don't take it seriously."

"Even after what happened today?"

"Stipe betrayed the fans, not me," Mills said. "They got the guy they were angry with. I'm just a hired gun doing his job, which is making a TV show that will reach the widest possible audience."

"They might not see the distinction," I said.

"They do. I'm an outsider. I don't know anything about the *Beyond Earth* culture and I don't care. They know that. I'm exactly who they think I am. They don't have anything invested in me," Mills said. "But they were devoted to Stipe. They listened to his stories again and again and again and supported him for decades with

146

their comic book money. They thought he was one of them, that he lived in their same little world and was as passionate about it as they were. Well, somebody finally noticed that he wasn't, it was all an act, and *Beyond Earth* was just a paycheck to him. That's certainly all it is to me, too."

"Speaking of money," I said, "if *Beyond Earth* succeeds you won't have to share the credit or the money with him now that he's dead."

"I wouldn't have shared the credit anyway," Mills said. "Stipe was, and would have remained, a has-been. He had a pay-or-play deal, so the salary checks come whether he's alive or dead and the back-end profit formula doesn't change, either. The money will just go to his estate now."

"So who controls his estate?" I asked.

Mills shrugged. "I don't know. We didn't talk about his personal life. Actually, we didn't talk at all. I told my secretary to ignore his calls."

Monk stood up and carried away his bowls of sorted nuts and pretzels.

"Hey," Beck said, "where are you going with those?"

"I'm putting them into individual Baggies, sealing them, and throwing them away, of course."

"Why?" Beck said.

"Because the nuts are contaminated," Monk said.

"No, they aren't," Beck said. "They've been right here in the bowl."

"Mixed together," Monk said gravely.

"To put it in *Beyond Earth* terms," I said, "it's like mixing matter with anti-matter."

"If that wasn't bad enough, countless numbers of strangers have touched those nuts with their bare hands," Monk said. "Who knows where those hands have been and what they've been doing?"

Monk shuddered at the thought. So did I. When he put it like that, the idea of eating those nuts did sound pretty disgusting.

"But I'm hungry," Beck said. "I haven't finished eating them."

"It would be healthier to eat a bowl of rat droppings," Monk said while walking away with the bowls. "You'll thank me later."

Beck stared after him. "What's his problem?"

"He's just being authentic," I said. "Authentically Monk."

CHAPTER THIRTEEN:
MR. MONK
AND THE EYE

Kingston Mills and Judson Beck left and while I ate my lunch, Monk went from table to table, gathering up the bowls of mixed nuts, sorting them into Baggies, and throwing them all out.

This did not go over well with the patrons, the waitresses, or the bartender. Someone called security, but I guess the guards had been briefed that Monk was with the police, so the bartender was told to let it drop.

Monk, however, felt it was his duty to instruct the bar staff and the security guards in the proper procedure for distributing nuts to diners, which is as follows:

Each type of nut or cracker must be in its own bowl. The bowls can be shared as long as all the patrons at the table are wearing rubber gloves.

"It's your duty to rigorously enforce this," Monk told the security staff. "For the good of humanity."

The security guards didn't look to me like they were ready to shoulder the burden of protecting humanity. And rather than follow Monk's draconian rules, the bartender chose not to offer nuts and pretzels at all, at least not while Monk was in the building.

It was a wise decision.

I didn't intercede in the fracas because I was tired, hungry, and wanted to eat my late lunch in peace.

But I couldn't observe what was going on with the complete detachment I desired and, even though I wasn't directly involved in the dispute, I felt my neck and shoulder muscles tighten with stress anyway.

Stottlemeyer and Disher came down and joined me, which drew Monk back to my table and gave the bar staff a reprieve.

"We arrested Roger," Disher said. "He was in room 717 in the midst of selling his diamonds to some local jewelers when we crashed his party. He was stunned to see us."

"Roger was sure that he'd committed the perfect murder," Stottlemeyer said.

"But he made the crucial mistake of underestimating the legendary brilliance of the San Francisco Police Department," Disher said proudly.

"I'd say Roger's estimate of our legendary

brilliance was pretty accurate. He just didn't figure on Monk." Stottlemeyer looked at Monk. "So, did you solve any other murders while we were gone?"

"Was there another one?" Monk asked. "Between the dead bodies and the mixed nuts, it's a miracle this hotel is still in business."

"I was talking about Stipe." Stottlemeyer reached for one of my leftover fries, but before his fingers could get to my plate, Monk pushed it out of reach.

"You should be wearing gloves," Monk said.

"The fries aren't evidence," Stottlemeyer said.

"Have you washed your hands lately?"

"I was only going to touch the fry that I intended to eat."

"So you'd just be poisoning yourself instead of yourself and others," Monk said. "Are you a man or an ape?"

"Never mind," Stottlemeyer said. "I shouldn't be eating fries anyway."

Disher reached into his coat pocket and handed me a DVD. "I had this made for Monk. It's a copy of the security camera video of Stipe's shooting."

"Thank you," Monk said.

"Don't let this DVD out of your sight,"

Disher said. "The press would love to get their hands on this."

"We'll guard it with our lives," I said.

"Don't bother," Stottlemeyer said. "I'm sure the footage will be all over the news tonight. The clerk at the hotel probably knocked off a copy before we got there and is auctioning it off to the highest bidder as we speak."

"You're awfully cynical," I said.

" 'Cynical' is just another word for 'realistic,' " Stottlemeyer said. "Did you get any leads from Kingston Mills or Judson Beck?"

"Not really," I said.

"On the contrary," Monk said. "We discovered another motive for Stipe's murder."

"We did?" I said.

"Conrad Stipe's consulting producer salary and his profits from the show," Monk said. "If we follow the money, it could lead us to the killer."

I guess I didn't do such a bad job of questioning them after all.

"You think someone made it look like a fan killed Stipe to distract us from the real motive?" Stottlemeyer asked. "That would certainly explain why Stipe was shot in broad daylight, in front of witnesses, and in full view of security cameras."

"Or the killer was a drug-crazed freak," Monk said.

"It sounds to me like we should have a talk with Arianna Stipe," Stottlemeyer said. "And her divorce lawyer, Howard Egger."

"Do you need me for that?" Disher asked.

Stottlemeyer gave him a look. "You have a pressing engagement somewhere else?"

"There are some leads I'd like to follow on the Lorber desecration before the trail gets cold," Disher said. "It's been my experience that the first two days are critical in cases like these."

"You've never had a case like this," Stottlemeyer said.

"I'm talking about the experience I'm having now," Disher said. "I can feel the chill."

"You're feeling my cold, stony gaze," Stottlemeyer said. "What have you got so far?"

Disher eagerly whipped out his notebook and flipped through several pages to refresh himself.

"The key card that the shooter used to enter and exit the Burgerville headquarters was registered to Brandon Lorber, who was issued only two cards, one for himself and one for his wife, Veronica," Disher said. "She says that she still has hers and that her husband reported his key card missing two weeks ago. He was issued a new one by Archie Applebaum, their security guy, right away."

"Did you find Lorber's new key card?" Monk asked.

"It was on his desk, beside the financial documents he was reading when he died. Our forensic accountant is taking a look at those documents now."

"Why?" Stottlemeyer said.

"Maybe there's a clue in the figures that could lead us to a motive and whoever shot Lorber," Disher said. "We have to find him before he strikes again."

"Before he shoots someone else who is already dead," Stottlemeyer said.

"That's only how it appears," Disher said.

"Lorber was definitely dead before he was shot," Stottlemeyer said. "The medical examiner confirmed it."

"Maybe the shooter thought Lorber was sleeping and didn't want to wake him before killing him," Disher said.

"That's your theory?" the captain asked.

"It's one of several that we're working on."

"We?" Stottlemeyer said.

"Last month a consumer group announced that Burgerville secretly used beef extract to add flavor to their French fries," Disher said. "The revelations infuriated the thousands of vegetarians who have been gobbling up the fries for years."

"You think he was shot by a homicidal vegan?" Stottlemeyer asked.

"They get pretty riled up when they eat flesh," Disher said.

"But if he was already dead," Monk said, "why bother shooting him at all? And why with the cold precision of a professional assassin?"

"To show that you can't escape their wrath," Disher said. "Even if you're dead."

"Are those your only suspects?" Stottlemeyer said.

"Last year, a guy bought coffee at the drive-thru window at a Burgerville in Pleasanton and spilled it on his crotch," Disher said. "He sued the company, claiming the scalding liquid neutered him. He lost and vowed to get even."

"Uh-huh," Stottlemeyer said. "So you're looking for either a deranged vegan or a vengeful eunuch."

"We have other theories," Disher said. "But I think it would be premature to go into them until I've had a chance to follow up on some other leads."

"Fine, you go do that," Stottlemeyer said. "We'll just muddle along here without you."

"Thank you, sir. If you get in a bind, or

just want to run stuff by me, you can find me at the SDU command center."

"You mean your desk," Stottlemeyer said.

"That was before," Disher said. "Now it's a command center."

Disher hurried away. Stottlemeyer sighed and waved a waitress over to the table.

"What's a guy got to do to get some nuts in this bar?" he said.

Monk and I took the stairs to Arianna Stipe's fourth-floor suite. Stottlemeyer took the elevator and got there ahead of us to handle all the introductions.

When we walked in, Howard Egger, the former Mrs. Stipe's lawyer, had his back to us and was making some drinks at the wet bar.

Arianna stood in the center of the room with her hands on her hips and faced the captain in her Juicy Couture T-shirt, Free City hooded sweat-jacket, and True Religion jeans. Her casual outfit was more expensive than most wedding dresses. The clothes were also intended to be worn by women a good thirty years younger and thirty pounds thinner than she was.

"I don't know what I can possibly do to help," she said with a slight lisp. "I was in flight to San Francisco from LA when

Conrad was killed."

I could understand why she was lisping. It must have been a real struggle for her to speak. Her lips looked like they'd been removed from the world's largest salmon and implanted on her face, which had apparently been peeled by an industrial laser, pulled taut over the top of her skull, and paralyzed into marble firmness with enough botulinum toxin to wipe out a city.

Her eyebrows had been tweezed away and replaced with arched tattoos that gave her a permanent expression of someone who sat on something very, very cold. Her straightened teeth were capped an unnatural, gleaming white that seemed to capture and reflect all the light in the room. Her breasts were as large, round, and hard-looking as NBA regulation basketballs. Perhaps they were.

I guessed her age to be about sixty, though it was hard to tell. The inside-out aliens on *Beyond Earth* looked more human than she did.

I tried hard not to scream.

"Most people don't usually start a conversation with me by offering an alibi," Stottlemeyer said. "Guilty conscience?"

"I like to get right to the point," she said.

"So do I." Howard turned around, carrying a drink for himself and one for Arianna. "Do you regard my client as a suspect?"

He was younger than his client by a decade, trim and tailored, wearing a crisp pin-striped double-breasted suit and a black patch over his left eye. He could have stepped right out of a glossy magazine advertisement for Jack Daniel's.

Monk ducked behind Stottlemeyer like a frightened child.

"Your client doesn't seem very heartbroken by her husband's murder," Stottlemeyer said, glancing over his shoulder at Monk.

"Ex-husband," Arianna corrected and sipped daintily at her drink.

"They are legally divorced," Howard added.

"But you were married for some time," Stottlemeyer said, sidestepping away from Monk, who followed him.

"I was a devoted and loving wife for thirty years, through good times and bad, through his adultery, drinking, chronic unemployment, and countless other embarrassments and betrayals. The last few years were especially hard when all we were living on was the proceeds from his *Beyond Earth* convention appearances. I finally had enough. I had my needs."

She stopped sipping so daintily and drank

half the contents of her glass.

"So why did you come here?" I asked.

"To kill him," she said.

"She means that figuratively, of course," Howard said.

Stottlemeyer took another step to one side, but Monk shadowed him again. Annoyed, the captain turned to look at Monk, who shielded his eyes with his hand.

"There's an entire hotel room here, Monk. Do you really have to stand right behind me?"

"Yes," Monk said.

"Do you mind telling me why?"

Monk gestured to the lawyer. "He's wearing a patch over one eye."

"I lost my eye in a car accident," Howard said.

"You should go and look for it," Monk said. "Right now. Don't come back without it."

"I'm afraid it's long gone, Mr. Monk," the lawyer said. "The accident happened twenty years ago."

Stottlemeyer faced Arianna, and Monk ducked back behind him again.

"Why did you want to kill your ex-husband?" Stottlemeyer asked. "Figuratively speaking, of course."

"Two weeks after our divorce was final I

opened up the *Hollywood Reporter* and there was a big article announcing that UBS Network had signed a multimillion-dollar deal to bring *Beyond Earth* back as a new TV series," she said. "Conrad never mentioned that anybody was interested in reviving the show while we were dividing our assets and negotiating our divorce settlement. He waited to close the deal until our divorce was final so he could cheat me out of my fair share of the windfall."

"He perpetrated a fraud," Howard said. "We came here to apprise him of that fact and attempt to reach an amicable financial settlement."

"And failing that?" Stottlemeyer asked.

"We'd sue his scrawny ass into oblivion. For the last twenty years, his career was in the sewer. Nobody in the business returned his calls. All he had was *Beyond Earth* and those fans who thought he was some kind of god," Arianna said. "I knew he was sleeping with Earthies at those conventions. I put up with it because it was the only thing keeping him going, the only way he could maintain his self-respect. But I've got self-respect too and it reached the point where I had to walk away from the marriage to keep it."

The point probably came when she realized that no amount of plastic surgery would make her as attractive to her husband as an adoring Earthie. And, of course, the more she went under the knife, the more conventions he had to attend to pay for it all, and the more Earthies he'd bed down.

It was a sad story that was written all over her body.

"I'll tell you this," she said. "I didn't put up with Conrad for all those years to get screwed when the galactic gravy train finally docked at our space station."

Arianna finished her drink and held out her empty glass to Howard for a refill. He dutifully took the glass from her and went to the wet bar.

Monk peeked out from behind Stottle-meyer now that Howard's back was turned to us.

"Have you considered wearing a patch over your other eye?" Monk asked the lawyer.

"No," Howard said as he poured Arianna another drink.

"You should," Monk said.

"But I wouldn't be able to see anything," Howard said.

"Maybe you could get one of those see-through patches."

"There aren't any."

"Then I guess you're out of luck," Monk said.

"I'm not the one with the problem," Howard said, returning with Arianna's drink. "*You* are."

"I have both of my eyes," Monk said, ducking back behind Stottlemeyer. "You don't and the rest of us have to see it. Try to show some sensitivity to others."

"*Me?*" Howard said.

"Ignore him, Mr. Egger," Stottlemeyer said and looked over his shoulder at Monk. "Just once, I would like to conduct an interview without being constantly inter-rupted because you're distracted by some minor detail like a can of 7-Up or an eye patch. It throws me off my game."

"That's exactly what they want," Monk said.

"You think he plucked out his eyeball just so you'd be distracted and irritate the hell out of me?"

"He's a lawyer," Monk said. "They're cunning. And who knows how far he'd go to protect his lover from a possible murder charge?"

"I didn't murder anyone and we're not lovers," Arianna said.

"So why are your lip balm and hand cream on one nightstand?" Monk said.

"And the suction cup and hydrogen peroxide he uses for removing and cleaning his acrylic eye, the one he's chosen not to wear right now, on the other side of the bed?"

We all turned to look at the bed. I don't know how Monk noticed all that from behind Stottlemeyer's back.

"She is legally divorced," Howard said indignantly. "Who she sleeps with isn't relevant to your investigation."

"But the fact that she's a liar is relevant and so is the fact that you've decided to wear that patch instead of your fake eye just to unnerve me," Monk said. "What are you hiding?"

"We were in a plane at the time of the murder," Arianna said. "*That's* a fact."

"So you keep telling us," Stottlemeyer said. "You could have hired a Snork to kill your ex-husband for you."

"That's an absurd and inflammatory accusation," Howard said. "She would have had nothing to gain from Conrad Stipe's death."

"I'm recently divorced too," Stottlemeyer said. "It just occurred to me there's still one thing I haven't gotten around to taking care of."

"What's that?" I asked, just to be helpful.

"Changing my will," Stottlemeyer said to

me. Then he glanced at Arianna. "If I catch a bullet on the job, my wife is still the sole beneficiary, which is okay by me, since we've got kids and she'd have to raise them. You don't have kids, but I bet your ex-husband didn't change his will yet either. He probably didn't see the need, since he was in good health and planned on being around a whole lot longer. Gee, I wonder who gets all his money now that he's dead?"

"I wouldn't know," Arianna said.

"Roll over in bed tonight and ask your lawyer," Stottlemeyer said. "I'm sure he could tell you."

"Don't say anything more, Arianna," Howard said. "This courtesy interview is finished."

"Just when it was getting interesting," Stottlemeyer said. "What a shame."

The three of us walked out and Howard slammed the door behind us. The captain faced Monk in the corridor.

"Would you have been any less unnerved by a fake eye instead of a patch?" Stottlemeyer asked him.

"Not really," Monk said.

"I didn't think so," the captain said.

CHAPTER FOURTEEN:
MR. MONK
AND THE SECRET

Ambrose was waiting for us at the front door when we arrived at his house. He looked distraught.

"Please tell me that you're investigating Conrad Stipe's murder," Ambrose said as we came in.

"How did you know about that?" Monk asked.

"I don't leave the house, but I'm not living in a cave," Ambrose said. "I know what's going on out there. The news is all over the Internet."

"So you know who Conrad Stipe is," Monk said.

"Of course I do," Ambrose said. "I'm devastated. He was a great man, an original thinker, and a true visionary. You have to find whoever killed him, Adrian."

Monk narrowed his eyes at his brother. "Do you have something you want to tell me?"

"About what?"

"About your shameful secret life," Monk said.

"I don't have a secret life," Ambrose said. "Shameful or otherwise."

"When nobody is around, do you wear a rubber elephant trunk?"

"There's never anybody around," Ambrose said. "And if you're referring to Mr. Snork's olfactory appendage, you're revealing your ignorance, Adrian. It may resemble an elephant's trunk, but everybody knows it's anatomically different in many significant ways."

"So you admit you're one of those Earthie freaks," Monk said.

"Mr. Monk," I began, but Ambrose held his hand up to stop me.

"It's okay, Natalie," Ambrose said, then turned to Monk. "We prefer to be called Earthers. 'Earthie' is a derogatory term, especially when combined with 'freak.' "

"How many years have you been hiding this from me?"

"I haven't hidden anything from you."

"You never told me that you were a member of a cult," Monk said.

"It's not a cult," Ambrose said. "It's a group of creative, open-minded people who enjoy the show, love the characters, and

166

embrace the ideals at the heart of Conrad Stipe's vision of the future."

Monk nodded. "How long have you been dropping acid?"

"Acid?" Ambrose said.

"You know what I'm talking about," Monk said. "Boomers. Electric Kool-Aid, Purple Haze. Yellow Sunshine. Momma's Pudding."

"Momma's Pudding?" I said.

"You heard me," Monk said. "Jungle Juice. Blue Cheer. Satan's Candy. Window Pane. The Frisco Speedball. Walking the Ugly Dog."

"You think I'm taking LSD?" Ambrose said, then turned to me. "That's short for lysergic acid diethylamide, an extremely potent hallucinogen."

"Thanks for clearing that up for me," I said.

"I don't know what to think anymore, Ambrose," Monk said. "God only knows what twisted acts of madness and depravity you're engaged in."

That didn't exactly narrow the field of possible behavior. Monk believed that eating at a salad bar was an act of depravity.

"Just because you don't understand something doesn't make it wrong," Ambrose said. "There's nothing illegal, immoral, or shameful about enjoying a work of art in all of its detail and complexity and sharing that experience with others."

"If it's all so innocent," Monk said, "why haven't you ever told me about this before?"

"You never asked," Ambrose said.

"But now your secret is out."

"My interest in *Beyond Earth* is hardly a secret," Ambrose said. "I've written half a dozen books about the show, its mythology, and its culture. If you had the slightest interest in my life, you would know that. But you don't care, Adrian. You never have. What do you really know about me?"

"Now I know that you're a freak," Monk said.

"I like *Beyond Earth*," I said. "Does that make me a depraved freak too?"

"Do you speak Dratch?"

"No," I said.

Monk motioned to Ambrose. "He does. It's a fictional language."

"It's not anymore," Ambrose said. "Hundreds of people speak Dratch, more than there are speaking Sanskrit these days. If you knew anything about *Beyond Earth,* and what it means to me, you wouldn't be so dismissive of it."

"It's a TV show," Monk said.

"It's much more than that to me," Ambrose said.

"How could it be?"

"Look around, Adrian. This is my world, the walls of this house. But *Beyond Earth* takes me away to a galaxy of wonder and adventure, to distant planets full of fascinating cultures and amazing creatures. Thanks to Conrad Stipe, I've traveled to places I could never have imagined."

"You haven't gone anywhere," Monk said. "It's not real. It's a fantasy."

"The ideals aren't," Ambrose said. "The community isn't. I have lots of friends out there, thanks to *Beyond Earth.* They talk to me all the time. They read my books. They are more a part of my life than you are. How can you tell me that's not real? It's very real to me."

"You need to get out more," Monk said.

Ambrose turned and marched into the kitchen, slamming the door behind him. I looked at Monk. He looked at me.

"What?" he said with a shrug.

"Don't you think you were a little hard on him?" I asked.

"He's one of *those* people, Natalie. He's probably in the kitchen right now drinking a 7-Up and calling for an appointment with a plastic surgeon. Next time we see him, he'll have pointed ears."

"He's your brother."

"That's what's so shocking. How could we have grown up in this house together and turned out so different?"

"Ambrose is a very sweet, sensitive man," I said. "So what if he loses himself in a TV show? He's all alone here. Can you really blame him for having a rich fantasy life? It's not like he has a lot of people to talk to."

"The front door is right there," Monk said. "There's nothing stopping him from walking outside."

"If that was a revolving door, you'd be a prisoner inside this house, too."

"No one would put a revolving door in a house."

"You're missing my point."

"You haven't made one."

I sighed and decided to take a different approach. "When was the last time you called Ambrose?"

"I'm not much of a phone person," Monk said. "It's not safe."

"Phones are perfectly safe, Mr. Monk."

"Haven't you ever heard of communicable diseases?" Monk rolled his shoulders. "Phones. That's where the communication starts."

"Okay," I said, resisting the almost irresistible compulsion to strangle him to death.

"When was the last time you read one of his books?"

"I've never had to assemble a dollhouse, repair a dishwasher, or learn to speak a fictional language spoken by freaks."

"I really wish you'd stop saying that about your brother."

"Why are your hands at your side and clenched into fists?"

"Never mind that," I said. "Ambrose is a versatile and talented author, which you would know if you'd ever read one of his books. I've read lots of them. He's got a real gift, Mr. Monk. He's great at explaining things and making even the most difficult ideas and tasks seem easy to understand. In a way, he's just like you."

"I don't see how."

"To a lot of people, installing a new piece of software or a new component into their home stereo system can be just as baffling as an unsolved homicide. But Ambrose solves the mystery for them. Maybe he can help you solve this one."

"Ambrose doesn't know the first thing about homicide investigation."

"But he knows everything about *Beyond Earth* and you don't," I said. "He could save you from having to spend a lot more time at that convention. Besides, Conrad Stipe meant a lot to him and helping to solve this murder could give him a positive way to work through his grief. You and I both know how important that is."

"It's no use. The investigation is out there." Monk tipped his head towards the door. "Ambrose won't leave the house."

"So we bring the investigation to him." I reached into my purse and took out the DVD that Disher had given me. "We can start with this."

"I don't know," he said.

I threw the DVD at him. It hit him squarely in the chest. He fumbled with it, catching it before it landed on the floor.

"That hurt." He rubbed his chest.

"Good," I said. "I was beginning to think you didn't have any feelings left."

He saw me glaring at him and shuffled off to the kitchen without another word.

Monk slowly opened the door. Ambrose sat at the table, spraying a bottle of Lysol with Lysol and wiping it clean with a paper towel. Until that moment, I had never seen anybody disinfect their disinfectant before.

"Doing a little housework?" Monk asked.

"It's not like I have an assistant to do it for me," Ambrose said. "We can't all live a life of luxury."

"I could use your help," Monk mumbled.

"Did you say something, Adrian?"

Monk cleared his throat. "I could use your expertise on the Stipe investigation."

"You aren't ashamed of me?"

"I'm not ashamed of you, Ambrose," Monk said. "As long as you promise not to wear an elephant trunk in public."

"I'm never in public."

"Then we're good," Monk said.

"I'd like to help," Ambrose said.

"Even though Stipe sold out and Kingston Mills is 'reimagining' everything about *Beyond Earth*?" I asked.

"I'm not happy about the new show, but that's all it is, a *new* show with the same name. They are starting from the beginning, not picking up where the original show left off, and they're using new actors. So it doesn't really change anything. Those original episodes still exist. They always will."

"You weren't mad at Conrad Stipe?" Monk asked.

"I'm sure he had his reasons for letting the studio and Kingston Mills do a new version of the show," Ambrose said. "Who am I to judge him?"

"I think you may be in the minority," I said.

"On the contrary," Ambrose said. "Most of the fans are glad to see the show coming back in any form, because it will renew interest in the original series. The Galactic Uprising speaks for a minority. You have to remember there were a lot of fans who were vehemently against the animated version of *Beyond Earth* and now it's considered canon."

"Canon?" Monk said.

"Part of the official *Beyond Earth* mythology and timeline," Ambrose said.

"Who decides whether it's 'official' or not?" Monk asked.

"It arises from a consensus among fans, experts, and Conrad Stipe, of course."

We went into the den. I sat next to Ambrose on the couch in front of the TV. The complete boxed set of *Beyond Earth* episodes and a box of tissues were on the coffee table. I figured that Ambrose must have been having a little *Beyond Earth* marathon as a tribute to Stipe.

Monk began by explaining what we knew and who our suspects were.

"Right now, we think Stipe was killed either by a disgruntled fan or by a disgruntled ex-wife. But so far, we don't have any evidence except this security camera footage, which was taken from four different security cameras mounted around the parking lot and convention center at the San

Francisco Airporter Motor Inn."

He put the DVD into the player and hesitated before pressing the PLAY button on the remote.

"What you're about to see is a murder, Ambrose. It's not an act. It's real," Monk said. "Are you sure you're ready for this?"

Ambrose bit his lip and nodded.

Monk hit PLAY.

Even though I'd already seen the footage and knew what I was going to see, it was still startling and shockingly violent. The screen was divided into quarters, and in each one was a different view of sudden death.

The taxi pulled up. Stipe got out. Mr. Snork emerged from behind the Dumpster, shot Stipe in the chest, and ran into the convention hall.

This time I focused mostly on the quarter that showed Stipe's face and the horrifying mix of shock, disbelief, and ultimately profound sadness on it as he dropped to his knees and then pitched forward, dead.

Monk and I looked at Ambrose. Tears welled up in his eyes.

"Excuse me," he said hoarsely. He got up and hurried out of the room.

Monk glared at me. "Happy now?"

"Of course not, Mr. Monk."

"This was your idea," Monk said. "All we've done is hurt him more."

"I thought it might help him," I said.

"To see someone he admired shot dead?" Monk said. "What was I thinking listening to you? This was wrong, Natalie. Very, very wrong."

I had to agree. I felt terrible.

Monk bent down and ejected the DVD. He was putting it back in the jewel case when Ambrose returned.

"What are you doing, Adrian?"

"We're done," Monk said. "I should have known better. I'm sorry you had to see that."

"Me too," Ambrose said, sitting down beside me. "Play it again."

"You can't be serious," Monk said.

I was surprised, too.

"I have to see it again, Adrian. I was overcome with shock and emotion the first time. I probably will be again, but I'm going to keep watching it until I know every detail by heart."

I put my hand on Ambrose's knee. "You don't have to do this."

"Yes, I do, Natalie. The killer is on that tape. And we're going to catch him."

CHAPTER FIFTEEN:
Mr. Monk
and the Details

Each time we watched the footage, I tried to concentrate on the events playing out in just one of the four quarters of the screen, but I couldn't stop myself from glancing at the others.

We watched the shooting again and again without comment. Each time the tape ended, either Monk or Ambrose would say "again" and one of them would hit PLAY on the remote.

The more Ambrose watched the tape, the less emotional he became, until he was sitting on the edge of the couch like Monk. I could really see the family resemblance in their faces, in the intensity of their concentration.

Finally, Monk rolled his shoulders and tipped his head from side to side, trying to work out that psychosomatic kink in his neck that reflected a glitch in his mind, a piece of information that refused to fit in.

"This doesn't make sense," he said, freezing the picture on Mr. Snork raising the gun and about to squeeze the trigger.

"It seems pretty straightforward to me," I said. "It's a shooting. You've had much stranger cases."

"But look at Mr. Snork when he shoots Stipe —" Monk began.

"That's not Mr. Snork," Ambrose interrupted.

"That's who he's dressed up as, so for the sake of discussion let's just call him Mr. Snork."

"Mr. Snork would never violate the Cosmic Commandments of Interplanetary Relations," Ambrose said. "He wrote them."

"That isn't Mr. Snork the fictional character. It's someone dressed like Mr. Snork," Monk said. "He just steps up and without hesitation shoots Stipe right in the heart."

"He's defiling the uniform," Ambrose said.

"Mr. Snork didn't hesitate, didn't aim — it was a perfect shot," Monk said, ignoring Ambrose.

"Maybe he's a hunter," I said. "Or has some experience target shooting."

"The uniform," Ambrose said, pointing at the screen. "Look at his Confederation uniform."

Monk shook his head dismissively. "It's

not the same as shooting a human being. He didn't even wince at the blood spatter or the sound of the gunshot. It's like he's done it a thousand times before."

"It's an orange shirt with the silver starburst insignia," Ambrose pointed out as he rose from his seat and went over to the TV. "That's from the first season."

"And if he's an angry fan, where's the emotion?" Monk said. "Why is he so calm?"

"Adrian," Ambrose said, tapping the screen with his finger, "he's wearing a season-one shirt."

"So what?" Monk snapped at him.

"But he's got season-two ears," Ambrose said significantly. "Take a good look. It's so obvious, I feel like a fool for not noticing it from the start."

"That's another thing," Monk said. "We have a totally unobstructed view of Mr. Snork. I'm sure there are a hundred places in San Francisco where he could have assassinated Stipe with less opportunity to be seen by witnesses and virtually no chance of being photographed. Instead he happened to choose the one spot where he could be seen clearly by not just one camera but *four* of them. It's almost as if he wanted to be absolutely sure that he was seen. Why would a murderer take such an enormous risk?"

"To make a statement," I said. "Which makes sense if he's a member of the Galactic Uprising."

"Or if that's what Arianna Stipe wanted us to think," Monk said. "Either way, the killer is wearing the perfect disguise."

"That's just it, Adrian. It's not perfect. It's all wrong," Ambrose said. "In season two, the network demanded that the producers make Mr. Snork's ears less pointy. They were afraid he looked too scary and unsympathetic. In fact, they wanted Stipe to change them to puppy ears so Snork would be more lovable, but he refused. They had to explain the ear change by having Mr. Snork suffer from a rare disease."

"That's an interesting story, if you have no life and never leave your house," Monk said. "It's also totally irrelevant."

"There's more —" Ambrose began.

"Please, God, no," Monk said, rubbing his temples.

I was suddenly reminded of what Stottlemeyer looked like most of the time he was around Monk. And me, too. There was more than a little poetic justice in this moment, and I savored it.

"In season two, they made the Confederation insignia on the uniform gold instead of silver," Ambrose said. "There's a lot of discussion about why that particular decision was made, but the actual facts have never emerged. Sadly, there's no paper trail and memories have faded with time."

"What does that have to do with anything?" Monk asked.

"The killer is wearing a season-one uniform with season-two ears!" Ambrose said. "Aren't you listening to a word I'm saying?"

"No, not really," Monk said. "This is a murder investigation. The first thing you learn is how to prioritize information. You can't be distracted by insignificant details that simply don't matter."

I had to remember that comment for the next time Monk wanted Stottlemeyer and Disher to stop their work to do something like contribute lint to a murder victim's pocket.

"A member of the Galactic Uprising would never make that mistake," Ambrose said. "They know and respect *Beyond Earth* too much — that's why they are fighting so hard against the new version. And surely Arianna Stipe, the wife of the creator of the show, would never let someone, even a hired killer, wear the wrong uniform with the wrong ears. The killer is violating canon and that's just going too far."

"Who cares?"

"I do," Ambrose said. "Any Earther would."

"Listen to yourself, Ambrose. You're obsessing over meaningless things that just don't matter. Follow my example and focus on what's important. Prioritize. That's how you solve cases."

"I'm telling you, Adrian, it's a season-one shirt with season-two ears," Ambrose said. "It's a very big deal."

"I think we're done for tonight," Monk said, turning off the TV and taking the DVD out of the player. "There's only so much we can do now. Maybe the captain will have more information for us to work with tomorrow."

"Thanks for the help, Ambrose," I said gently, trying to smooth things over.

"I tried," Ambrose said, then shot a glare at Monk. "But he can be so stubborn. Good night, Natalie."

"Good night, Ambrose," I said.

Ambrose walked away. Monk looked after him and shook his head.

"How sad," he said. "Imagine going through life getting hung up on such meaningless little things."

I looked Monk right in the eye. "You certainly aren't anything like that."

"That's because I'm a seasoned man of the world," Monk said. "Ambrose is just a man of the house."

I went home, too exhausted by the long day to do anything but soak in a hot bubble bath. It was warm, cozy, and relaxing, but I felt like I was squandering my vacation from parental responsibility. I should have been doing something exciting, edgy, and fun that I couldn't do on an ordinary night with my daughter at home.

Instead, I was playing with the bubbles and thinking about why someone would shoot a dead man three times, why someone would dress up like a TV character and shoot a man in full view of security cameras, and why the Monk brothers were so incredibly messed up.

I couldn't solve any of those mysteries, of course, but I couldn't get them out of my head either. They were too compelling.

But the one mystery that took center stage in my thoughts was the one closest to my heart.

The Monks.

I knew the other two cases would be solved, but the mystery of the Monks was probably something that psychologists could ponder for decades and still not figure out.

They were raised by a very cold, controlling woman who drove their father away. She didn't show her sons any affection whatsoever or teach them how to deal with the simplest of social interactions.

It's no surprise that they both developed debilitating psychological disorders. Monk was obsessive-compulsive. Everything had to fit his personal sense of order. His brother was agoraphobic, unable to cope with anything outside of his carefully controlled environment.

Both were trapped in their own worlds, worlds with rules that they created and rigidly followed, even if it meant alienating everyone around them.

I found it almost unbearably sad.

And yet both men were sweet and honest and astonishingly brilliant. They both had an eye for detail that allowed them to see with remarkable clarity things that the rest of us found confusing, mysterious, and downright impossible to understand. They could see how things worked and explain it to the rest of us so we could see it, too.

It was, Monk liked to say, a gift and a curse.

It was also a tragedy and a mystery.

The more I thought about it, the more I wondered about Mrs. Monk. Who was she?

What was her childhood like? What hopes and dreams did she have for her two children and did they achieve them?

I probably found her so fascinating because I was a mother and because, as much as I wanted time to myself, I missed my daughter and she was never far from my thoughts. By thinking about Mrs. Monk and her son, I was also thinking about Julie without directly thinking about Julie.

I believe that our children are reflections of ourselves and we like that but we want them to emulate only our best qualities and values and none of our faults. We want a better life for them than we ourselves had. We also want them to develop their own unique personalities separate from ours and to explore their full potential.

I still remember the first time Julie expressed an opinion. She was four or five years old. She pointed to a woman on the street and said, "That's an ugly dress."

I was stunned, mainly because I thought it was a very nice dress. And I told her so.

She shook her head. "It's ugly."

Julie had looked at something, measured it against her own values and tastes, and found it unappealing.

Her own values and tastes. Not mine. *Hers.*

Wow. In that moment, she wasn't just my baby anymore. She'd become a person. I gave her a great big hug and smothered her with kisses. So, of course, for the rest of the day she called everything and everyone ugly, just to get more attention from me.

There's probably a lesson in that, but never mind. Let's stick to the Monks.

I couldn't understand how Mrs. Monk could be pleased by their social isolation, which I know began when they were children. I've seen some of their home movies. They are the saddest things ever captured on film.

I wanted Julie to be happy and free. And I certainly didn't want her to be alone, to be an outcast. I wanted her to have a rich life, full of family and friends.

She was only twelve, but I could already see that I didn't have to worry about that aspect of her life. She had lots of friends and could function in society, at least the dog-eat-dog society of the seventh grade.

But that didn't seem to be what Mrs. Monk wanted for her sons. Or was she just so frightened for their safety that she became overprotective and encouraged them to live in an ordered world of their own making that was intentionally unwelcoming to outsiders? A world where they would be safe *because* they were alone?

Like I said, I don't have the answers. But it was something to think about.

By the time I reached that profound conclusion, the bubbles had all popped and the water had turned cold. I dried off, put on some skin cream, and poured myself into bed. I was asleep the instant my face touched my pillow.

I don't remember much of what I dreamt that night, except that at one point I was in a stainless-steel room folding socks into pairs while Scooter watched me through an observation window. I couldn't hear him, but I could read his lips.

He kept saying, "You're so needy," again and again.

CHAPTER SIXTEEN:
Mr. Monk
and the Session

Captain Stottlemeyer was right. When I turned on the TV during breakfast, the first thing I saw was Mr. Snork aiming his gun at Conrad Stipe. The station at least had the good sense not to show the actual murder, but even without that the video was still disturbing.

The content hadn't changed, but the context had, making the footage disturbing in an entirely different way. I was seeing it now in a newscast, heavily edited and pumped up with dramatic graphics. The station was showing the shooting repeatedly in a brazen, calculated attempt to titillate viewers. The worst part was that it was probably succeeding.

I couldn't swallow my bagel. I'd lost my appetite.

The footage was followed by a live report from outside the county morgue, where hundreds of devoted fans had held a candlelight vigil. One of them, an overweight man in his forties in a too tight costume and a Snork trunk dangling sadly from his puffy-cheeked face, explained to the reporter, the bubbly Mindy Drake, what they were doing.

"We're waiting for him to rise again," the fan said.

Mindy was dumbfounded. Then again, I'd seen her dumbfounded by the meteorologist predicting rain.

"You mean like Jesus?" Mindy asked.

"No, of course not," the fan said. "Like Starella when she was reborn on Tryptonia."

"But we aren't on Tryptonia," she said. "We're on Earth."

"Tryptonia is Earth on a parallel plane of existence," the fan said.

"Oh," Mindy said solemnly. "I didn't know that."

She didn't know Sacramento was the capital of California either. She discovered that when she announced during the Begonia Festival in Capitola that she was reporting live from the state capital.

"Conrad Stipe chose to tell us about it in a fictional context because society wasn't ready to embrace the truth," the fan explained. "That's because he lived spiritually and creatively on both the parallel Earth and on our own. So now his presence there will cross over and revive his corporeal presence here so he can continue his important work, the same way it happened for Starella in that seminal episode."

"How do you know that's what will happen?"

"The best evidence will be when Conrad Stipe walks out that door."

The reporter turned to the camera. "And we'll be here when it happens."

She said it without a trace of sarcasm.

That live report was followed by a taped interview with producer Kingston Mills, who sat in front of a poster for the new *Beyond Earth*.

He said that "the industry lost a giant and a true pioneer" but that he had lost "a colleague, a dear friend, and an inspiring mentor."

Mills wiped away a tear and then reminded viewers not to miss the reimagined *Beyond Earth* because that would be "the best way to honor Conrad's memory and his lifetime of creative achievement."

I was tempted to hurl my TV out the window, but then I remembered what they cost and took the less expensive approach of simply turning it off.

As I drove to Ambrose's house, I began to wonder if maybe Mills had killed Stipe so he could hog all the credit for the show and get a massive amount of free publicity right before the premiere. The more I thought about it, the more devious and possible it sounded to me.

Maybe I've been spending too much time around murderers the last few years.

I rushed up to the front door of Ambrose's house, eager to pitch my theory to Monk. I knocked on the door. Ambrose answered it, muttered a quick hello to me, then hurried back to the dining room. He seemed tired and distracted.

I followed him and was surprised by what I saw. He'd taken the security video, digitized it, blown up several frames of the shooter, and printed them out. He'd mounted the pictures on poster boards along with various blowups and drawings of Confederation uniforms, insignias, and Snork ears. He'd then connected them all with arrows and all kinds of handwritten notations.

He must have been up all night working on the presentation.

"What is all this?" I asked.

"Irrefutable proof that the assassin was

wearing a season-one shirt and season-two ears."

"I don't think anyone doubted you," I said.

"Adrian did," Ambrose said.

"I didn't doubt you," Monk said, coming up behind me. "I said it didn't matter."

"Oh, but it does," Ambrose said.

He took out a pointer and began his presentation. "The particular season-one uniform that the killer is wearing is modeled on the distinct design of the wardrobe from the pilot episode, which differs from the uniform used in the subsequent episodes, because the original production designer was unavailable for the series. You can see it most clearly here in the trim around the collar and cuffs."

Monk shook his head. "Nobody cares."

"Ursula Glemstadt does," Ambrose said.

"Who is Ursula Glemstadt?" Monk asked.

"She makes and sells Confederation uniforms for the fan community," Ambrose said. "And she is the only one who insists on using the original designs from the pilot, down to the exact stitching of the seams."

"You think she sold the uniform to the killer," I said.

"I know she did," Ambrose said. "And she's got a booth at the convention."

"That's a real lead, Mr. Monk," I said.

Monk sighed and looked at his brother. "How many of those uniforms do you think she has made and sold over the years in person and through mail order?"

"Hundreds," Ambrose replied.

"The killer could be any one of those customers," Monk said. "That doesn't really help us."

"But if you look at the fraying, or lack of it, and the vibrancy of the color, I'd say it's a brand-new uniform and has never been washed. He could have bought it in the last few days at the convention."

"Or bought it years or months ago and is wearing it for the first time."

"It's worth checking out," I said.

"Not really," Monk said.

"I've also studied the ears," Ambrose said. "I think I've narrowed them down to three possible molds and the craftspersons who manufactured them."

Monk rolled his eyes. "That's a big help. Let's go, Natalie, or we'll be late for my regular appointment with Dr. Kroger."

Ambrose started gathering up his boards. "Wait. Aren't you going to take these?"

"What for?" Monk said.

"To show your colleagues in the police department."

"They won't be interested."

Monk walked out, but I stayed behind.

"Of course we'll take them, Ambrose. I know that Captain Stottlemeyer will appreciate your work very much."

He smiled gratefully and gave me the poster boards and a manila envelope.

"I've attached contact information on how to reach Ursula and the three ear-makers, along with a letter of introduction to them from me. That should smooth the way for the detectives."

"Thank you, Ambrose," I said. "I'll be sure the captain gets everything."

Monk was waiting for me at the car, his arms crossed. He watched me load the posters into the car.

"You shouldn't encourage him," Monk said.

"Why not?" I said. "He's just trying to help."

"You're only reinforcing his ridiculous obsession with insignificant details," Monk said. "How is he ever going to learn to function in life if he continues to focus on meaningless minutiae? He needs to loosen up in a big way."

I stopped and stared at Monk, a man who won't sit at a table that has only three chairs and counts the parking meters whenever he walks down a street.

"Have you ever heard the phrase 'the pot calling the kettle black'?" I asked him.

"That makes no sense. Pots are inanimate objects that don't talk, and if they did, why would they talk to a kettle?"

I just shook my head and got into the car. While I drove Monk to his psychiatrist's office, I pitched my theory about Kingston Mills and his possible motive for murdering Stipe.

"You might be onto something," Monk said.

I was flattered. "You really think so?"

"No," Monk said.

"Then why did you say it?"

"Say what?"

"That I might be onto something," I said.

"You might be," Monk said. "Of course, by that I mean no way in hell."

"Why don't you just say that instead?"

"I don't want to be insensitive," Monk said.

"But you have no problem telling a one-eyed man to find his eyeball or calling your own brother a drug-addicted freak."

"What's insensitive about that?"

I gave him a look to see if he was joking, but then I remembered that Monk doesn't have a sense of humor. He was serious. All

195

the time.

We arrived at Dr. Kroger's office precisely four minutes early. That's because we always get there eight or ten minutes early, wait outside on the sidewalk until it's four minutes before the appointment, and then go in.

Dr. Kroger was a trim and fit fiftysomething, much like the late Brandon Lorber, and had a golfer's tan. I don't know if he actually played golf, but he looked like someone who did.

He had an enormously calming presence, which I suppose is a necessary quality for someone in his profession, but if you're already calm, which I am most of the time, you run the risk of slipping into a coma while you're talking to him.

There was no one in his waiting room when we arrived, and as soon as Dr. Kroger opened his inner-office door, Monk marched in without so much as a greeting.

The office was clean and contemporary and looked out on an inner courtyard that had a fountain that trickled down one of the concrete walls and into a bowl of damp, glistening stones.

If I ever needed to see a shrink, I'd want his office to be warm and cozy and inviting, like a family room. Dr. Kroger's office was sterile and almost cold enough to keep food fresh. No wonder Monk felt comfortable there.

"We've got a psychiatric emergency to deal with," Monk said, taking his customary seat.

Dr. Kroger raised an eyebrow. That's about as worked up as he ever got. "We do?"

"It's not me, of course," Monk said.

Dr. Kroger nodded sagely. I think he even picked his nose sagely. He was that kind of guy. "It's everyone else."

I was walking out when Monk called to me. "See, Natalie?" Monk said. "He gets it." I couldn't let that remark go without an explanation.

"Mr. Monk is talking about his current case," I said. "He's investigating the murder of Conrad Stipe, who created a TV show called *Beyond Earth,* which has a cult following."

"These are deeply disturbed individuals," Monk said. "They walk around with their internal organs on the outside of their bodies."

"Is that so?" Dr. Kroger said, as if that was something he saw every day. He sat down in his chair beside Monk and motioned to me to stay. I stood at the door, feeling awkward.

"Yesterday, we visited a *Beyond Earth* convention where the fans dress up as characters from the show," I said and sat down on the couch facing Dr. Kroger and Monk. "One of the characters is an inside-out alien being."

"I see." Dr. Kroger glanced at Monk. "And you find this behavior unnatural and distressing."

"They need to be institutionalized," Monk said. "You can commit them, can't you?"

"Not unless they are my patients and I believe that they present an imminent danger to themselves or others."

"What if we were talking about a member of my family?" Monk asked.

"Are we?"

"My brother, Ambrose, is one of them," Monk said. "He's a member of the cult."

"It's not a cult, Mr. Monk," I said.

"You said yourself that the show has a cult following," Monk said.

"I didn't mean that kind of cult," I said. "I meant the good kind."

"There's no such thing as a good cult," Monk said. "Before you know it, you're sacrificing goats, dancing naked in the woods, and selling cookies door-to-door."

"You think the Girl Scouts is a cult?"

"Haven't you seen the vacant look in their eyes?"

"Everyone eventually gets that look around you, Mr. Monk."

"I thought Ambrose never left the house," Dr. Kroger said.

"He doesn't," Monk said. "He's crazy at home."

"I think it's great that Ambrose is a member of this fan club. You should encourage his participation," Dr. Kroger said. "This is a very positive step for him."

"They speak a fictional language!" Monk said.

"It's a harmless bonding ritual and, in Ambrose's case, quite healthy and perhaps even essential for his mental and emotional well-being."

"Harmless?" Monk said. "They save breakfast cereal for thirty years. Some of them have even had plastic surgery to give themselves pointed ears."

"Granted, that might be going too far, but it's not necessarily a sign of a mental illness," Dr. Kroger said. "Human beings have an instinctive need to belong to some kind of social group for their emotional and physical well-being and survival. They will go to extreme lengths to achieve this. Even you, Adrian."

"I don't think so," Monk said.

"Your dream is to become part of the police department again," Dr. Kroger said. "That's a reflection of your need to belong to something."

"It's a job," Monk said. "It's not a TV show."

"It's a social group with its own culture, code of conduct, belief system, shared values, and common goals. Everyone wears a uniform or carries a badge so that they can be recognized as members of the group to their own members and to 'outsiders.' It's not unlike the costumes that the science fiction fans wear. And like the fan club, they also provide an essential support system for their members."

"The police department enforces the law and maintains order," Monk said. "That's what they are supporting."

"They are also supporting each other," Dr. Kroger said. "Just look at how Captain Stottlemeyer and Lieutenant Disher have supported you over the years. It's because you are one of their own. Who supports Ambrose?"

"Me," Monk said.

"Like you did this morning?" I said. "You completely dismissed his efforts to help."

"Because they were wasted efforts and

no help."

"Everyone needs to belong to something," Dr. Kroger said. "I have my family, I have friends, and I have my profession. That's what defines me, gives me identity and a sense of belonging. Ambrose never leaves the house, so his desire to be part of something must be even more intense and even more difficult to achieve. I'm glad that he's apparently found something."

"Why do you think Ambrose is so attracted to *Beyond Earth* and its fan following?" I asked.

"Science fiction is a highly imaginative genre that isn't restricted by reality or any of the rules of modern life. It has broad appeal but it's especially attractive to people who, for whatever reason, have been marginalized or ostracized by society at large for their perceived physical, mental, or social imperfections. For them, it's much easier to fit into a rich fantasy world where anything is possible than a real one that excludes them. I'm not at all surprised that Ambrose is drawn to it. It's not just a support system, it's also a means of escape."

I told Dr. Kroger about the reimagining of the show and the fervent opposition to it by the Galactic Uprising.

"Do you think a fan would kill Stipe over

the changes to *Beyond Earth*?"

"I think people will kill over just about anything," Dr. Kroger said. "But especially something or someone who threatens to totally destroy what they believe in."

"It's a TV show," Monk said.

"To you and me it is, Adrian. To them, it's their way of life."

"How do we rescue Ambrose from their clutches?" Monk asked.

"It's simple, Adrian. Become more involved in his life. The more he's involved with you and others, the less he will need what the fan club gives him." Dr. Kroger looked at his watch. "I'm afraid our time is up for today."

"We haven't even started," Monk said.

"Not only have we started," Dr. Kroger said, standing up. "We've finished."

"But Natalie was here," Monk said. "It doesn't count."

"Think of it as a group session and a very productive one, too. Thank you for participating, Natalie."

"My pleasure," I said.

"But we didn't talk at all about me," Monk said.

"It was all about you, Adrian."

"I don't see how," Monk said.

"Think about it," Dr. Kroger said, leading

us to the door and opening it. "It will give us something to discuss at our next session."

"You're not going to charge me for this," Monk said.

"Of course I am," Dr. Kroger said.

"You're lucky I'm not a police officer," Monk said.

"Why?" Dr. Kroger asked him.

"Because I'd arrest you for robbery," Monk said and walked out in a huff.

CHAPTER SEVENTEEN: MR. MONK SPEAKS UP

Captain Stottlemeyer and Lieutenant Disher were starting their day at a crime scene at the foot of the Filbert Steps, so that's where we had to go to tell them about our new leads.

Filbert Street dead-ends at the base of Telegraph Hill, where a concrete and steel stairway crisscrosses the weedy cliff up to Montgomery Street. From there, wooden steps climb the rest of the way among cottages and a lush, beautiful garden that's home to wild parakeets.

It's a place I usually associated with solitude and beauty. But today, the dead end was living up to its name and casting its shadow over everything else.

Seeing a corpse in the morning puts a damper on my entire day, but unfortunately it was becoming increasingly typical for me. Even so, I wasn't getting so blasé about it that I could stand over the corpse and sip my morning coffee, which was exactly what Stottlemeyer and Disher were doing. They both held Starbucks cups in their hands. Stottlemeyer had a little foam in his mustache.

The corpse was in a narrow, weedy patch beside the steps between the sheer face of the hill and a windowless side of an office building that abutted it.

There was an empty taxicab double-parked at the curb near the lot, the driver's-side door ajar, which led me to brilliantly deduce that the victim was the cabbie.

Monk and I stepped over the yellow crime scene tape and joined the captain and Disher beside the body. The victim was lying faceup, his legs curled underneath him in an unnatural way. He appeared to me to be in his early thirties. He'd been shot once in the head.

"Good morning," Stottlemeyer said.

"It's hard to feel good about it when you're looking at a dead man," I said.

Stottlemeyer nodded and took a sip of his coffee. "If I let every murder get to me, there wouldn't be any of me left."

"And if you don't," I said, "are you still the person that you want to be?"

"That's the last time I'm ever going to say good morning to you," Stottlemeyer said.

"What brings you here?"

I wiped my upper lip. Stottlemeyer got the message and dabbed at his mustache with a napkin from his pocket. "The Stipe case," I said.

"Who is the victim?" Monk asked, walking carefully around the body, looking at it from various angles.

"His name is Phil Bisson," Disher said. "He's a cabbie. A tourist walking down the Filbert Steps spotted the body two hours ago and called 911. The ME puts the preliminary time of death around one a.m."

Monk looked up at the staircase, then back down at the body.

"What do you think happened?" I asked Disher.

"A robbery-homicide," he replied.

Monk cocked his head from side to side. He was processing the information. It wasn't tracking for him. He was a man whose body language gave away just about everything he was thinking and feeling. It's a good thing he never played poker.

"Here's what we think happened," Disher said. "The cabbie gets flagged down by a guy, who pulls a gun on him and forces him out of the car. The guy leads the cabbie over to the lot behind the building, out of sight of the street, and shoots him. The robber takes the cabbie's cash and runs."

I tried to imagine what this dead end must have looked like at one a.m. under the dim glow of the streetlight with the office buildings empty and the street deserted. It was a nice area but I still wouldn't stop my car here under those conditions.

"The cabbie must have been desperate for a fare to stop here," I said.

"Or new at the business," Stottlemeyer said. "Or fatally stupid."

Monk rolled his shoulders. "You're assuming the cabbie was driving along Sansome Street when the robber caught his attention."

"Yeah," Stottlemeyer said.

"Are you sure the cabbie wasn't responding to a call?" Monk asked.

Disher nodded. "We checked with his dispatcher. There was no call. And the cabbie didn't call in that he was picking someone up. The dispatcher says that's not unusual. The cabbie wouldn't have called in until he knew his destination."

Monk stepped back over the police tape, went to the sidewalk, and looked to his right at Sansome Street, Levi Plaza, and the bay beyond.

"If someone tried to flag the cab down from here, the cabbie wouldn't have been able to see him," Monk said. "The robber would have had to be standing on the corner."

"Okay," Stottlemeyer said, "so he was at the corner."

"But look at how the cab is parked," Monk said. "The driver pulled in and turned around so he'd be facing the street again. Why would he do that if he was picking someone up at the corner?"

The three of us stepped over the police tape and joined Monk on the sidewalk.

"Simple. The cab was going the opposite direction when the robber flagged him down," Stottlemeyer said. "While the cab was making the U-turn to pick him up, the robber walked back here."

"Wouldn't that have made the cabbie suspicious?" Monk asked.

"It should have," Stottlemeyer said. "Apparently it didn't and he paid for his mistake."

Monk frowned. Stottlemeyer frowned. So did Disher.

I was pretty sure that they were each frowning for very different reasons.

Monk was frowning because something didn't seem right to him about the murder.

Stottlemeyer was frowning because he thought he had it all figured out and he didn't want Monk complicating things.

And Disher was frowning because if Monk made things more complicated it would mean more work for him and more time away from investigating the Lorber case.

Monk held out his hand to me. "Baggie, please."

I reached into my purse and gave Monk one. I carry around a lot of Baggies in my purse for disposing of his used wipes and for collecting any evidence that he finds at crime scenes.

He walked back to the lot and disappeared behind the building. I turned to Stottlemeyer and Disher.

"Have you come up with any new leads in the Stipe investigation?" I asked.

"I wouldn't call them leads, but we have some interesting information." Disher referred to his notebook. "A writer named Willis Goldkin filed a lawsuit a couple of days ago against Stipe, claiming half the profits from the show."

"On what grounds?"

"That he co-created it and that Stipe ripped him off," Disher said. "Now that Stipe is dead, Goldkin might stand a better chance of winning."

"Why did he wait so long to sue?"

"There wasn't any money in it before,"

Stottlemeyer said. "Now there is."

"That's not all," Disher said. "Stipe was granted a restraining order a month ago against Ernest Pinchuk, the leader of the Galactic Uprising, for stalking him and sending him threatening e-mails."

"Were they in English or Dratch?"

"What's Dratch?" Stottlemeyer asked.

That was when we heard a loud pop that sounded like a gunshot. The sound came from the vacant lot. Two uniformed officers instinctively reached for their guns. We hurried over to find Monk standing beside the body, holding the Baggie, which was now torn.

"What the hell are you doing?" Stottlemeyer asked.

"Proving a point," Monk said.

"You could have gotten yourself shot," Stottlemeyer said.

"There's a big echo in this pocket created by the building and the side of the hill. If blowing up a plastic bag and popping it made that much noise with all the traffic on Sansome, imagine what a gunshot would have sounded like last night. But none of the residents up there along the Filbert Steps reported hearing anything, did they?"

"No, they didn't," Stottlemeyer said with a groan.

"So the robber used a silencer," Disher said.

Stottlemeyer shook his head. Monk walked over to the taxi. Stottlemeyer sighed with resignation.

"We've got to face it, Randy," Stottlemeyer said. "This wasn't a robbery. It was staged to look like one."

"Why do you say that?" Disher asked.

"Because robberies like this are done by desperate people, and they don't usually carry around silencers," Stottlemeyer said. "I knew I shouldn't have taken decaf this morning. I'm sleep-walking through this investigation."

Stottlemeyer was often too hard on himself for missing the things that Monk saw. I'm sure the captain would have come to the same conclusion as Monk. It just would have taken him a lot longer.

"My coffee is caffeinated," Disher said. "What's my excuse?"

"I don't know, Randy," Stottlemeyer said. "Maybe you were distracted by the demands of the Special Desecration Unit."

"Yeah," Disher said. "That must be it. I don't need to tell you how overwhelming a command position can be."

Stottlemeyer turned to Monk, who was walking around the cab, a scowl of disgust on his face.

"Thanks, Monk. We'll take it from here."

"This car is filthy," Monk said. "When was the last time the cabbie washed it?"

"I don't know, but I promise you that we'll wash it when the lab guys are done."

Monk took out a handkerchief and used it to open the rear door of the car.

"There's no need to do that, Monk. I appreciate your help, and for setting us on the right track, but we'll handle this one ourselves. I need you to concentrate on finding Conrad Stipe's killer."

But Monk ignored him and leaned into the backseat of the taxi.

"That's why we're here," I said. "We've got some new leads."

"You do?" Stottlemeyer said, looking hopeful.

"The uniform that the killer was wearing was from season one," I said. "But his ears were from season two."

The hope I saw in Stottlemeyer's face disappeared. "How is that a lead?"

"I'll show you," I said.

I led them over to my car, opened the back door, and pulled out the poster boards. I pointed to one of the blowups of the killer.

"Look closely and you'll see that it's not just any season-one uniform. It's from the pilot episode. There's only one person making and selling uniforms with that design. Her name is Ursula Glemstadt and she has a booth at the convention."

I pointed to the photos that Ambrose had arranged to illustrate the typical fading of a uniform over time and multiple washings. As I did, I noticed a tiny footnote referencing Ambrose's book *The Encyclopedia of Confederation Uniforms and Other "Beyond Earth" Clothing.*

"Based on the color and lack of fraying on the killer's uniform," I said, "there's a good chance he's wearing it for the first time."

"Meaning he could have bought it a day or two before the shooting," Stottlemeyer said, catching on. The expression of hope was back on his face. "Randy, contact this Ursula woman and see if she can tell us anything about her recent customers. Bring a sketch artist with you."

"I'm on it," Disher said.

Stottlemeyer looked at me. "It's pure Monk to come up with a lead based on when someone last laundered their clothes, but I've never seen him do a presentation before."

"He didn't," I said. "His brother did."

"Ambrose?" Stottlemeyer said. "Since

when does he help Monk on investigations?"

"Ambrose is an expert on *Beyond Earth.*"

"He's an Earthie?" Disher said.

"Earther," I corrected.

Stottlemeyer grinned. "Monk must love that."

Monk emerged from the back of the cab. "I know who killed this cabdriver."

We all turned around, shocked.

It wasn't the first time Monk had solved a case at the crime scene — we'd seen him do it yesterday at the Belmont — but it still never ceased to be startling.

"You do?" Stottlemeyer said.

"It's the same person who shot Brandon Lorber," Monk said.

"You solved my desecration case, too?" Disher said, a tinge of disappointment in his voice. "They're connected?"

"Without a doubt," Monk said.

"Wait a minute," Stottlemeyer said. "You're saying that whoever murdered this cabbie and made it look like a robbery also snuck into Burgerville headquarters two nights ago and put three bullets into a dead man?"

"That's what I am saying."

"That's saying a lot," Stottlemeyer said.

"There's more," Monk said.

"Don't tell me," Stottlemeyer said. "You know who did it."

Monk didn't say anything. He just looked at us.

"Well?" Stottlemeyer prodded.

"You just said not to tell you," Monk said.

"It's an expression, Monk. It means 'tell me.' "

"How can 'don't tell me' mean 'tell me'? Wouldn't it make more sense to *say* 'tell me'?"

"Tell me!" Stottlemeyer said.

Monk didn't say anything.

"I'm waiting, Monk," Stottlemeyer said. "Spit it out already."

"You said not to tell you," Monk said.

"I just said 'tell me,' " Stottlemeyer said.

"If 'don't tell me' means 'tell me,' then doesn't it follow that 'tell me' means 'don't tell me'?"

Stottlemeyer massaged his temples. "If you don't reveal the name of the killer this instant, I am going to tie one of my shoes in a double knot and leave the other one in a single knot for the rest of the day."

Monk gasped. "Okay, okay, there's no need to do anything drastic. If this is what happens when you give up caffeine, don't do it again. It makes you crazy and irrational."

"Who killed the cabbie and shot Brandon Lorber's corpse?" Stottlemeyer demanded.

Monk paused for dramatic effect. I think he savors these moments and wants them to last as long as possible.

"Mr. Snork," he said.

CHAPTER EIGHTEEN:
MR. MONK
CONNECTS THE DOTS

Remember how I said before that we were shocked when Monk declared that he'd solved the cabbie's murder? Well, after Monk said it was Mr. Snork who did it, we were super-shocked. Our jaws were hanging open because we had lost the motor skills to keep them shut.

"Mr. Snork?" I repeated, just to be sure I'd heard him right the first time.

"You know, the guy with the elephant trunk and pointed ears," Monk said.

"We know who Mr. Snork is," Stottlemeyer said. "What we don't know is what makes you think that the same person shot Brandon Lorber's corpse, shot Conrad Stipe, and shot this cabbie."

"I can tell you now that the bullets removed from Lorber don't match the bullet removed from Stipe," Disher said. I think he didn't want to see his Special Desecration Unit disbanded before it had even closed its first case.

"I don't need ballistic evidence," Monk said. "I have something much more damning and convincing."

"What?" Disher asked.

"Gum," Monk said.

"Gum," Stottlemeyer repeated.

We repeated what Monk said a lot. I think Stottlemeyer, like me, just wanted to assure himself he'd actually heard Monk say the unbelievable thing that we'd just heard him say.

Monk pointed to the backseat of the cab. "There's a two-day-old wad of chewing gum under the seat."

"Meaning what?" Stottlemeyer asked.

"Conrad Stipe was in this taxi."

"Anybody could have stuck gum under the seat," Disher said. "I'm sure there are gobs of wads under there."

"There are," Monk said, looking a little sickened. "But this one is in the same place that Stipe put his gum in the other cab. It's also the same color and consistency as the other wad of gum and it's approximately two days old."

"How do you know it's two days old?" Stottlemeyer said.

"I have great gum instincts," Monk said.

"Gum instincts?" Disher repeated.

"I honed them during my years on the streets," Monk explained.

"So while you were walking the beat as a uniformed cop, you were studying the gum on the sidewalks?" Disher asked.

"Long before that, my friend. I've been watching for gum on the sidewalks since birth. It's a blight on society," Monk said. "If you run a DNA test on the gum under the seat of this cab you'll see that I'm right that Stipe is the culprit. We should be scraping gum off all the sidewalks in San Francisco and having it tested, too."

"Why would you want to do that?" I asked.

"To prosecute the offenders," Monk said.

"People who spit out their gum on the streets?"

"It's about time justice was served on those despicable monsters," Monk said. "Finally we have the technology to do it."

"Just because Stipe rode in that cab while he was in town doesn't mean the same shooter killed him, killed the cabbie, and desecrated Brandon Lorber," Stottlemeyer said.

"The candy wrapper does," Monk said.

He took a pair of tweezers from his pocket, leaned inside the cab, and came out holding a tiny gold foil wrapper.

"I found this on the floor of that filthy cab. It's from the coffee candy in the bowl on Lorber's desk," he said. "The shooter must have helped himself to a piece the same way you and Lieutenant Disher did."

Monk motioned to me for a Baggie.

"That brand of coffee candy is sold all over the country," Disher said. "Tens of thousands of people buy it. How do you know that wrapper came from a piece of candy in Lorber's bowl?"

I took a Baggie out of my purse and held it open so Monk could drop the wrapper inside. He paused before he dropped it in so he could squint at the writing on the wrapper.

"The lot number is the same," Monk said. "So is the twisting flaw."

Stottlemeyer sighed. "What flaw?"

"Ordinarily, the candies are individually wrapped with the foil machine-twisted in the same direction on both ends," Monk said. "But the ends were folded in opposite directions on these candies, causing a tiny tear at the seam. You can also see it in the wrinkle pattern at the ends of the open wrapper."

"You may see it," Stottlemeyer said, "but no other human being can."

"Even if the same man shot the cabbie

and Brandon Lorber's corpse," Disher said, "you still haven't connected it to Conrad Stipe."

"Lorber's shooter was in the cab," Monk said. "Conrad Stipe was in the cab. Now Lorber, Stipe, and the cabbie have all been shot. That's too big of a coincidence to be a coincidence."

There was a long silence, which Stottlemeyer finally broke with a sigh of resignation.

"You're right," Stottlemeyer said. "So what's the connection between Lorber, Stipe, and the cabbie?"

"Only one thing so far," Monk said and pointed to the taxicab. "That rolling garbage can."

The taxicab was towed back to the forensics lab so it could be taken apart for clues and, if Monk had his way, thoroughly cleaned and disinfected. We went back to the station with Stottlemeyer and Disher.

Monk had the evidence and the crime scene photos from Lorber's office brought to one of the interrogation rooms. While he sorted through it, Disher made some calls to find out more about the cabbie and his activities over the last few days.

There wasn't much evidence to look at,

just the papers that were on Lorber's desk when he died and the bullets that were removed from his body. There was also the bloody chair that Lorber had been sitting in, but thankfully Monk hadn't asked for that to be brought in.

Monk examined the items without removing them from their evidence Baggies.

I browsed through the crime scene photos and passed them along to Monk, who compared them to what was in the evidence bags. I wasn't sure what I was supposed to be looking for, but I didn't see any *Beyond Earth* books or toys on the shelves.

And that was when I remembered something.

"Mr. Monk, do you remember the lady with the *Beyond Earth* cereal?"

"She will haunt me forever," he said.

"I don't know if this means anything, but she was selling some *Beyond Earth* toys that Burgerville gave away in their kid's meals thirty years ago. That's a connection, I suppose."

"It is," Monk said. "But I don't know if it means anything."

"Have you found anything?"

"A paper clip irregularity," Monk said.

"Is that serious?"

He laid out the Baggies on the table. "All

the papers on Lorber's desk were attached with color-coded paper clips. He had some kind of paper clip system for organizing his work. But the financial documents he was reading when he died were held together with a regular paper clip."

"Maybe that was part of his system," I said.

"There were no other documents on his desk bound with a colorless paper clip," Monk said. "And if you look closely at the paper, you'll see that it's badly streaked. There are lines going across the page every eighth of an inch or so."

"Maybe it's a bad photocopy," I said.

"That's exactly what it is," Monk said. "It's a bad photocopy of a document that was shredded and then reconstructed from the strips. The streaks aren't from the photocopying process. They are from the blades."

"I wonder what was so important about this document that Lorber had it reconstructed from shreds," I said. "Maybe what we're looking at is evidence of industrial espionage. Maybe this was something he had stolen from a rival's trash."

At the mere mention of the word "trash," Monk instinctively recoiled.

"The forensic accountant should be able

to tell us what the numbers mean," Monk said. "But whatever it is, I don't think Lorber was reading it when he died."

"Then what was it doing on his desk?"

"Someone wanted us to believe that Lorber was reading it when he was killed. Whoever it was would have fooled us if only he hadn't used the wrong paper clip."

Color-coded paper clips. Dried gobs of chewing gum. Coffee candy wrappers. *Beyond Earth* uniforms. They weren't the sexiest clues in the history of criminal detection, but they added up to something.

But what?

All we knew was that three men were dead.

Brandon Lorber was the CEO of a chain of burger restaurants and was shot three times after he'd already died of a heart attack. The shooter had a piece of coffee candy and, at some point, got into a taxi driven by Phil Bisson.

Conrad Stipe was the creator of *Beyond Earth,* which was being remade into a new TV series. He chewed gum and stuck some under the seat of the taxi that took him to a *Beyond Earth* convention, where an assassin dressed as Mr. Snork shot him to death. Sometime in the last two days Stipe also rode in Phil Bisson's taxi.

Phil Bisson was a cabbie who drove both Conrad Stipe and his killer in his taxi. Were Stipe and the killer in the cab together? Was that why the cabbie was murdered, because he could testify that the two men had met and he could identify the killer?

I shared my thinking with Monk.

"It's a good theory," Monk said.

"So in other words," I said, "it's a bad theory."

"If I thought it was a bad theory, that's what I would have said. Unlike Captain Stottlemeyer, who is in the throes of caffeine withdrawal, I don't say the opposite of what I mean. The only question I have about your theory is where does Brandon Lorber fit in?"

"Maybe he doesn't," I said. "Maybe you're wrong about the wrapper."

Monk shook his head. "Impossible."

"Surely you've been wrong once or twice," I said.

"Not on something as significant as how a candy wrapper is twisted," Monk said.

That ridiculous comment gave me an opportunity to confront Monk with his own hypocrisy in a way he might actually understand.

"How is the way that a candy wrapper is twisted more significant than whether some-

225

one is wearing a first-season Confederation uniform with second-season Snork ears?"

"There's a big difference," he said.

"Which is?"

"A candy wrapper is real and *Beyond Earth* is fiction," Monk said.

"The uniforms are real," I said. "The killer was wearing one. It was as real to him as the candy he put in his mouth. You can't dismiss what's significant to Ambrose just because it's not important to you."

"Or to any sane, well-adjusted human being," he said.

"But you believe that people care how the ends of a coffee candy wrapper are twisted."

"They do if they are sane, well-adjusted human beings and not druggie freaks."

I would have pursued it further, perhaps to the death, but Monk got up and headed for the door.

"Let's go talk to the forensic accountant," he said. "And find out what the shooter wanted so badly for us to know."

CHAPTER NINETEEN:
MR. MONK AND A
THOUSAND SUSPECTS

The Forensic Accounting Unit of the San Francisco Police Department was in the basement, but what it lacked in windows and views it more than compensated for with high-tech toys. The dark offices were bathed in a blue glow from the dozen ultra-thin flat-screen monitors that seemed to cover every surface except the ceiling and the floor.

Two men and one woman sat at their desks, working at their keyboards, the soft, springy clicking of the keys like a chorus of electronic cicadas. There was no clutter whatsoever on the desks — no coffee cups, no paperweights, no loose papers, and no family photos or personal items.

The temperature down there, emotionally and physically, was very chilly, but I could tell that Monk liked it. There was no cleaner space in the entire police department.

All three of the accountants were young,

attractive, and dressed in stylish, perfectly fitted black clothes that made them almost entirely disappear into the shadows around them. They were like ninjas but with personal stylists and health club memberships.

The woman rose from behind her two flat-screen monitors and glided towards us. She was probably around my age and had short blond hair and very pale skin. I guess she didn't see much sunlight. But what struck me most about her was the big gun in the holster on her belt.

It was comforting to know that she was armed in case a spreadsheet resisted arrest. She probably carried around those razor-sharp silver ninja stars in a pouch somewhere in case things really got tough.

She introduced herself to us as Lieutenant Sylvia Chase, the commander of the Forensic Accounting Unit. I guess she already knew Monk by reputation within the department, because she didn't bother offering him her hand. Or maybe she was just as cold as the room.

"Welcome to the cutting edge of law enforcement," she said with a nod.

"I had no idea this department even existed," Monk said, glancing appreciatively around the room.

"We solve financial crimes the same way

they are committed," she said. "Quietly and in the shadows."

I think the ninja accountant was taking that last part too literally. If her skin hadn't been so pale, I wouldn't have been able to see her at all.

"I like your office," Monk said. "It's very clean and inviting."

"Thank you," she said. "I believe in an orderly environment."

"Me too," Monk said. "Can I work here?"

"I'm aware of your skills as a homicide investigator," she said, "but do you have any advanced accounting experience?"

"No," Monk said. "But I like even numbers and I am very clean."

"I'm afraid that's not good enough," she said.

I couldn't see Monk's face too clearly, but I was pretty sure he looked like he was about to cry.

"What makes this unit 'the cutting edge'?" I asked.

"Murder is a Stone Age crime, Ms. Teeger. It hasn't really changed over the centuries," Chase said. "But finance is the future of crime. You can steal millions of dollars and destroy the lives of tens of thousands of people with just a few keystrokes on a computer in the privacy of your own home.

You can topple a corporation, perhaps even a government, with your PDA."

"Could I just hang out here?" Monk said. "My apartment is being recarpeted."

"There was a coffee stain," I said.

Monk nudged me hard. Apparently I'd revealed too much.

"Don't worry, Lieutenant Chase. I wouldn't bring coffee in here," Monk said. "I'm not drinking it ever again. I'm not even thinking of coffee. Coffee is banned from my existence."

"I appreciate that," she said. "But I'm afraid this is a restricted area. You probably shouldn't even be here now."

"My wristwatch has more RAM than the computers that the detectives are using upstairs," I said. "How come you get all the cool stuff down here?"

"Combating financial crime takes a different breed of cop, entirely new methods of investigation, and the latest technology," she said. "The resources we receive are in direct proportion to the amount of revenue we've brought in."

"I thought you were supposed to enforce the law," I said. "I didn't realize you were supposed to turn a profit, too."

"Last year we recovered nearly twenty-two million dollars in cash, stocks, and other assets earned by various criminal enterprises," Chase said. "After the cases we investigate are adjudicated and any victims are reimbursed for their losses, a significant percentage of what remains of those ill-gotten gains is apportioned to the police department to fund our continuing law enforcement efforts."

"Why can't some of that money make its way upstairs to Homicide?" Monk said. "Particularly for the housekeeping budget."

"I'm sure some of it does," she said. "But we need these tools to do our job effectively and keep up with the technological strides made by the criminals we pursue," she said. "That costs a lot of money."

"It takes money to make money," I said.

"Or to follow money," Chase added.

"It doesn't seem fair," Monk said. "Everybody in the building should be able to enjoy this blissful environment. Especially me."

"I'm assuming you two didn't come down here to debate how the police department allocates its resources," Chase said.

"We'd like to know what you've learned from the document that was found on Brandon Lorber's desk," Monk said. "It's just numbers to us."

Chase smiled at Monk. "It is far more than mere numerals on a page. Numbers are a lot like people. They each have a story. They interact with one another. They entertain. They inform. They deceive. They can create happiness or inflict enormous pain. You have to know how to get them to talk."

I could have cheered. She was helping me reinforce the argument I tried to make to Monk at Ambrose's house and in the interrogation room. Maybe hearing it from her, someone he obviously admired, would have some impact on him. But I wanted to make sure he didn't miss the point.

"In other words, Mr. Monk," I said, "she's saying that what's insignificant or meaningless to you can have great importance to someone else. Numbers are her second-season ears."

Chase and Monk both looked at me quizzically. Or gave me withering stares. I don't know for sure. It was hard to tell in that light, but even in the nearly pitch-dark room it was obvious to me that neither one of them saw my point with the same startling clarity as I did.

"Never mind," I said. "Lieutenant Chase, what did those numbers have to say to you once you got them into the interrogation room and beat them with a phone book?"

Chase shook her head and turned to Monk.

"Ears and a phone book?" she said. "What do they have to do with anything?"

Monk shrugged. "She's been babbling nonsense like that all day. Please go on, Lieutenant Chase."

"To put it simply, that document is a secret internal financial report that reveals that years of financial irregularities, mismanagement, and impropriety are about to catch up to Burgerville. The company is on the verge of total collapse."

"But it's one of the biggest fast-food chains in the country," I said. "They've got restaurants everywhere."

"That aggressive expansion has cost a lot of money in the midst of a downturn in popularity of their product. The company has been trumpeting its success but the truth is that average store sales have been plummeting for years. They fell twenty-one percent in the last fiscal quarter alone. The company is generating a pitiful cash flow and will take a net loss of more than a hundred million dollars this year."

"They hid all of that from the public?" Monk asked.

"And from their investors and the government," Chase said. "But the real crime is what will happen to the employee pension plan, which was sponsored by Burgerville and was made up almost entirely of company stock."

"When word gets out about their financial problems, the value of the stock will nosedive," I said. "Thousands of lives will be ruined."

"It's Enron all over again, only on a smaller scale," Chase said.

"It won't seem small to the people who've lost their life savings," I said. "It's catastrophic. How could this happen without anyone noticing?"

"What's going on is no secret from the Justice Department. They've been quietly building a case against Burgerville for months," Chase said. "But it was a secret from the employees."

"Maybe not to all of them," Monk said. "There was at least one person who knew."

"A person with a gun and a message for Lorber," I said.

Monk nodded. "Only he got there a little too late to deliver it."

Lieutenant Chase went on to tell us more about Lorber's financial misdeeds. He convinced the company to buy out the seven restaurants of a Burgerville regional franchisee for far more than the market value. It turned out the franchisee was his brother-in-law.

She also told us that Burgerville over-charged franchisees for supplies and misappropriated the money that the restaurants contributed to a marketing and promotion fund.

The list of financial irregularities seemed to go on and on, and the shredded document on Lorber's desk was the Rosetta stone to discovering it all.

Now that Lorber was dead, attention would focus on Andrew Cahill, the company's longtime chief financial officer, who had been named acting CEO after Lorber died.

It was clear that Brandon Lorber had been on the verge of being outed as a greedy, dishonest scumbag who'd ruthlessly plundered the futures of his employees for his own personal gain. He was facing public humiliation, criminal prosecution, and the fury of thousands of employees.

It was no wonder, then, that he'd had a heart attack or that someone wanted to kill him.

The desecration made sense to me, too. I could see why someone who'd lost everything would fire a few bullets into the body of the guy who was responsible. He did it from fury and frustration at the cruelty and unfairness of being cheated yet again — this time cheated out of the opportunity for justice or revenge.

I didn't see how Burgerville's financial problems and Lorber's death — and subsequent desecration — fit in with Conrad Stipe and the cabbie, but we now had thousands of possible suspects in the shootings.

I just wasn't sure whether that made the case easier to solve or a whole lot harder.

We went back upstairs to share what we had learned with Stottlemeyer and Disher.

The contrast between the Homicide Department and the Forensic Accounting Unit was startling. The squad room was bathed in the off-white glow of fluorescent bulbs and the diffused sunlight streaming through the dirty windows and crooked blinds.

The light made the stained white walls look yellow and somehow made the gray metal desks seem even more dented, scratched, and old than they were. The big, cumbersome computer monitors on all the paper-cluttered desks appeared bloated, beat-up, and fifty years old.

Yes, I know desktop computers haven't been around that long, but somehow when electronic equipment becomes dated, it seems far older than it actually is. Of course, most electronic equipment becomes dated two months after it comes out, but you get my point.

Even the people in Homicide seemed older, fatter, wearier, and less organized than the black-clad ninja accountants in the basement.

Monk looked depressed. "This is a cesspool."

"You never minded it here before," I said.

"That was before I glimpsed heaven," he said. "Now there's no going back."

I'm sure most of the cops in the Homicide Department would feel the same way. Maybe the real reason that the accountants carried weapons was to protect themselves from the fury of their jealous coworkers.

Disher was sitting at his desk. He'd replaced the placard with his name on it with one that read SPECIAL DESECRATION UNIT.

"Where have you been?" he asked.

"Talking with Lieutenant Chase," I said. "Have you ever been down to her office?"

Disher lowered his voice. "They're not real cops, if you catch my drift. They are stuck in some windowless pit in the basement. I had her come up here and visit the big boys so she'd realize just how important this assignment was."

"I'm sure it was very exciting for her," I said.

"She got the message," Disher said. "That's what counts."

"When did you start playing office politics?"

Disher tapped his new nameplate. "It comes with the job, baby."

I didn't see the point of reminding him that his unit had been effectively disbanded the moment Monk deduced that the desecration was part of a homicide case. Disher deserved to enjoy his new position for as long as it lasted. I even let him get away with calling me "baby" — that's how sensitive I was being.

"It's a good thing you're here," Disher said, rising from his seat. "The captain and I have lots of news for you."

"We have some for you, too," I said and we followed him into Stottlemeyer's office.

"You were right, Monk," the captain said from behind his desk. "Stipe was in that cab."

"You got the DNA back on the gum already?" Monk asked.

"We took the low-tech approach," Stottlemeyer said. "We went through Stipe's personal effects again."

"We found a taxi receipt in his wallet for

the ride from the airport to the Belmont Hotel," Disher said. "It was from Phil Bisson, the cabbie who was shot."

"You were also right about the candy wrapper," Stottlemeyer said. "Lorber's shooter was in that cab, too."

"You confirmed the lot number and twist of the wrapper?"

"I checked with the dispatcher and got all of Bisson's fares for the last week," Disher said. "The cabbie picked someone up two blocks from the Burgerville headquarters the night of the shooting and took him to the airport, where the cabbie picked up Stipe and took him to the Belmont."

"And you were onto something with those *Beyond Earth* uniforms," Stottlemeyer said.

"I was?" Monk said.

"Ambrose was," I said.

"The seamstress remembers selling uniforms during the convention to Morris Hibler, the convention organizer, and Ernest Pinchuk, the leader of the Galactic Uprising," Disher said. "She sold a dozen to other people she didn't know, so we've got her looking at photos of convention attendees and we're going to sit her down with a sketch artist."

Monk rolled his neck and shoulders and smiled. I knew that smile. We all did.

It got us smiling, too.

"You've got it all figured out," Stottle-meyer said. "Don't you?"

"Yes," Monk said. "I do."

CHAPTER TWENTY:
MR. MONK AND THE DEADLY TRIANGLE

This was the part that I liked best, when everything about the case seemed so clear and I felt stupid for not seeing how everything fit together. But Monk was taking his sweet time getting to it.

"I owe you an apology, Lieutenant," Monk said.

"For what?" Disher asked him.

"You were way ahead of me on this one," Monk said.

"I was?" Disher said.

"I was still so emotionally disturbed by my stained carpet that I wasn't thinking clearly enough to appreciate that you'd seen the key to the whole case."

"It's completely understandable, Monk," Stottlemeyer said. "Who among us wouldn't be completely rattled by a coffee stain on the carpet?"

"Thank you, Captain," Monk said, totally missing that he was being patronized.

"So what was it that I saw?" Disher asked.

"The deadly triangle — the two shots to the chest and the one to the head," Monk said. "You noticed right away that Lorber was shot by a coldly efficient, professional killer."

"So I was right," Disher said.

"Yes, you were," Monk said.

"I actually solved a case before you," Disher said proudly, then glanced at Stottlemeyer. "Have you ever done that?"

"It doesn't make sense," Stottlemeyer said.

"I don't like to flaunt my deductive skills. That way people will underestimate me and let their guard down," Disher said. "But beneath the surface thrives a keen intellect. I'm like Columbo, only without the overcoat, the cigar, and the glass eye."

Stottlemeyer glared at Disher. "What I meant was that a professional killer would have known that Lorber was already dead."

"That's why he shot him," Monk said.

"I don't follow you," Stottlemeyer said.

"Have you had some caffeine?" Monk asked.

"It won't help," Stottlemeyer said.

"Here's what happened," Monk said. "The hit man was hired to kill Lorber. He was to be paid half up front and half when the deed was done. But when he got there,

Lorber was already dead, cheating the killer out of his payday."

"So he made it look like a man who died of natural causes was actually murdered," I said.

"Exactly," Monk said.

"Isn't it usually the other way around?" I said.

"That's why nobody would have questioned that it was murder," Monk said.

"You did," I said.

"But nobody else would have, including me and Columbo over there," Stottlemeyer said, glancing at Disher. "When we find the corpse of someone who has been shot twice in the chest and once in the head, it's usually a safe assumption that it's murder."

"Not anymore," Disher said sadly. "Now the easy ones aren't even going to be easy."

"We'll just have to count on your keen intellect to see us through," Stottlemeyer said. "Does anyone know besides us and the medical examiner that Lorber died of natural causes?"

"No," Disher said.

"Let's keep it that way," Stottlemeyer said.

"I'm confused and I've had plenty of caffeine," I said. "What do Stipe and the cabbie have to do with it?"

"They were in the wrong place at the

wrong time," Monk said. "After shooting Lorber, the hit man walked a few blocks away and hailed a taxi to the airport. The same taxi then picked up Stipe and took him to his hotel."

"We know all that," Stottlemeyer said. "What we don't know is why the hit man came back from wherever he went and killed the cabbie and Stipe."

"The cabbie could identify him," Disher said.

"But Stipe couldn't," I said.

"I think that the hit man left something incriminating behind in the cab," Monk said. "Something that both the cabbie and Stipe saw and that could tie the hit man to Lorber's murder."

"But Lorber wasn't murdered," I said. "The hit man killed the cabbie and Stipe just so they couldn't tie him to a murder that never happened."

"Yes," Monk said.

"But he knew the Special Desecration Unit would be relentlessly pursuing him," Disher said, "and that once we took him down, he would do hard time. That was too terrifying for him to contemplate."

"What was the incriminating thing that the hit man left behind?" Stottlemeyer asked.

"I don't know," Monk said. "But he somehow found out that the next rider in the cab was Conrad Stipe and that he was in town for a *Beyond Earth* convention. So he disguised himself as Mr. Snork and made sure he was seen shooting Stipe in front of cameras and witnesses. He wanted to be sure we'd go looking for the killer in the wrong direction."

"Let me get this straight," Stottlemeyer said. "You're saying the whole *Beyond Earth* thing was nothing but a distraction and that Stipe was killed simply because he picked the wrong cab to take him to his hotel."

"It's all about Brandon Lorber," Monk said. "We need to find out who wanted him dead and hired a hit man to do the deed."

"But there are so many people with a reason to want Stipe dead," Disher said.

"The hit man got lucky," Monk said.

"If the hit man hadn't killed Stipe and the cabbie, the worst thing he could go down for would be desecrating a corpse," Stottlemeyer said.

"That's a big crime," Disher insisted.

"Not as big as murder," Stottlemeyer said. "We're making a lot of leaps here, based on nothing but chewing gum and candy wrappers, especially without the incriminating item you're guessing is at the center of all this. Are you sure you're right?"

"Always," Monk said.

If the shooter was a professional killer, it certainly explained why Mr. Snork looked so relaxed when he shot Stipe and why his aim was so good. But it also proved something else that struck Monk a lot closer to home.

"Not always, Mr. Monk," I said. "Lieutenant Disher isn't the only person you owe an apology. You owe Ambrose one, too."

"I don't see why," Monk said.

"Ambrose gave you an important clue and you ignored it."

"What clue was that?" Disher asked.

I looked sternly at Monk. If he didn't tell them, I would and he knew it.

"The hit man was wearing a season-one *Beyond Earth* uniform with season-two ears," Monk said. "The reason they didn't match was because the killer didn't know any of the insignificant details about the show."

"Isn't that how you usually solve cases, by noticing the seemingly insignificant details the killer missed?" I said.

"That's different," Monk said.

"No, it isn't. This uniform mismatch proves that the killer wasn't a real *Beyond Earth* fan. Ambrose also noticed that the uniform was new, which helps prove that the killer bought it the day of the shooting."

Monk glared at me. "Thanks for pouring extra antiseptic in my wound."

"The correct phrase is 'rubbing salt in the wound,' " Disher said.

"Nobody would ever rub a wound with salt," Monk said. "It doesn't clean or disinfect."

"But it would be extremely painful," Disher said.

"So would hacking off your arm with an ax," Monk said. "But I don't see what that has to do with Natalie trying to embarrass me in front of my employer."

"That's not what I was doing," I said. "I was standing up for your brother."

"Is he here?" Monk asked me pointedly.

"Of course not," I said. "He never leaves the house. That's why I had to stand up for him."

"I see," Monk said. "So are you working for him now or for me?"

I had never seen that look in Monk's eyes before, at least not directed at me. It was pure anger. I realized that I'd crossed a line with him.

"For you," I said. "I hope."

My pulse quickened. I might have just smart-assed my way right out of the best job I'd ever had.

But Monk didn't say anything to relieve my anxiety. He just turned and walked out of the captain's office.

"What did I just do?" I asked Stottlemeyer and Disher.

"Relax," Stottlemeyer said. "You weren't any harder on him than Sharona was."

"She was a real hard case," Disher said. "She didn't let Monk get away with anything."

"And now she's gone," I said.

"Monk didn't fire her," Stottlemeyer said. "She escaped."

"That doesn't mean he won't fire me."

"Monk has his insecurities — thousands of them, in fact — but he also has an enormous ego," Stottlemeyer said. "It's healthy for him to be reminded that he can't ignore other people's feelings and that he isn't the center of everybody's world."

"I'm sure there are a lot of bosses that need to hear that." I turned to Disher. "When was the last time you told the captain he was insensitive and wasn't giving somebody else enough credit for their work?"

Disher shifted his weight uncomfortably. "I don't need to because he's never done that."

"Kiss-ass," I said.

"Monk needs you, Natalie, and not just to drive him around and hand him disinfectant wipes," Stottlemeyer said. "He knows that."

"I hope you're right," I said and went out to look for my boss.

I caught up with Monk outside, where he was walking down the street, tapping each parking meter that he passed.

"Where are you going, Mr. Monk?"

"I'm wandering aimlessly to Burgerville headquarters."

I didn't bother to point out that if he knew exactly where he was going he wasn't wandering or aimless. A half hour ago I would have.

"What's there?"

"Andrew Cahill, the company's acting CEO," Monk said. "I want to talk with him."

"I could drive you," I said. "We'd get there a lot faster."

"So you can embarrass me in front of a possible suspect in the murder scheme?" Monk said. "I don't think so."

"I didn't mean to embarrass you, Mr. Monk," I said. "And if I did, I'm sorry."

"You're supposed to watch my back," Monk said. "Not stab it. You know how vulnerable I am now that I've been uprooted from my home and thrust into the unknown."

"You're staying with your brother," I said. "How is that the unknown?"

I'd spoken without thinking and immediately regretted my confrontational tone.

Monk stopped. "There you go again, questioning everything I do, contradicting everything I say."

"I do not," I said.

He gave me a look and started walking again. I caught up with him.

"Okay, right then, yes, I contradicted you, but I don't do it all the time. I only said what I said in the captain's office to help you."

"How could pointing out my failings in front of the people who pay me to be perfect possibly help me?"

"First off, they don't expect you to be perfect. You put that pressure entirely on yourself," I said. "I was trying to bring you closer to your brother."

"I didn't hire you for that," he said.

"You hired me to be your assistant and to make life as easy for you as possible. At least I *think* that's what I'm supposed to do, though you've never come out and said it.

That's left me pretty much on my own to figure out how best to do that for you."

"I've given you lists," he said.

"Of your phobias," I said. "Knowing that you're afraid of throw pillows, diving boards, and dust bunnies doesn't give me a whole lot to go on. I believe that one way of making your life easier is by improving your relationship with your brother."

"We get along great," he said.

"You never see each other."

"That's why," he said.

"He needs you, Mr. Monk, and I believe you need him."

"So now you're a family therapist," he said.

"I know you're both lonely and that you don't have to be," I said. "It hurts me to see that."

He stopped again. "It does?"

"Of course it does, Mr. Monk."

"Why?"

"Because I don't like to see the people I care about unhappy," I said.

"You care about me?"

"You're much more than just a boss to me," I said. "Assuming I still work for you."

"Of course you do," Monk said.

I sighed with relief. "Thank you, Mr. Monk."

"But I'm glad to know I'm much more than a boss to you," he said.

"Because I'm more than an employee to you?"

"Because this isn't just a job," Monk said. "It's a lifetime commitment."

CHAPTER TWENTY-ONE:
MR. MONK GOES
TO BURGERVILLE

Monk faced the revolving door as if confronting an old enemy. He squinted at it and jiggled his arms at his sides. There was no way he was going through that doorway again.

"You look like a marshal staring a gunfighter down and waiting to draw your gun," I said.

"I should have known when I saw this that Brandon Lorber was the kind of man who'd rip off his employees and destroy their futures."

I waved to Archie Applebaum, who was sitting at his guard desk in the center of the lobby. He got up and came over. He held up his security card key for me to indicate that he knew I wanted him to let us in.

"Because he had a revolving door in his lobby?" I asked Monk.

"He clearly enjoyed the suffering of others," Monk said. "What other purpose would there be for making people endure that?"

"Maybe so that they could get in and out of the building faster and he could conserve the heat and air-conditioning in his lobby."

Monk snorted. "You're so naïve."

Archie slid his card through the reader on the security door, held it open for us, and motioned us inside.

The security door was only used after hours and for the handicapped, but it was the only way Monk was going in or out of the building.

"Welcome back," Archie said. "Leland called and said you might be coming down. What can we do for you?"

"We'd like to talk to Andrew Cahill," I said.

"I'll call up and see if he's willing to see you," Archie said.

"Up?" Monk said.

"He's on the tenth floor," Archie said.

"Please ask him if he'll come down to see us," I said.

"No," Monk said. "We want to go up."

"That's a lot of stairs, Mr. Monk," I said.

"I want to see him in his office."

Archie went to his desk, made the call, then came back over. "He'll be glad to see you."

He walked us over to the stairs, unlocked the door, and held it open.

"You're awfully security-minded here," Monk said.

"This is the corporate headquarters of a national chain," Archie said. "We attract a lot of kooks."

"Does everybody have a shredder in their office?" Monk asked.

"Of course," Archie replied.

"What happens to the shredded documents?"

"The custodians pick them up, put them into a separate bin, and bring it down here," Archie said. "I lock it in a special closet until the document disposal service gets here."

"There's a service for that?"

"They come once a week," Archie said. "They take the shredded paper away and incinerate it."

"I also lock my garbage in a special closet," Monk said.

"You do?" Archie said.

"He does," I said.

"Doesn't everybody?" Monk said. "I wonder if they would come to my house each week, pick up my garbage, and incinerate it."

"You'd have to ask them," Archie said, "but I don't think they would."

"Who has keys to that closet?" Monk asked.

"Mr. Lorber, the building manager, and I share a set with the two guards who work the other shifts. Why do you ask?"

"I'm fascinated by shredded documents," Monk said. "I like putting things back together that have been taken apart."

"You'd enjoy reconstructing a shredded document?"

"I'd love it," Monk said and started up the stairs.

By the time we reached the tenth floor, I was aware of every muscle in my body and the full capacity of my lungs to draw in air.

Judging by the way Monk was breathing and the pained expression on his face, he wasn't any better off than me, but somehow he'd mastered the ability to control his sweat. There wasn't a bead of moisture on his skin. It was amazing.

I had to get him to teach me how to do that.

I wondered what other uncontrollable body functions he'd controlled. Could he also manage the moisture in his eyes and the production of saliva in his mouth? Maybe he even controlled the growth of his hair.

As I was trying to remember the last time Monk had had a haircut, a secretary met us at the stairwell with bottled water.

The water wasn't Sierra Springs, so Monk refused it. I gladly took both bottles and guzzled them down as the secretary led us to Cahill's corner office.

Cahill looked like a man who could bench-press my car. His muscles rippled under his tailored business shirt like the surface of the ocean. I don't know whether they were moving or I was just swooning from my trek.

His office was furnished identically to Lorber's, right down to pictures on the wall of himself standing outside of various Burgerville restaurants across the country. The only difference was a Lucite paperweight on his desk with a butterfly in it.

"It's good to meet you, Mr. Monk," Cahill said, offering Monk his hand. "I want to help you any way I can in your investigation."

I gave Monk a disinfectant wipe before he had a chance to ask for it. I was eager to please after our little tiff.

"I can assure you my hands are clean," Cahill said with a smile. "In every respect."

"It sounds like you're honing your denial skills for the trial," I said. "The smile might just work on the jury."

"I didn't murder Brandon Lorber," Cahill said. "I was at a Burgerville opening in Chula Vista."

"Lorber was killed by a professional hit man," Monk said. "An alibi doesn't clear you as the one who hired him. But I believe my assistant was referring to the criminal trial for all the fiscal shenanigans here."

"I don't know what you're talking about," Cahill said.

People said that a lot around Monk.

In the context of a murder investigation, it was usually a lie.

In the context of observing one of Monk's rules about things, like the proper way to rake leaves, it was the truth.

But we weren't talking about raking leaves. We were talking about raking in cash and committing a murder to hide it.

"Then you are one terrible CFO," I said. "The police forensic accountants have put you under an electron microscope. We know all about the overpriced buyout of franchises that were secretly owned by Lorber's brother-in-law and the pillaging of the marketing fund, among other things. It's your job to know where the money is going around here, isn't it?"

"What I meant to say was that I wasn't

involved in any financial irregularities," Cahill said. "It was all Brandon's doing. He manipulated the figures I was given, he lied to me, and he paid off my subordinates to feed me inaccurate information. I was shocked by the extent of his criminal activities, which is why I've been cooperating fully with the Justice Department for the last few months."

Monk walked over to Cahill's desk and examined the shredder.

"So you're going to blame all the shenanigans on Lorber when the crimes here become public," Monk said. "I can understand why you would. Lorber won't be here to defend himself or to point the finger at you instead."

"Lorber takes the fall, you take the company," I said. "His murder has worked out well for you."

Cahill started to speak, but Monk interrupted him.

"Nice shredder," Monk said. "May I try it?"

"Go ahead," Cahill said and pointed his finger at me. There appeared to be more muscles in his finger than in my leg. "You think I'm coming out of this unscathed? I'm going to be pilloried in the press. I'm going to lose millions of dollars in stocks and everything I had in the employee pension plan."

Monk took a piece of blank notepaper off of Cahill's desk and fed it into the shredder, which spit it out in tiny strips. Cahill pointed to the shreds with his big finger.

"That might as well be my future as a CFO," Cahill said, "unless I can somehow save this company. But the odds aren't in my favor."

Monk took two of the shreds, held them up to the light, then dropped the strips back in the trash.

"It could be worse," Monk said. "You could be going to jail."

"Not likely," Cahill replied. "I have immunity from prosecution in return for my testimony."

"I'm sure that immunity doesn't extend to murder," Monk said.

"If you're looking for someone with a motive to kill Brandon, you don't have to look any further than his own house," Cahill said. "His wife gets everything, and now that Brandon is dead, nobody can take it from her. If he was alive, he would have been prosecuted and his assets would have been seized. She'd have lost the Pacific Heights mansion, the yacht, the Gulfstream, the house in Hawaii, the house in Vail, and the his-and-hers matching silver Bentleys. She would have had to go back to strutting her surgically sculpted ass on the catwalk."

"She was a model?" I asked.

"She was a stripper," Cahill said. "Brandon met her in a Dallas strip club fifteen years ago and left his wife for her. She was a gold digger. She has very expensive tastes, which I doubt Brandon would have been able to afford once the government got through with him."

"Do you think she'd kill to keep it?" I asked.

"She loves her Bentley a hell of a lot more than she loved him," Cahill said. "Gold diggers don't stick around once the gold is gone. They go looking for a new place to dig."

"I don't know why people would pay to see someone take off their clothes," Monk said as we went back down the stairs. I could have told him, but he didn't give me the chance. "I would pay a naked person to put their clothes on."

Now *that* was interesting. "Would you watch them do it?"

"I wouldn't even be in the same zip code," Monk said. "And I would still cover my eyes."

"Then what is it you'd be paying for?"

"Peace of mind," Monk said. "I would know that there's one less naked person in the world."

"I didn't know nudity was a big problem," I said.

"Huge," Monk said. "Bigger than global warming."

"Maybe they're taking off their clothes because it's getting so warm."

But I could tell from the contemplative look on his face that my flip remark wasn't going to put an end to his musing on this issue.

"Why would someone marry a naked person?" he asked.

This was like having a conversation with my daughter. She was always asking me weird questions that weren't so easy to answer. Not too long ago, she asked why we couldn't put sick people to sleep like dogs. My daughter is very pragmatic when it comes to death, which scares me a bit, since she's likely to be the one taking care of me in my old age.

I answered Monk the way I would have answered Julie if she'd asked me the same question.

"Everybody is a naked person," I said.

"I'm not naked," Monk said.

"Not now," I said. "But you can't be dressed at every moment."

"Of course you can," Monk said.

"At some point during the day even you have to take your clothes off, Mr. Monk."

"No, I don't."

"How's that possible?"

"It's required in a civilized society. You're supposed to dress and undress in stages," Monk said. "You always leave one piece of clothing on at all times throughout the process. Didn't you read the manual?"

"What manual?"

"The one my mother gave me and that your mother gave to you, of course," Monk said. "You might want to brush up on your skills by reading the revised edition that you gave Julie. A lot of things have changed since you and I were kids."

"I didn't give Julie a manual."

Monk looked at me in horror. "What kind of mother are you? You'd better get one before child protective services finds out."

His mother gave him a manual for dressing? She must have written it herself. I thought it would be fascinating and more than a little horrifying to read.

"Maybe I could borrow your family's copy," I said.

"I wish you could," Monk said, "but it's

long gone."

"What happened to it?"

"Trudy asked to read it once," Monk said. "I haven't seen it since. It's a mystery."

It wasn't to me.

If I'd been Monk's wife, and loved him as much as she did, I know what I'd have done with that manual. I'd have burned it. I wondered if it was really such a mystery to Monk, who had solved much more complicated riddles than that.

"So if you don't ever completely undress," I said, "how do you shower?"

Monk blushed. "Don't you think you're getting a little personal? I'm your boss, after all. You shouldn't be thinking about me in the shower."

"I'm not," I said.

"I don't even want to think about me in the shower," he said.

Monk stopped at the fifth floor, took a deep breath for courage, and dashed out. For him, being on an odd-numbered floor was like walking on a rope bridge over a deep gorge, so he must have had a good reason for doing it.

I followed after him to Lorber's office.

"What are we doing here?" I asked.

"Conducting an important test," Monk said.

He took a piece of blank paper from Lorber's desk and fed it into the shredder.

"If you're trying to figure out which machine the shredded document came from, you can forget it," I said. "The shredder in here is identical to the one in Cahill's office."

"No two shredders are identical," he said.

"It's the same brand, the same model, and the same blades."

"That's where you're wrong." Monk picked up two shreds and held them up to the light. "They get dull and chipped in different places. All it takes is one document with a staple in it to put an almost imperceptible groove in the edge of a blade."

"*Almost* imperceptible?" I said. "You'd need a microscope to see it."

"I can see it," Monk said.

"You can?"

Monk dropped the shreds back in the trash. "The shredded document came from Cahill's office. I just wanted to double-check."

"So he knew exactly what was going on and instead of going straight to the authorities, he shredded the evidence," I said. "He's a liar."

"Most murderers usually are," Monk said. "Is he one?"

"I don't know," Monk said. "Yet."

I admired the unshakable confidence behind the way Monk said "yet." In every case he investigated, there was never any doubt in his mind that he would find the killer.

There was just one exception, and it was the case that mattered the most to him.

Trudy's murder.

I looked forward to the day that changed.

CHAPTER TWENTY-TWO:
MR. MONK AND THE
HOUSE OF HORRORS

I'm not sure why people draw a distinction between so-called old money and new money. Money is money. Either you have it or you don't. It's how you spend it that counts.

I know from personal experience what it's like to be rich and poor. I came from a very wealthy family that made their fortune in the toothpaste business.

"Everybody has teeth and they don't want to lose them," my grandfather used to say. "It's the most secure business on earth."

It was a business my grandfather almost lost after it was revealed that he'd laced the original formula for his toothpaste with sugar to appeal to his customers' "sweet tooth," thus hastening their dental decay. The business miraculously recovered from the scandal, diversified, and thrived, becoming the global conglomerate that it is today.

I had whatever I wanted when I was growing up except maybe a little insecurity. My life was too safe, too pampered, too restricted.

I know what you're thinking: oh, boo-hoo for the rich girl. Believe it or not, money isn't all that it's cracked up to be. Not only does money not buy you happiness, but it doesn't necessarily give you freedom either. Sure, you have freedom from the fear of starvation or homelessness. But when everything comes easy, and you live in a rarefied world, it doesn't really feel like you're living.

So I rebelled. I disavowed my family's money and I eloped with a man who was rich in character but cash poor. It was the happiest time of my life, and I have Julie to always remind me of it.

I've been struggling financially ever since. It's no treat being a single mother. It would be easier to just give in and take my father's money, but then I wouldn't be surviving on my own, and what lesson would my daughter take from that? And I wouldn't have met Monk, and my life would be considerably less unpredictable and exciting.

Knowing what it is to be rich and poor means that I'm not impressed by wealth or the people who have it. Monk isn't either, but for entirely different reasons. He's socially illiterate. He's unaware of the deference, envy, and feelings of inferiority that are expected of you by those who have more money than you do.

In fact, Monk didn't know the appropriate behavior in any situation. He made his own rules and was surprised when nature and humankind didn't follow them.

So neither Monk nor I was intimidated by Brandon Lorber's Victorian mansion in Pacific Heights and its commanding, IMAX view of the Golden Gate, Marin County, and Alcatraz Island.

Pacific Heights has been the Mount Olympus of San Francisco's elite since the 1800s. Merchants and robber barons flush with their gold, sugar, and railroad riches needed a high place where they could live above the riffraff they exploited and be certain that everyone could see the monuments to their success.

That's still true today, whether your money is old or new or just on paper.

Stottlemeyer and Disher, being poorly paid civil servants, would have been uneasy around so much money and power, which is probably why they opted to let us see Veronica Lorber on our own. I think the captain believed that a black-sheep rich girl and a socially clueless detective would be more effective with the widow Lorber than they would be. Money and influence are kryptonite for people whose livelihoods depend on the whims of politicians.

So I parked at the cul-de-sac at the end of Broadway, where the street met the lush forest of the Presidio and the top of the Baker steps that led down to the Marina District.

I saw two painters with their easels standing at the top of the Baker Street steps facing the spectacular view. One artist was painting a picture of the bay, the other was painting the painter who painted the bay.

I looked over my shoulder as we walked to the Lorber mansion to see if maybe there was someone else above us perhaps painting a picture of a painter painting a picture of a painter painting the bay. I bet you can't say that four times fast.

There were two stone lions, each with one paw on a stone ball, on either side of the Lorbers' front gate. Monk was troubled by this; he liked the symmetry of the matching lions but felt they should have a ball under each paw.

He didn't say that, but I could tell. I'd been with Monk a long time. And like I said before, he's not real good about hiding his feelings.

I wasn't wild about the lions either. Lots

of rich people had them and I had no idea what they were supposed to symbolize. Why lions? And why did they have their paws on stone balls?

The front door, the size of the entrance to Oz, was opened by a uniformed butler. He looked like a turtle who'd evolved into a man fifty years ago and traded his shell for a tuxedo.

"Your lions only have one ball," Monk said.

The butler raised an eyebrow. "Excuse me?"

"This is Adrian Monk and I'm his assistant, Natalie Teeger," I said. "Captain Stottlemeyer of the San Francisco Police arranged an appointment for us with Mrs. Lorber."

"Indeed," the butler said, stepping aside. "She'll see you in the study. This way, please."

We stepped inside and followed him down a marbled corridor. My grandfather was right about everybody having teeth, but it looked to me like there was more money to be made in selling the food they chewed with them.

The butler led us into a massive room with a ceiling high enough to accommodate the space shuttle.

Monk staggered back from the study in horror and revulsion. I've seen him do the same thing when confronted with a bowl of granola.

It wasn't the ceiling that freaked him out, it was the decor. It looked like the trophy room of a hunter's lodge. The walls were crowded with mounted fish and the decapitated heads of deer, elk, antelopes, bears, and God knows how many other creatures. There were animal skins on the floors and draped on the furniture. An enormous stuffed bear stood in one corner in an eternal snarl at a glass-eyed tiger across the room.

I wondered if Brandon Lorber had personally shot every cow that Burgerville used for its beef. But he didn't limit his killing to the animal kingdom. There was even a colorful collection of butterflies spread out in display boxes on a few of the tables.

Veronica Lorber sat in a chair beside the bear. She was probably the only trophy Lorber had bagged that wasn't dead and stuffed.

If Dolly Parton fell into a vat of Ben & Jerry's Chunky Monkey ice cream and ate her way out, she'd look like Brandon Lorber's widow.

Her eyes were red, her cheeks tear-streaked. She clutched a balled-up tissue in her fist like a lifeline. It was a good thing the tissue was in her hand and not on the floor or Monk might have called in a strike team from the Centers for Disease Control in Atlanta.

The butler announced us as if we were arriving at some grand ball. "Mr. Adrian Monk and Ms. Natalie Teeger are here to see you, madam."

"Thank you, Maxwell," Veronica said.

The butler gave a slight bow and shuffled away.

"Do come in, Mr. Monk," Veronica said with a sniffle.

"I can't," Monk whispered to me.

"Just a moment, please," I said to Veronica with a smile, then turned to Monk. "What's wrong?"

"What isn't?" Monk said.

I looked back at the room and tried to see it from Monk's point of view. Animal heads of all sizes, shapes, and species everywhere. Nothing matched.

In Monk's worldview, it was complete chaos. If they were going to have deer heads on the wall, there should have been an even number of the same size heads lined up in a neat row, not mixed with elk and antelope. Every animal should have had its own row.

And don't get me started on the butterflies. They shouldn't even have been in the same room.

"I know that it's a mess, Mr. Monk, and that the deer shouldn't mingle with the elk and the butterflies," I said, "but you can do this."

"Who cares about the mess?"

"You do," I said. "You *always* do."

"That's the least of the problems," Monk said.

"Is it her sniffling that's bothering you?"

"Open your eyes, woman!" Monk pointed into the room. "It's a slaughterhouse!"

"What did you say?" Veronica asked.

"He says it's a beautiful house," I said, then lowered my voice to Monk. "Please keep your voice down. It's just a trophy room."

"I don't see any trophies. All I see are body parts splattered everywhere," Monk said, raising his voice again in his exasperation. "The walls are dripping blood."

"Did he say something about dripping blood?" Veronica asked. "What blood?"

"You must have misheard him. He said 'ripping good.' It's a British expression, a compliment. We need another moment," I said and pulled Monk out of her earshot.

I couldn't believe that he was so rattled by

some animal heads. He was a homicide detective. He'd seen a lot worse. And since I'd become his assistant, I had, too.

"What's the big deal?" I whispered. "You see dead bodies every day."

"I've never been in a room where hundreds of mutilated corpses were nailed to the walls, spread out on the floors, and draped over the furniture. It's revolting, not to mention extremely unsanitary."

"What about the morgue? You love it there. And there are bodies, and body parts, everywhere."

"But they are clean bodies and body parts that are meticulously organized in a sterile environment," he said. "Clean, organized, and sterile. The way everything in life should be."

I groaned and leaned back into the study.

"Would you mind if we moved this discussion to a different room?" I asked Veronica. "It seems that Mr. Monk is allergic to elk."

"I'm staying right here," Veronica said. "I haven't left this room since I got the awful news that Brandon was killed. I may never leave."

"Why not?" I asked.

"When I sit here," she said, "I feel close to him."

"Is his head on the wall, too?" Monk asked.

Veronica gasped and so did I.

"Mr. Monk!" I said, then turned back to Veronica, who had the same startled look as the deer on the wall. "Please forgive him. He's not himself today."

"That's because I'm choking on the overwhelming stench of death," he said.

Veronica's face turned bright red. Her cheeks puffed with fury. She looked like a terrified blowfish with collagen injections.

"This was my husband's favorite room in the house. The only reason I don't have Maxwell throw you out right now is because I know you are a brilliant detective and that you will find my husband's killer," she said. "So tell me, Mr. Monk, what's your problem? Are you one of those animal rights wackos who picket outside our restaurants because we serve beef?"

"No," Monk said.

"Then I don't understand how you can be so cold and insensitive," she said. "I've just lost my husband in a brutal murder. Do you have any idea how I feel right now?"

"I do," he said. "That's why I can't understand why you'd want to surround yourself with death. You're even sitting on an animal skin."

"It's leather," she said.

"You shouldn't sit on it," Monk said. "You should bury it."

We were off to a very bad start, and we hadn't learned anything that would be useful to our investigation. At least I didn't think we had. Maybe there was an animal hair or something that would prove decisive. Even so, I thought it best to try to save this disastrous meeting from getting any worse.

"Since you two can obviously carry on a conversation without being in the same room together, I suggest that Mr. Monk stay out here in the hall, you stay in the study, and we discuss the homicide. Finding your husband's killer is, after all, our common goal."

"It's easy," she said. "Arrest Andrew Cahill."

"What makes you think he killed your husband?" Monk asked.

"Brandon discovered that Andrew was running some sort of devious financial scheme and was going to expose him this week."

"The evidence suggests that it was the other way around," Monk said.

"Of course it does," she said. "Andrew was the CFO. He was in the best position to manipulate the numbers to tell any story he wanted. I told Brandon not to say a word to Andrew and just go straight to the authorities. But once my husband has a target in his sights, he always pulls the trigger."

"But Cahill wouldn't really gain anything by killing your husband," Monk said. "He's already been granted immunity in exchange for his testimony. The only one who would gain is you."

"I've lost my husband," she said.

"But you've kept his fortune," Monk said. "And you will probably get to keep whatever remains of Burgerville after all the lawsuits and prosecutions are settled."

"Money means nothing to me compared to what I have lost," she said. "My husband's love was priceless."

"So why were you sleeping with Andrew Cahill?" Monk asked.

"How can you say such a thing!" she exclaimed, rising to her feet.

"Because of the evidence," Monk said. "You collect butterflies; your husband didn't. The butterfly in the paperweight on Cahill's desk is a rare Panamint swallowtail, like the one in the collection on that table beside you. The Panamint swallowtail is so rare that even the National Museum of Natural History doesn't have one. But you gave one to Cahill. It's not something you would give to a man you loathed. Quite the opposite. I'll bet Cahill didn't dare put it on his desk until after your husband's body was wheeled out of the building in a body bag. And if it meant that much to him, his feelings for you must be pretty strong, too."

"You are an awful little man," she hissed.

"I'm not the one sitting on dead flesh in a room full of animal heads," Monk said. "I hope you're at least going to wash your hands."

"If you and Cahill didn't hire a hit man to kill your husband," I asked her, "then who did?"

"There are those awful little animal rights wackos," she said. "And there was that awful little man who spilled coffee in his lap and blamed my husband for it. And there are those awful little environmentalists who accuse us of polluting the environment with our packaging materials. The world is full of awful little people."

Hearing her talk, I imagined this mass of angry elves carrying torches and marching towards her house.

"None of those people hired an assassin to kill your husband," Monk said.

"How would you know?" Veronica snapped.

"They wouldn't have had access to your

husband's security key card," Monk said. "But whoever hired the hit man did and knew exactly when the security guard would be on patrol and away from his desk in the lobby. That person was someone close to Brandon Lorber. And no one was closer to him than you."

Her lower lip quivered with rage — or perhaps the collagen had suddenly drained out into her chin, which would explain why she had two of them.

"Get out," she said.

"Gladly," Monk said. "Would you be offended if we ran?"

"It's far too late to be concerned about offending me," she said. "You awful little man."

I'm tall, but as we hurried out of Veronica Lorber's house of horrors, I couldn't help wondering if I would always be remembered by her as that "awful little woman."

CHAPTER TWENTY-THREE:
Mr. Monk
and the X

Once we were outside, I asked Monk a few questions that were bugging me.

"How did you know that the butterfly collection was Mrs. Lorber's and not her husband's?"

"It was an educated guess," Monk said. "I have a hard time believing that a man who likes to shoot things would run around chasing butterflies with a net. And if Brandon Lorber was going to give Cahill a trophy, it would be an animal head, not a colorful insect."

"How did you know which butterfly that was?"

"The Panamint swallowtail has a chemical composition that will make any animal that swallows it regurgitate immediately," Monk said. "I want to know about anything that will make me regurgitate. Throwing up is about as close as you can get to dying without already being dead."

"What are the odds of a Panamint butterfly taking a wrong turn and flying into your mouth?"

"You never know," Monk said and seemed to notice the two artists at their easels for the first time.

He glanced at their works-in-progress as we passed the two men on our way to my car. The artist painting the bay was doing the kind of rudimentary work you find at those traveling art shows that pop up on weekends in shopping center parking lots.

But the other artist, the one doing a painting of the painter, had real skill and a sense of humor. He'd even managed to capture the amateurish quality of the painting his subject was working on.

Monk seemed very interested in this painting, too. But before he got too distracted, I still had a few more questions for him.

"If Veronica Lorber and Andrew Cahill are sleeping together, why did he put the blame for Brandon Lorber's murder on her and why did she put it on him?" I asked. "Are they so cold and self-centered that they would betray one another right away?"

"They did it to cancel each other out," Monk said, looking over the artist's shoulder.

"Cancel each other out? What does that mean?"

"They figured if they each accused the other of murder, we would never suspect the two of them of having an affair and conspiring together," Monk said. "But it backfired. We see them as the calculating and greedy people that they actually are."

"So with Brandon Lorber dead, and Cahill's immunity, they can both walk away from the financial scandal with their assets more or less intact," I said. "That's a pretty good motive for murder."

"Money and sex usually are," Monk said.

They were certainly the things that were driving Arianna Stipe and Veronica Lorber. They were both selfish, greedy, man-hungry predators.

Granted, Arianna had just gone through a bitter divorce, so I couldn't really fault her for sleeping with her lawyer and pursuing her share of Conrad Stipe's money. But I still didn't like her.

Veronica Lorber at least put on a show of grief, but that's all it was. She'd betrayed her husband while he was alive and might even have paid for his murder so she could get all his money.

The two women had a lot in common.

I was sure that if I introduced them to

one another they would become good friends — at least until they inevitably stabbed each other in the back over money or men.

While I was musing about that, Monk cleared his throat to attract the artist's attention.

The painter was a very thin man whom I guessed to be in his forties, with a weather-beaten face that attested to all the time he'd spent outside. He was wearing a paint-spattered T-shirt. There were flecks of paint tangled in the hairs on his tanned hands.

"Excuse me," Monk said, "but you've made a mistake."

The painter turned. "There is no right and wrong in art, sir."

"That's also a mistake," Monk said. "There's always right and wrong. The artist you are depicting is clearly wearing a checked shirt with twenty-four squares on his back. But you have only fourteen squares in your painting. He's not wearing anything on his head, but you have given him a sailor's cap. It's inaccurate."

"This isn't a photograph," the painter said. "It's an artistic interpretation. I'm painting it the way I see it."

"Then you need glasses," Monk said. "And you're delusional."

The painter took his brush and, without any warning at all, painted a blue X over Monk's mouth.

Monk staggered back, sputtering and yelping and flailing his arms as if he were being attacked by a swarm of bees. He waved his hands in front of his face because he reflexively and desperately wanted to wipe the paint off but didn't dare do it for fear of getting it on his hands or clothes. He was in agony.

The two painters and several passersby stared at him.

"Relax, Mr. Monk," I said, reaching into my purse for a wipe. "I'm coming."

He hopped in place as I tried to remove the paint with the wipe.

"Stand still, Mr. Monk, or I'm going to get the paint all over you."

He immediately froze. He didn't speak or move a muscle while I worked, terrified that he might get paint in his mouth. The silence was nice. I subtly positioned him so I could admire the view at the same time.

It took a whole package of wipes and about twenty minutes, but I finally managed to get all the paint off his face. Luckily, none of it had gotten on his clothes.

By the time I was done, the painter who'd put the X on Monk had packed up his things and left for the day. I'm sure that watching the felon escape and not being able to chase after him was frustrating for Monk.

I managed to talk Monk out of calling an ambulance for himself and taking a trip to the emergency room. I reminded him that the dangers he faced at the hospital were far worse than any posed by the paint that had been on his skin.

Instead we headed back to the police station so Monk could marshal the full resources of law enforcement to, and I quote, "hunt down that psychopath like a ravenous dog."

As soon as we arrived at police headquarters, it was obvious to me from the expression on Stottlemeyer's face that he was already in a bad mood — and Monk hadn't even opened his mouth yet.

"We need to launch a manhunt," Monk declared as he marched into Stottlemeyer's office.

The captain sighed wearily. "Who are we manhunting?"

"A drooling, paint-covered psychopath," Monk said. "We need to form an impenetrable dragnet around this entire city until we arrest him."

I didn't recall the painter drooling, but I

didn't say anything.

"On what charge?" Stottlemeyer said. "Or is it the drooling that's bugging you?"

"He attacked me with a deadly paintbrush," Monk said.

"You look fine to me."

"Only because Natalie was there to provide immediate lifesaving measures," Monk said and then, almost teary-eyed, he turned to me. "I am eternally grateful."

I thanked Monk and then briefly explained to Stottlemeyer what had happened in what I like to think was an objective, nonjudgmental way. The account seemed to lighten the captain's mood considerably. I could see him fighting back a smile.

"He could be the Zodiac killer," Monk said when I was done.

"The guy would have to be at least in his sixties to be the Zodiac killer," the captain said.

"If he's not the Zodiac killer, he's another killer," Monk said. "He's the paintbrush killer."

"Who has he killed?"

"I don't know," Monk said. "But if he hasn't killed somebody yet, he will. He's covered in paint."

"He's a painter," Stottlemeyer said. "It goes with the job."

"The hell it does," Monk said. He was getting pretty worked up. "He's a psychopath and that proves it. It's a reflection of his disordered mind. You can ask the profilers at Quantico."

"You want me to bring the FBI into this?"

"It's a matter of national security," Monk said.

"I'm not calling the FBI, the National Guard, or the CIA, but I'll be sure to alert all my patrol units to be on the lookout for him, okay?" Stottlemeyer said. "In the meantime, how about telling me how it went with Andrew Cahill and Veronica Lorber."

"The usual," Monk said.

"That much I know," Stottlemeyer said. "I've already heard from their lawyers, the chief, and an aide to the mayor. Did you really ask her if she had her husband's head on the wall?"

"She's a nut job," Monk said.

I looked at Monk. "Did you just say 'nut job'?"

"Did you see the room she was in?" Monk said.

"I've never heard you use that phrase before," I said.

"I've never been in a room like that before."

"Technically, you still haven't," I said. "You stood out in the hall."

"Tell me that one of them hired the guy who killed Brandon Lorber," Stottlemeyer said.

"I can't," Monk said. "At least not yet."

"That's a shame," Stottlemeyer said. "It would make it a lot easier for me to deal with the pressure I'm getting from my superiors if I could say that one of the people complaining about you is guilty of murder."

"One of them is a nut-job adulteress, the other is a liar and embezzler," Monk said. "Who cares about their complaints?"

Stottlemeyer nodded. "You've got a point there, Monk."

Disher rushed in carrying a sheaf of papers. "I've got the artist renderings of the people who bought *Beyond Earth* uniforms at the convention."

He laid some of the drawings out on Stottlemeyer's desk. We leaned over to look at them. None of the faces looked familiar to me.

Disher glanced at Monk. "Did you really tell Lorber's grieving widow that she was sitting on dead flesh that should be taken out and buried?"

"Yes," Monk said.

"I wish I could have been there to see her reaction to that," Disher said.

"No," I said. "You don't."

Disher laid out the rest of the sketches that he was holding. "These are descriptions of customers who bought second-season Mr. Snork ears from the vendors that Ambrose told us about."

Monk tapped one of the drawings of one of the rubber-ear buyers, a guy who looked vaguely like a wax figure of Jude Law, and found an almost identical drawing from among the costume customers. He put them side by side.

"This is the same man," Monk said.

"I noticed that, too," Disher said. "I ran the sketches through the various criminal databases and came up with nothing."

Monk held up the pictures in front of me. "Take a good look at these."

"I am," I said.

"Now imagine him covered with paint and wielding a brush of doom," Monk said. "Do you think it could be the same man?"

"No," I said. "I don't."

"Are you sure?" Monk said.

"Positive," I said. "The painter looked completely different."

"What painter?" Disher asked.

Stottlemeyer dismissed Disher's question

with a wave of his hand.

"Maybe it was a cunning disguise," Monk said. "We know the assassin likes disguises."

"Why would the hit man who shot Brandon Lorber, killed Conrad Stipe, and gunned down the cabdriver be standing outside Mrs. Lorber's house today disguised as a painter?" I asked.

"I don't know," Monk said. "But all the paint in the world can't hide that man's black soul."

"What's James Brown got to do with this?" Disher asked.

"We're talking about a painter," I said, "not the Godfather of Soul."

"Not necessarily," Monk said. "There could be an organized-crime angle to this."

"It's been a long day, Monk," Stottlemeyer said. "My suggestion is that you get some rest and tackle this fresh tomorrow."

Monk squinted at the two drawings some more. "Maybe you're right. But tomorrow I may want to talk to this Godfather of Soul and see what he knows."

"I'll keep that in mind," Stottlemeyer said.

CHAPTER TWENTY-FOUR:
Mr. Monk Makes
a Mistake

I took Monk back to Ambrose's house. On the way, I thought about reminding Monk of the large contribution his brother had made to the investigation. But then I remembered how close I'd come to being fired and decided to keep my mouth shut for a change. Monk was right when he chewed me out — he wasn't paying me to meddle in his personal life.

Monk let himself in without bothering to knock. We found Ambrose in the kitchen, sitting at the table with two open cans of 7-Up in front of him, reading the newspaper. On the front page was a picture of Mr. Snork aiming his gun.

"Hello, Natalie," Ambrose said. "It's a distinct pleasure to see you again."

It was nice to know I was distinct. "Thank you, Ambrose."

"I've already had dinner," Ambrose said. "But I've saved some linguine for you both.

There's eighty-eight noodles left for you. You could split it evenly."

"That's a very tempting offer," I said, "but I'm afraid I have plans for dinner."

My plan was not to eat it with the Monks.

"Forty-four noodles is more than enough for me," Monk said. "I don't mind sharing."

"No thank you, Mr. Monk," I said, heading for the door. "I should really be getting on my way."

"How did your investigation go?" Ambrose asked.

I stopped. I had to hear how Monk answered this.

Monk looked at me, then at his brother. "Thanks to you, Ambrose, it went very well."

"Me?" Ambrose said. "What did I do?"

"You saw what nobody else did, that the killer had made a big mistake. He wore a first-season uniform with second-season ears. It helped us to discover that Stipe's murder had nothing to do with *Beyond Earth*. We approached the sellers you identified and were able to generate a sketch of the killer without his Mr. Snork disguise."

"Tell me everything." Ambrose sat up straight in his seat. "Talk slowly and don't leave out a single detail."

I couldn't leave now. So I sat down, took the two 7-Ups that Ambrose offered me, and listened as Monk recounted the events and developments of the day.

Ambrose listened attentively to every word and even took notes. I looked at his work and was surprised to see that it included annotated footnotes referencing various publications and the dates and times of previous conversations with Monk and me regarding the investigation. I don't know why he was doing it, except that he was a Monk and they have this thing about noting the details.

"You made some amazing deductions, Adrian," Ambrose said when Monk was finished.

"I could have made them a lot earlier if I'd listened to you," Monk said. "You're a great detective."

"I'm not really sure what I am, but I'm certainly not a detective," Ambrose said. "I don't have your worldly experience, adventurous spirit, or fearless, devil-may-care attitude towards life."

Monk was fearless?

I have a list somewhere that he gave me of the 222 things he's afraid of. Number 222 on the list is: *Having a list that ends on the number 221 or 223.*

But I didn't think this was a good time to contradict Ambrose's impression of his brother, not if I wanted to keep my job.

"You have all those same qualities," Monk said. "You'd discover it for yourself if you'd just leave the house and go out into the world."

Ambrose shook his head. "I'm not you, Adrian. I don't have your strength."

"I'm not strong," Monk said.

"I could never go through what you have," Ambrose said, then looked at me. "Or you. I'd be destroyed."

"We are," Monk said.

"A piece of us, maybe," I said. "But it was worth it, Ambrose. Love always is."

Ambrose shook his head. "No, you're both special people. Especially you, Adrian. You're the best detective on earth and I'm proud of you."

Monk stared at him as if seeing his brother for the very first time. "You are?"

"Of course I am," Ambrose said. "Who wouldn't be? I'm sure there are thousands of people who look up to you. I'm just one of them."

"No, you're not," Monk said. "You're my brother."

"That doesn't mean I can't admire you, does it?"

I leapt out of my chair and hugged Ambrose and then I hugged Monk. It was like hugging two mannequins, but I couldn't help myself. It was such a great turning point for them and I wanted them to feel it.

They both looked a little shocked by my show of affection.

"Why did you do that?" Monk said.

"I'm your surrogate hugger," I said. "I gave you both the hugs that you two should have given each other."

Ambrose looked at Monk. "Is she okay?"

"She has been acting irrationally all day," Monk said. "I really think she needs some rest."

Ambrose looked at me. "Are you pregnant?"

"No," I said. "Absolutely not. What would make you think that?"

"I've read that women get irrational and emotional when they're pregnant," Ambrose said.

"Well, I'm not. But Mr. Monk is right. Some relaxation is exactly what I need," I said. "I'll see you both tomorrow. Shall I come a little later than usual?"

"Sure. Let's sleep in and rest up," Monk said. "I'll see you at nine-oh-five."

That was his idea of sleeping in?

"That extra five minutes is going to make

296

all the difference, Mr. Monk. Thank you."

"There's no need to thank me," Monk said. "You've earned it."

Monk and Ambrose walked me to the door.

"I didn't bring anything with me to read," Monk said to Ambrose. "Which one of your books would you recommend?"

"You'd like to read one of my books?" Ambrose asked.

"What better way is there to spend an evening at home than to read a good book?" Monk replied.

As I walked out the door, I looked back to see Ambrose handing Monk a book.

"This is my manual for the Akita Multi-Standard VCR and DVD Burner Combination Player-Recorder. It won the Pritiker Award for Technical Writing for Electronic Audiovisual Components," Ambrose said. "I've been told it's a very compelling read, particularly the German version."

"It sounds great," Monk said, as he put the book under his arm and gave his brother a sincere smile. "Why would anyone want to toast a DVD? Are they edible?"

I was on my way home when I got a call from Firefighter Joe, my "friend-with-benefits." He had finished his shift at the firehouse and wanted to know whether I might be free for dinner.

I tried not to sound too enthusiastic when I said yes, but I think I gave myself away when I said I would meet him at his house in five minutes.

He made reservations at his favorite Italian restaurant in North Beach, but we never got there. I walked through his front door and into his arms, and that's where I stayed.

I won't go into detail about what happened the rest of the night, but let's just say that it was sweet and tender and that by morning I was beginning to seriously rethink my strict policy against ever getting seriously involved with another man in a dangerous profession.

This friends-with-benefits thing had its pluses, that's for sure, but I think we both felt unsatisfied on a fundamental, emotional level. I knew that he did and I pretended like I didn't. He never brought it up, but I could feel it. I also knew that I could lose him if a woman came along who was as cute and lovable as me but was more willing to let him into her life.

It wasn't just my life, or I would probably have taken the risk. I had to think about Julie's heart, too, and what she would feel every time Joe Cochran went back to work at the firehouse. She'd lost her father and I didn't want her to go through anything like that again.

I didn't want to either.

Yes, I know you can't protect yourself or those you care about from heartbreak, not if you want to enjoy all the wonderful things that come from close relationships with other people.

But I felt I could lower the chances of Julie's experiencing that kind of pain again by consciously avoiding close relationships with anyone who regularly and intentionally put his life in jeopardy.

So that's what originally led me into that friends-with-benefits thing with Joe, which, by the way, I kept secret from Julie.

But that night, after my experience with Scooter, and seeing the solitary lives that Monk and Ambrose led, and observing the lengths to which the *Beyond Earth* fans went to belong to something, I was reevaluating my thinking. I certainly appreciated what I had with Joe Cochran that night a whole lot more than I had before.

I thought about what I'd said to Ambrose.

It was worth it . . . love always is.

Maybe that's what I was needy for.

Even so, I wasn't brave enough to change my arrangement with Joe just yet. I was, however, about to show him just how much I appreciated him when I got a call very early in the morning.

I rolled over in bed and knocked my cell phone off his nightstand when I tried to reach for it. I practically tumbled out of bed scrounging around for the phone on the floor.

"Hello?" I said.

It was Captain Stottlemeyer. "Sorry for the wake-up call, but I need to see Monk. And you'd better prepare yourself for a very bad day."

"It's not the first day that's started off for him with a corpse," I said. "Or for me either."

"I thought I was pretty lively," Joe whispered. I poked him in the chest and almost broke my elbow. He's that buff.

"This homicide is different," Stottlemeyer said. "It proves that everything Monk said yesterday about the murders of Brandon Lorber, Conrad Stipe, and the cabbie was wrong."

"Monk is never wrong about murder," I said.

"He is now," Stottlemeyer said.

CHAPTER
TWENTY-FIVE:
Mr. Monk and the
Strange Thing

A visit to the San Francisco Airporter Motor Inn is a bleak and depressing way to start your day even if there isn't a dead body involved.

I can't imagine what it must be like to stay there, even for a one-night stand. I've never had one, but from what I've heard from my friends it's miserable enough waking up next to someone you'd rather forget without it also happening in a place where you wish you'd never been.

Then again, it's not a whole lot better when you're there to see a bullet-riddled corpse.

Monk and I were once again at the rear of the convention center, which was once again a crime scene, where once again we found a car, a distraught driver being interviewed by Lieutenant Disher, and two morgue guys with a body bag to be filled and zipped.

The victim they were waiting to bag was

producer Kingston Mills, who was sprawled facedown in the parking lot behind the black Lincoln Town Car that presumably had delivered him to the hotel. His aloha shirt didn't look quite so festive soaked with blood.

There were wounds in his back and his right leg and a trail of blood leading from the open rear door of the limo to the producer's body.

"This isn't right," Monk said.

"Murder never is," I said. I was glad I hadn't had breakfast before I left Joe's place.

There was a crowd of *Beyond Earth* fans being kept a safe distance away by a couple of uniformed officers, who'd stretched some yellow crime scene tape between several lampposts. It was odd to see people dressed up as four-breasted women, aliens with external internal organs, and elephant-trunked aliens watching us as if we were what was unusual.

Stottlemeyer was leaning into the limo talking to Judson Beck, who was sitting inside wearing a new Confederation uniform, which I noticed had the same insignia but a much more militaristic look than the original.

"You're going to have to leave the vehicle now, Mr. Beck," Stottlemeyer said.

Beck shook his head. "No way."

"I'm sure the killer is long gone," Stottlemeyer said.

"He could be hiding in the brush, just waiting for me to come out so he can finish the job."

"There is no brush and you are surrounded by armed police officers," Stottlemeyer said, opening his jacket to show Beck the gun in his shoulder holster. "I assure you that you are perfectly safe."

Beck folded his arms across his chest and shook his head again. "No."

"This limo is a crime scene and we need to collect evidence from it," Stottlemeyer said.

"The killer was out there, not in here," Beck said. "This is where I am staying. You can drive me straight to the airport and then do whatever you want with this car."

Stottlemeyer sighed and walked over to us.

"I guess this experience was a little too authentic for him," he said. "Hard to believe that guy is an action hero."

"He only plays one on TV," I said.

"He must be a hell of an actor," Stottlemeyer said. "Would you like to guess what happened here this morning?"

"The limo arrived, Kingston Mills got out,

and Mr. Snork popped up from behind the Dumpster and shot him," I said.

"You're a natural. You should enroll in the police academy immediately. Beck closed the door, locked it, and called 911 on his cell phone," Stottlemeyer said, then turned to Monk. "This pretty much blows away your hit man theory."

"I don't see why," Monk said.

"Because some guy dressed like Mr. Snork just murdered another producer of the new *Beyond Earth*."

"The reimagined *Beyond Earth*," I said.

"Whatever," Stottlemeyer said. "We've got this one on tape, too."

"I'm sure you do," Monk said. "That was the point."

"You've lost me," Stottlemeyer said. "As usual."

"There are two explanations for this killing," Monk said. "Number one, the hit man learned that we've discovered the Lorber connection and wanted to lead us astray again. Or, number two, this is a copycat killing by someone who is taking advantage of the publicity surrounding Stipe's murder."

"Or number three, you were wrong and there's no connection between Stipe's killing and the desecration of Lorber's body," Stottlemeyer said. "It's just a coincidence that Stipe rode in the same taxi as the cabbie who was killed the other night."

"I suppose you think it's also a coincidence that the same cabbie picked up a fare near the Burgerville headquarters the same night that Lorber was shot."

"Sure, why not?" Stottlemeyer said. "Stranger things have happened."

"Give me some examples," Monk said.

"I don't have any off the top of my head," Stottlemeyer said and looked over at Disher. "Hey, Randy, tell me something strange that you've heard about."

"I read this morning about a goat born with two noses," Disher said.

"There you go," Stottlemeyer said to Monk. "That's strange."

"It's not a coincidence," Monk said. "It's a birth defect."

"Okay, how about this?" Disher said, closing his notebook and joining us. "I read about a woman here in San Francisco who has been searching for the birth mother who gave her up for adoption in Boston twenty years ago. It turns out that they've been working together as waitresses in the same restaurant for the last three years."

"That's one coincidence," Monk said. "This case has at least three. There's no comparison."

"Wait a minute, Monk," Stottlemeyer said. "You asked me to give you some examples of strange things and I did and now you're changing the rules. Why don't you just admit that you were wrong?"

"I'm not," Monk said. "We have the gum and the candy wrapper."

"I've got a video that shows the same guy who killed Conrad Stipe shooting another *Beyond Earth* producer in exactly the same spot. I think my evidence trumps yours."

"I don't see how," Monk said.

"Maybe because you don't want to see it," Stottlemeyer said. "You're blind to anything that goes against the way you think things should be."

"The way I think things should be happens to be the way things should be," Monk said. "So it's okay."

"I've got news for you, Monk. A gob of dried gum and a wrinkled candy wrapper aren't enough to build a homicide case on, much less *two* of them, not even for you."

"The fact is that somebody hired a hit man to murder Brandon Lorber," Monk said. "But then Lorber died of natural causes before he could be killed."

"There you go," Disher said. "That's a strange thing."

Monk ignored him and continued. "So the

hit man shot Lorber three times, in a manner consistent with a professional killer, in order to collect his full fee."

"The deadly triangle," Disher said.

"The hit man took a taxi to the airport, the same one that picked up Conrad Stipe," Monk continued. "But the assassin left something incriminating behind, so he killed Stipe and made it look like a fan did it, and then he killed the cabbie and made it look like a robbery."

Stottlemeyer sighed. "Yes, so you've told me already. And now that I've heard it all again, I'm asking myself how I could have bought it the first time. Do you really think it's plausible that a guy would kill two people on the possibility that somebody might come after him for shooting a corpse?"

"He did it so he wouldn't forfeit the money he was earning for the assassination," Monk said. "It was motivated by greed."

"That explanation doesn't make the theory sound any more plausible to me," Stottlemeyer said.

"It's not a theory and I can prove it," Monk said. "Could you turn the body halfway over for me?"

"Sure," Stottlemeyer said and looked at

Disher. "Go ahead."

"Why me?" Disher said.

"Because I'm the captain and these are new shoes," Stottlemeyer said. "I don't want to get blood on them."

Disher put on a pair of rubber gloves, leaned down, and gingerly lifted Mills enough so Monk could see the front of the body.

Monk crouched beside Disher. "As you can see, Kingston Mills has been shot in the shoulder, the back, and the leg."

"So?" Stottlemeyer said.

Monk stood up.

"Here's what happened. When Mills got out of the limousine, the shooter emerged from behind the Dumpster and shot him in the shoulder. The bullet spun Mills around and he started to flee towards the hotel. The killer shot him in the leg and then once more in the back before escaping into the crowd in the convention center."

"Yes, I know," Stottlemeyer said. "I heard it from a dozen witnesses and I saw it with my own eyes on the security video."

"But Stipe was shot only once, right in the heart," Monk said. "Mills was shot three times and only the last bullet was fatal."

"So what?"

"The man who killed Stipe was a crack

shot. The man who killed Mills was not."

"Or the killer got lucky the first time," Disher said, rising to his feet again.

"Either the hit man is trying to make it look like this is a copycat killing or that's exactly what it is," Monk said. "Either way, this doesn't change anything."

"It does for Kingston Mills," I said.

"I've got to go with the evidence, Monk," Stottlemeyer said.

"I'm glad you're seeing reason," Monk said. "So we're going back to looking for the hit man and whoever hired him."

"We're going back to our original notion that Conrad Stipe was killed by someone in the *Beyond Earth* community," Stottlemeyer said. "I'm betting that whoever did that also took out Kingston Mills. It's the simplest explanation."

"Simple isn't always right," Monk said.

"Nine times out of ten it is," Stottlemeyer said. "It's that tenth case that keeps you in business, Monk."

"Does this mean that the Special Desecration Unit is taking the lead again in the Lorber investigation?" Disher asked Stottlemeyer.

"It's all yours, Randy," Stottlemeyer said. "You can start by getting Judson Beck out of that limo."

"What does that have to do with the Lorber case?"

"Nothing," Stottlemeyer said.

"No problem. I can do that," Disher said. "All it takes is a little finesse."

"That's why I asked you," Stottlemeyer said. "Because you're so smooth."

Disher took a deep breath and marched over to the limo.

"Could I get a copy of the security video?" Monk asked. "I'd like to see it."

"I'm glad to hear that. I was afraid you might quit on me in a huff." Stottlemeyer reached into his jacket and handed me a DVD.

"I don't huff," Monk said. "Or puff. I've never puffed. I am firmly against all puffing."

"That's good to know," Stottlemeyer said. "I still need you on this one, Monk. We're back to trying to find a needle in a box of needles and you're the best man for the job."

We heard a scream from the limo. We turned to see Disher yanking Beck out of the backseat by the collar of his shirt and dragging him towards a police car.

"Finesse." Stottlemeyer smiled. "It works every time."

Monk headed back towards my car. I hurried to catch up with him.

"Where are we going?"

"Home," he said.

"Don't tell me you're giving up," I said. "The captain just told you how much he needs you."

"He certainly does," Monk said. "He's going in the wrong direction."

"Then why are you going home?"

"I need to consult an expert," Monk said.

CHAPTER
TWENTY-SIX:
MR. MONK
AND THE EXPERT

We sat down with Ambrose on the couch and watched the security camera footage of Kingston Mills getting killed. Watching it reminded me in an odd way of what was happening with *Beyond Earth.* The shooting of Kingston Mills was the shooting of Conrad Stipe, only reimagined and more authentic.

Like the previous video, the image was divided into four sections, each one giving us a different angle of the loading dock area of the convention center.

The limousine pulled up to the rear of the convention center. The back door of the car opened and Mills bounded out. Almost immediately, Mr. Snork emerged from behind the Dumpster, coughed, and shot him once in the shoulder.

Ambrose grimaced and made a notation on his yellow legal pad. I don't think he really had anything to write. The images were just too hard to take.

I didn't blame him for turning away. It's not easy watching real violence, pain, and bloodshed. The look on Kingston Mills' face when the bullet hit him in the shoulder was something I will never forget. It was raw, naked terror. Mills was a man who knew with absolute certainty that he was about to die a horrible death. And when you see something like that, you can't help but imagine yourself in the same situation and imagine all too clearly what it would feel like.

It gave me a shiver.

Things played out on the screen exactly the way Monk had described them to us at the crime scene. Mills tried to run, but Mr. Snork marched after him, continuing to fire, the coughing ruining his aim.

The second bullet hit Mills in the leg, knocking him off his feet. He tried to crawl away, but Mr. Snork walked up and put him down with a bullet in the back.

It was an execution.

I had to force myself to keep watching. It was one thing to show up at the scene of a murder; it was another to watch a human being die.

Mr. Snork coughed again and ran back into the convention center. That was where the DVD footage ended.

Monk rolled his shoulders, cocked his head from side to side, and turned to us. I knew the look. He was going to tell us whodunit.

"What do you think?" Monk asked.

I thought he knew who did it. But before I could answer, Ambrose spoke up.

"It's horrible," Ambrose said. "At least it was over instantly for Conrad Stipe. This was like torture."

"Maybe if he wasn't coughing so much his aim would have been better," I said.

"The number of times the victim was shot isn't the only difference," Monk said. "In the first shooting, Mr. Snork was perfectly centered in all four security camera views. But this time, there were instances where the shooter was partially or completely obscured by other objects."

"It didn't seem to me like he was avoiding the cameras," I said.

"He wasn't," Monk said, "but he wasn't paying close attention to how he was being photographed by them. This shooting wasn't tightly organized and choreographed. He also blinked."

"Blinked?" I said.

"He was startled by the sound of the gunshots," Monk said. "The other shooter wasn't."

"The other shooter?" Ambrose said. "This isn't the same man?"

"I don't think so," Monk said.

This was the point when Monk would ordinarily reveal who the killer was, but instead he stayed silent.

Ambrose chewed on his lower lip. "Could I see it again?"

"Of course," Monk said and replayed the DVD.

I wondered why Monk was being so reticent about announcing his conclusion. Did I misread his body language?

I watched the footage again. That time I noticed the blinking, too. But in every other way, this Mr. Snork looked just like the other Mr. Snork to me: the same basic build, the same color eyes, the same uniform, and, of course, the same elephantine trunk and pointed elfin ears.

"You're right, Adrian," Ambrose said. "It's not the same man."

"How do you know?" I asked.

It's a question clever people like the Monks get asked a lot by considerably less clever people like me.

"It's the same uniform that the first shooter wore, but he's wearing season-one ears," Ambrose said. "The nasal appendage is also the design from the pilot, not the more refined, less hairy one used in later episodes. This man is a *Beyond Earth* purist who is paying remarkable attention to detail. Notice how he's holding his gun. He's grasping it like a Confederation energy dissembler weapon instead of a conventional handgun."

"So I guess it wasn't his coughing that threw off his aim after all," I said.

"He's not coughing," Ambrose said.

"Then what is he doing?" I asked.

"He's speaking Dratch."

Once Ambrose mentioned it, I realized that what I'd thought was coughing was in fact the guttural hacking of Snork-speak that we'd encountered when we tried to talk to the leader of the Galactic Uprising.

"Congratulations, Ambrose," Monk said. "You've just solved the murder of Kingston Mills."

"I have? *Before* you could?" Ambrose asked incredulously.

He had good reason to be incredulous.

"You've revealed that the killer is Ernest Pinchuk," Monk said. "I never would have spotted that he was speaking Dratch without you."

I might not have, but Monk surely would have. In fact, I'm positive that he knew "whodunit" from the first moment he watched the security tape.

So this performance could mean only one thing: Monk was giving his brother a gift.

I don't know if he was doing it out of guilt for ignoring Ambrose's efforts to help before, or as a way of acknowledging the importance of *Beyond Earth* in his brother's life, but his reasons didn't matter.

It was the most selfless thing, perhaps the *only* selfless thing, I'd ever seen Monk do.

Ambrose beamed with pride. "Would you like to know what he's saying?"

"You can read lips?" I asked.

"Of course," Ambrose said.

"In Dratch?"

"And seven other languages," Ambrose said. "If you include pig Latin."

"Incredible," Monk said.

And useless.

How often did Ambrose get a chance to speak in pig Latin to anyone, much less have to read their lips?

Monk was overdoing it now, but Ambrose was too flattered to notice.

We watched the DVD again and stopped every few moments so Ambrose could jot down what Pinchuk was saying. When we reached the end of the video, Ambrose gave us the full translation.

"He's saying, 'Feel the hot kiss of my bullets of righteous justice, you miserable, greedy scumbag. You are guilty of unspeakably heinous crimes against humanity, the Confederation, the *Beyond Earth*–verse, and all of fandom. And for that unforgivable transgression you must die.'"

That was an awfully overwrought speech, even in Dratch.

Monk turned off the TV and smiled. "That sounds like a confession to me."

Monk called Captain Stottlemeyer on Ambrose's speakerphone and told him that the shooter was Ernest Pinchuk and that he'd identified him off the security video thanks to observations made by Ambrose.

What helped Stottlemeyer accept Monk's conclusion was that Pinchuk had a strong motive for wanting Mills dead, he could be placed at the scene of the crime, and he'd already been identified as one of the people who'd purchased a first-season uniform recently.

That, and the fact that Monk was, until that day, never wrong when it came to homicide.

But Stottlemeyer wasn't ready to accept Monk's conclusion that this was a copycat crime. He believed that Pinchuk was responsible for both killings.

"It's the same motive for the same shooting at the same location," Stottlemeyer said. "So the obvious conclusion is that it's the same guy."

"Except there are too many differences," Monk said. "There's the ears."

"And the nose," Ambrose said.

"And the way he was holding the gun," I said, just to be supportive.

"Maybe Pinchuk did all that just to throw us off," Stottlemeyer said, "to make it look like there are two different killers when there was actually only one."

"But you wouldn't have noticed and neither would I," Monk said. "The differences are obscure details that would only be noticeable and significant to the most ardent *Beyond Earth* fans."

"Which is why he did it that way," Stottlemeyer said. "He knew the security video would end up on TV. Wearing a baseball cap or something for the second killing would have been a difference that was too obvious. It wouldn't have fooled anyone."

"I don't think Pinchuk is that smart," Monk said.

"Don't underestimate the intelligence of *Beyond Earth* fans," Ambrose said. "One of them is a Nobel Prize winner in physics."

"It doesn't matter right now whether Pinchuk killed one person or two," Stottlemeyer said. "We can all agree that he killed Kingston Mills, and that's all I need to arrest him."

So Stottlemeyer hung up and sent Disher to arrest Pinchuk at the Airporter. But Pinchuk wasn't there. His girlfriend told Disher that Pinchuk feared he'd come down with Rigilian Fever and so he went back home to Berkeley. Rigilian Fever, she explained, is the stomach flu for Snorks.

Since the East Bay town was outside of the captain's jurisdiction, Stottlemeyer contacted the Berkeley police and arranged to meet them at Pinchuk's house to make the arrest.

We headed out to join them.

On the way there, I couldn't resist asking Monk about why he gave Ambrose the credit for cracking the Kingston Mills murder case.

"Because Ambrose solved the crime," Monk said.

"*After* you did," I said. "You just didn't say anything."

"Do you think he noticed?" Monk asked.

"He hasn't seen you solve enough crimes to recognize the visual tics," I said. "But I have. So why did you do it?"

"I wanted him to feel good about himself for a change."

"What makes you think he doesn't?"

"Because he's a Monk," he said sadly.

I'm sure the double meaning of those words probably wasn't intentional, but it wasn't lost on me.

"But you're a Monk and you feel good about yourself," I said.

"Rarely," Monk said.

"So when do you feel good about yourself?"

"When I solve a case," Monk said.

"That happens a lot," I said.

"Not often enough to keep me from dwelling in misery most of my waking life," Monk said. "It would take dozens of murders a week for me to feel really good about life."

"You do see the contradiction in that, don't you?"

"That hundreds of people would have to die for me to know true happiness and fulfillment?"

"Yes," I said.

"Now you know why I'm miserable," Monk said.

The front yard of Ernest Pinchuk's dilapidated house was strewn with weeds and littered with trash. It might as well have been surrounded by a moat, too, as far as Monk was concerned. There was no way he was crossing the yard to the sagging front porch.

So we stayed on the curb as Captain Stottlemeyer and a thirtyish detective from the Berkeley PD walked up to Pinchuk's door and Lieutenant Disher led a few local uniformed officers around the back.

The Berkeley cop knocked on the door while Captain Stottlemeyer stood off to one side, his gun in his hand.

"Ernest Pinchuk? This is Detective Hidalgo Rhinehart, Berkeley PD. We want to talk with you."

Hidalgo Rhinehart? With a name like that, he must have dropped from a branch of a very interesting family tree.

There was no answer. Rhinehart knocked again.

"Open up," he said.

I heard Disher yell "Halt!" from the backyard and then came loud shrieking, coughing, and gurgling.

Stottlemeyer stepped off the porch. "What the hell is that sound?"

"It's Pinchuk," I said. "He's spitting out some Dratch."

"He should have chewed it before trying to swallow it," Stottlemeyer said, holstering his gun.

"It's a language," I said.

"A fictional one," Monk added.

Disher led Pinchuk down the driveway to the street. Pinchuk was still in his Snork outfit and his hands were cuffed behind his back.

"You have the right to remain silent. Anything you say can and will be used against you in a court of law," Disher said. "Regardless of what language you speak it in, a real one or a TV one."

Pinchuk angrily gurgled and wheezed and snorted at us some more as Disher finished reading him his rights and put him in the back of a police car.

"You get some weird cases in Frisco," Hidalgo said.

"That's why we have Monk," Stottlemeyer said, offering his hand to Hidalgo. "Thanks for the cooperation today."

"My pleasure," Hidalgo said. "I'm always glad to kick one of our wackos across the bay. It's one less for me to deal with."

Disher joined us. "I got a look inside his house when he came out. You've got to see it."

"Okay," Stottlemeyer said and started ambling down the driveway. "But I'm telling you right now that I'm not going to take any decorating tips from a guy with an elephant trunk glued to his nose."

We followed the captain. Monk looked at his feet as he walked to avoid stepping on the cracks in the driveway. The backyard was as weedy as the front, but there was a concrete path from the driveway to the door at the rear of the house. Monk stuck to the path, concentrating on his balance as if he were crossing a bridge over a deep gorge.

The door was ajar. Stottlemeyer pushed it open the rest of the way and we stepped into another world, a couple of centuries into the future.

The living room was an exact replica of the command center of the starship *Discovery,* right down to the captain's control podium, the joysticks on the navigational console, and the panel of constantly blinking multicolored lights of the main computer, which always seemed to explode in a shower of sparks whenever the ship ran into a meteor storm or was attacked by aliens.

But on closer examination, there were a few things that didn't fit in, like the stack of junk mail on the communications console, the unlaced sneakers on the floor, the half-eaten bag of Doritos on the command podium . . .

. . . and the gun resting on the captain's stool.

"Beam me up, Scotty," Stottlemeyer said.

CHAPTER TWENTY-SEVEN:
MR. MONK
FINDS HIMSELF

Ernest Pinchuk sat at the table in the interrogation room, his arms folded across his chest, glaring defiantly into the mirror that he knew hid the four of us who were in the observation room watching him.

Monk studied Pinchuk as if the man was some weird creature on exhibit in a zoo.

"He hasn't said a word," Stottlemeyer said. "He just gurgles."

"That's Dratch," I said. "I've heard that it's hard to speak the language clearly with only one tongue."

"Why won't he speak English?" Disher asked.

"His girlfriend told us that he's protesting the changes to *Beyond Earth*," I said. "He's vowed to speak Dratch until they cancel the show or agree to do a version that's true to the original."

"You'd think now that Stipe and Mills are dead he'd feel he's made his point," Stottlemeyer said.

"Has the network announced that the show is canceled or that they'll be doing a loyal version?" I asked.

Stottlemeyer shrugged. "Not that I know of."

"Until they do, I don't think he's going to talk to us. At least not in English."

"Oh, he'll talk," Stottlemeyer said. "By the time I'm done, he'll confess and save us a lot of needless hassle in court."

"Why would he do that?" Monk said.

"He may not want to speak English, but he understands it. When he's confronted with the enormity of the evidence against him, he's going to want to make a deal."

"What do you have to offer him?" I asked.

Stottlemeyer smiled at us. "Watch and learn."

A few moments later, Stottlemeyer wheeled a TV/DVD combo into the interrogation room and closed the door. Monk, Disher, and I watched quietly.

The captain smiled at Pinchuk. "You are looking at a very happy man, Ernie. You want to know why? This is a dream case for me. I can get a conviction and a lethal injection for you without even making an effort."

Pinchuk sputtered and snorted.

"What's that you say? I have trouble understanding you with that thing on your nose. Maybe this will help."

Stottlemeyer yanked the trunk off of Pinchuk's face and tossed it in a corner.

Pinchuk shrieked, not in pain but like someone who'd been stripped naked in public. He covered his exposed nose with his hands as if it was a much more private part of his body.

I was shocked by what the captain did. I know it was only a rubber nose, but given who Pinchuk was, and what the trunk meant to him, it seemed like an act of brutality.

I'm sure that was exactly what Stottlemeyer intended.

"Is that better?" Stottlemeyer asked. "Can you breathe more clearly now?"

Pinchuk hissed and coughed and glugged.

"I guess not. But that's okay. There's nothing you have to say. The evidence speaks for itself."

Stottlemeyer turned on the TV. The security camera video of the Kingston Mills shooting played out on the screen.

"There you are, Ernie, in living color, killing Kingston Mills for ruining the show you love. Ballistics has matched the bullets recovered from the body to the gun we found in your house. Case closed. I just wanted to personally thank you for making my job so easy. I'm going to get home early tonight."

Pinchuk made some more disgusting noises. Stottlemeyer started to leave, then reconsidered.

"Oh, wait, I almost forgot. There's more. I wish all serial killers were as considerate as you about supplying us with ironclad evidence of their crimes. We've got your first murder on tape, too."

Stottlemeyer played the Stipe video. Pinchuk gurgled during the playback with such intensity that he was practically spitting.

Disher grinned. "This is so great."

I wasn't entertained. From the moment Stottlemeyer ripped off the trunk, I found the whole experience unsettling. I was seeing a side of the captain that I didn't like very much. Not that I was rooting for Pinchuk — he was a murderer. But he was still a human being.

"Gee, he's dead and you still can't stop hating Stipe for selling you all out," Stottlemeyer said. "Even without the gun on this one, it's an open-and-shut case. That's because you were thoughtful enough to wear the same new uniform that you bought this week in both killings. It would have been really nice if you'd worn a name tag, too. But, hey, I'm not criticizing."

Pinchuk was barking and huffing like a seal, perspiration forming on his brow.

"I think the jury is going to set a new record for the fastest delivery of a guilty verdict in U.S. history. What do you think? Will they be out in ten minutes? Five minutes? Or just thirty seconds? I guess it depends if they want the free lunch first or not."

Pinchuk's face was bright red. He was definitely under pressure now. He might even be having a stroke.

"He's going to crack," Disher said.

I glanced at Monk, whose head was tilted to one side, observing Pinchuk from a different angle. I wondered what he saw.

Stottlemeyer leaned across the table in front of Pinchuk.

"With all this evidence against you, you're going to get the needle, no question about it. But if you want to confess, and plead guilty, you can take a stand against the corporate bastards who ruined your show and then you can spend the rest of your life in prison, watching *Beyond Earth* reruns all day. That could be paradise. It's your choice. It makes no difference to me. I win either way."

Pinchuk burst out with a passionate stream of coughing, gagging, gurgling, barking, and mewling. He was saying something, and saying it forcefully.

Monk turned to me. "Call Ambrose."

I hit the speed dial on my cell phone and followed Monk, who marched out of the observation area and directly into the interrogation room.

Stottlemeyer looked up, obviously surprised to see us, especially since things were going so well.

"This isn't a good time, Monk," Stottlemeyer said.

Monk went to the TV, froze the image of Mr. Snork shooting Stipe, and looked at me. "Have you got Ambrose on the line?"

At that moment, Ambrose answered the phone.

"Hello, you've reached the Ambrose Monk residence. This is Ambrose Monk speaking."

"Hi, it's Natalie. Hold on a moment." I nodded to Monk, hit the SPEAKER button, and held up the phone. "He's on."

"Ambrose, we're with Ernest Pinchuk, leader of the Galactic Uprising, who has just been arrested for the murder of Kingston Mills." Monk faced him. "Did you also kill Conrad Stipe? Is that you on the security video?"

Pinchuk seemed to repeat the same saliva-spewing tirade that we'd just witnessed. Monk was careful to move out of the range of any spit.

Monk looked at the phone as if it were Ambrose himself in the room. "What did he just say, Ambrose?"

"He's saying that the gunman is wearing a first-season uniform with second-season ears, which we know is obvious. He says it's a violation, an abomination, and an insult to everything *Beyond Earth* stands for, and on a personal note, I would have to agree."

"Ambrose speaks Dratch?" Stottlemeyer asked.

"He can lip-read it, too," I said.

"If I look up 'pointless' in the dictionary after today," Stottlemeyer said, "that's going to be the new definition."

Pinchuk looked, and sounded, like he was choking on a hairball.

Ambrose spoke up again. "He's saying that Conrad Stipe betrayed himself, his principles, and all of fandom by allowing that snake Kingston Mills to ruin *Beyond Earth.* But whoever is wearing that mismatched uniform is doing the same thing. He says that man is besmirching Earthers everywhere and Mr. Pinchuk wouldn't do that. That is not him. He says he's an honorable man."

"You gunned down a guy in a parking lot this morning," Stottlemeyer said to Pinchuk. "I wouldn't call that honorable. That was murder."

Pinchuk did some more hacking and snorting while Ambrose did a running translation.

"He's saying that it wasn't murder, it was an execution for crimes against humanity. He's admitting that he shot Kingston Mills. In fact, he wishes that he could have shot whoever was wearing the wrong uniform when he murdered Stipe. He believes the shooter's purpose was to offend, belittle, and disrespect Earthers. His theory is that it was an act of aggression by someone from *Star Trek* or *Battlestar Galactica* fandom to turn the world against *Beyond Earth*."

"He's upset about the uniform," Stottlemeyer said. "But not the murder. I find *that* offensive."

Pinchuk kept talking, if you can call it that. Ambrose spoke up.

"Mr. Pinchuk maintains that he didn't kill Conrad Stipe. He was certainly angry enough to do it, but despite what Stipe did, he was still the creator of *Beyond Earth* and Mr. Pinchuk respects that."

"There you have it," Monk said. "This

man killed Kingston Mills but not Conrad Stipe."

"Let's step outside," Stottlemeyer said, motioning Monk and me to the door.

He led us out of the interrogation room and into the hallway, where Disher joined us.

"That was amazing," Disher said. "I've never seen an interrogation like that before."

"Neither have I," Stottlemeyer said, and gestured to my cell phone. "Could you tell Ambrose you'll call him back?"

"Sure," I said and did as he asked.

After I ended the call, Stottlemeyer turned to Monk.

"I didn't want to have this discussion in front of the murderer or your brother. You're embarrassing yourself, and it's painful to watch."

"I'm doing what I always do," Monk said.

"Yeah, that's the problem. You're refusing to acknowledge anything that doesn't fit the way you want it to."

"That's how I solve murders," Monk said.

"Not this time," Stottlemeyer said. "The guy in that room is nuts. You're taking his word, in some make-believe language, as some kind of gospel. It's not. It's the babbling of an idiot."

"I believe him," Monk said.

"Because he's playing you, Monk. He's telling you what you want to hear."

"I know this man," Monk said.

"You only met him two days ago," Disher said.

"He's me."

We all stared at Monk in disbelief. It certainly wasn't the first time, as you know. But this was a particularly outrageous statement for him to make.

Two days earlier, Monk was calling the *Beyond Earth* fans drug-addicted freaks. He was ready to disown his brother and have him committed for associating with them. And now he was joining their ranks?

Something was very wrong with Monk. Had he finally snapped?

"He's nothing like you," Stottlemeyer said.

"He's me," Monk said. "And he's my brother."

Stottlemeyer pointed at the door to the interrogation room. "He's got pointed ears and an elephant nose!"

"Ernie *had* an elephant nose," I said. "Until you tore it off of him in an act of police brutality."

Stottlemeyer gave me a withering look. "It's a rubber nose. I took it off of him, I didn't beat him with it."

"You might as well have," I said.

Stottlemeyer turned his attention back to Monk, dismissing my objections by showing me the back of his head.

"He lives in a house that's been remodeled to look like a spaceship," Stottlemeyer said. "He speaks a made-up language. He's not you or Ambrose."

"Technically, Ambrose does speak the language and knows the show inside out," Disher said. "So Pinchuk isn't Monk, but maybe he's a little bit Ambrose."

Stottlemeyer gave Disher the same withering look he'd given me, but before he could rip Disher's head off with his bare hands, Monk spoke up.

"Ernest Pinchuk is a messed-up, probably drug-addicted freak, no question about it," he said. "But in his deranged mind, he's living according to the natural order of his universe. His life fits. He's making sure every detail is correct. He wouldn't wear a first-season Confederation uniform with second-season ears any more than I would walk down the street with mismatched socks."

"You'd kill yourself first," I said.

"I'd have you change my socks and *then* kill me," Monk said. "I wouldn't want to be seen dead with mismatched socks either."

"But if you *were* buried with mismatched

socks, that would definitely be a desecration," Disher said. "And you have my word that the Special Desecration Unit wouldn't rest until we caught whoever did it."

"Is there a point here somewhere?" Stottlemeyer asked.

"Ernest Pinchuk is a lunatic but a man of principle," Monk said. "Look at what he's doing right now. He's sticking to his vow to speak Dratch, even when his life is at stake, because he believes it's a necessary step to restore the natural order of his world. I understand him because we're the same. Only I'm not insane."

This was a revelatory, life-changing moment for Adrian Monk. *That* was the point that Stottlemeyer was missing.

Monk had just taken a monumental step forward in understanding himself and others. Dr. Kroger would probably call it a breakthrough.

By comparing himself to Pinchuk, Monk was actually empathizing with someone whose beliefs and lifestyle were fundamentally different from his own.

It was incredible!

It was what I'd been trying to get him to do for years and even more intensely since this case began. I wanted him to see how similar he was to Ambrose, the Earthers, and other people he criticized for not being just like him.

And now he was getting it. Or at least he seemed to be.

I hoped this new understanding would stick, though I wasn't convinced by the argument he was making as far as the actual case was concerned.

"I'm telling you, Monk, you're being manipulated," Stottlemeyer said. "That guy probably knows all about you and is taking advantage of it."

"Even if that's true, he's admitted to one murder," Monk said. "If he did the other one, too, what would he have to lose by admitting it? That alone should indicate to you that your scenario just doesn't make sense."

"*Mine* doesn't? If I hold up the evidence for my theory against your gum, candy wrapper, and this guy's idiotic blathering, it's no contest which one adds up to the more convincing case," Stottlemeyer said. "Any reasonable person, and more importantly, any jury of twelve of my peers, would agree that I've got the shooter responsible for two murders."

"And they'd be wrong," Monk said. "Conrad Stipe was killed by a hit man."

"Who you think killed two people just so

he couldn't be pinned for shooting a man who was already dead," Stottlemeyer said.

"Exactly," Monk said.

"Desecration is a very serious crime," Disher said. "That's why we have a special unit to combat it. The assassin was terrified that we'd catch him."

"The unit didn't exist until Lorber was shot," I said. I didn't mind contradicting Disher. I didn't work for him.

"But the shooter anticipated that we'd form the special unit after we saw his crimes," Disher said. "That's how clever he is and why he's met his match in me."

"The hit man is still out there, free to kill again," Monk said. "And he will for the right price. We have to find him before he does."

Stottlemeyer rubbed his temples.

"We're done here, Monk," the captain said. "This homicide is closed and your services on this case are no longer needed."

"You're firing me?" Monk said.

"No," Stottlemeyer said. "I'm just telling you that this particular investigation is concluded and that we have our man."

"You have the man in one murder," Monk said. "Not two."

"Let it go, Monk. It's over. You misread the clues in this one. It was bound to happen sometime," Stottlemeyer said. "But I want you to know that it's okay. I still think you're the best detective I've ever met. I'll call you when another difficult case comes along."

"You're making a big mistake," Monk said and walked away.

Stottlemeyer looked at me. "You have to help him deal with this. Convince him the case is closed. If he obsesses over it, he'll only make things worse for everybody."

I didn't say anything one way or the other. I just turned and followed Monk out.

I had a lot of faith in my employer, and I wanted to be supportive, but I couldn't help feeling that maybe this time Stottlemeyer was right.

CHAPTER TWENTY-EIGHT:
Mr. Monk
Spreads the Word

When I got outside, I found Monk pacing in front of my car.

"Let's go," he said impatiently.

"Where?"

"Burgerville headquarters, of course."

I sighed. "Mr. Monk, the case is closed."

"Not for me it isn't," he said. "It's not done until the murderer has been caught."

I thought about what Stottlemeyer had just told me. "Maybe you ought to take a time-out."

"A time-out?"

"Step back from this for a day or two, relax a little, collect your thoughts. Afterwards you may see things differently."

"My thoughts are already collected," he said. "Indexed and color-coded."

"Color-coded?"

"It's an integral part of my thought filing system," he said.

"You have a thought filing system?"

"You don't?" Monk said.

I shook my head.

He nodded knowingly, as if some other great mystery had finally been solved.

"That explains so much," Monk said. "I've had a real breakthrough today."

"I think so, too," I said. "You're understanding people now in a way you never have before."

"That's so true," Monk said. "I can't imagine how anyone could go through life with their thoughts spread out all over their psyche. I see you in a whole new light, Natalie. Your mind is a mess. You can't hold a thought if you can't find it first."

"I was talking about Ernest Pinchuk and how he's really no different than you."

"I'm glad you can see that although he's crazy, his thoughts are organized. It's the first step in your rehabilitation. If you can organize your thinking, you'll be a lot more rational," Monk said. "But we don't have time to straighten out your life right now. We have to save the captain from making a mistake that could destroy his career."

"But what if he's right?" I said. "Then all you'll be doing is antagonizing powerful people who could get him fired. And if he's gone, you'll lose the only champion you have in the San Francisco Police Department."

"He's not right," Monk said. "And I can prove it."

"With gum and candy wrappers?"

"With the hit man himself," Monk said.

"You can do that?"

"I can," Monk said.

Archie Applebaum saw us coming, so he got up from behind his security desk in the lobby of Burgerville headquarters and opened the after-hours employee door for us.

"You really ought to try the revolving door, Mr. Monk," he said. "It's fun."

"That's what people say about skydiving, too."

"For some people it is," Archie said as we followed him back to his donut-shaped desk.

Ernest Pinchuk would have been happy in Archie's seat. It wasn't Captain Stryker's command podium, but the console looked a lot like the navigational station of the *Discovery* bridge. There were lots of buttons and several screens that showed alternating views from the cameras in various corridors and stairwells.

"Maybe there are people who enjoy setting themselves on fire, drinking rat poison, and stabbing themselves in the heart with a butcher knife, too."

"That would be suicidal," Archie said.

"So would jumping out of an airplane and going through a revolving door."

"It's a door," Archie said. "Not a buzz saw."

I knew that it was futile arguing with Monk about something like this, or just about anything else, but I couldn't blame Archie for trying.

It's human nature, I suppose.

"We'd like to see Andrew Cahill," Monk said.

"Let me call up and see if he is available," Archie said.

He picked up the phone, told the secretary that Monk was downstairs, and then he waited for her response. I judged by the way his expression hardened that the news wasn't good.

Archie hung up and looked at Monk. "Mr. Cahill doesn't want to see you. In fact, he asked me to escort you out of the building and never allow you in again."

"I see," Monk said. "Then would you mind passing along a message to him for me?"

"Sure," Archie said, and took out a pen.

"You can give it to Mrs. Lorber, too,"

Monk said. "The medical examiner has determined that Brandon Lorber wasn't murdered. It was natural causes."

Archie looked up from his notepad. "The guy was shot three times."

"Yes," Monk said.

"Twice in the chest and once in the head," Archie said. "That's not natural. Even if I wasn't a cop before, I'd know those were fatal shots."

"They would have been if he wasn't already dead when he was shot," Monk said. "He died of a heart attack before he was shot."

"Why would anyone shoot a dead person?"

"I don't know, but you can tell Mr. Cahill and Mrs. Lorber that it's no longer a homicide investigation," Monk said. "It's a desecration case."

"I'm sure that Mr. Cahill and Mrs. Lorber will be relieved to hear that," Archie said, jotting down some notes. "So do the police even care about a corpse shooting?"

"The Special Desecration Unit is on it," I said.

Archie raised an eyebrow. "There's a unit for that?"

"There is," I said.

"Wow," he said.

■ ■ ■ ■

We walked back to my car, Monk tapping each parking meter that we passed, keeping a silent count. I never understood why he did that. I mean, I got the counting part but not the touching. Didn't he realize how many hundreds of people had touched those parking meters? How many birds must have crapped on them?

But I didn't bring it up. I didn't have enough patience, Advil, or Pepto-Bismol in reserve at that moment to deal with it.

"Where to now?" I asked.

"Nowhere," he said.

I wasn't sure what that meant. "So are we going back to your place to check on the carpets? They should be done by now. Or are we going back to Ambrose's house?"

"We're going back to the car and staying here until something happens."

I glanced back at the Burgerville building. "We're doing a stakeout?"

"Yes, we are."

We got into my car, which was parked at the corner of a side street. It gave us a pretty good view of the lobby and the entrance to the underground parking garage.

"What are we waiting to see?" I asked.

"The hit man," Monk said. "Whoever hired him is going to be pretty upset that he paid for nothing. He is going to want his money back."

"Do you really think the hit man is going to give him a refund?"

"We'll see," Monk said.

Thank God for National Public Radio and Starbucks.

If it weren't for *All Things Considered,* I would have had to spend the next few hours talking to Monk instead of listening to thoughtful left-wing news and liberal commentary, though I could have lived without the constant pleas for pledge money. They should just install coin slots in car radios and be done with it.

If it weren't for the Starbucks two doors down from my car, I would have gone thirsty, hungry, and had no restroom to use. But after all the coffee I drank, I was so wired by nightfall that my hair was practically standing on end and I could pick up the NPR broadcast without turning on the radio.

Even so, the hours crawled by very slowly. And I had to stay alert the whole time.

It wasn't because I had to do my part in the surveillance of the building. It was because I had to keep my eye on Monk.

I had to stop him from going out and chastising drivers for not parallel parking properly.

I had to stop him from giving some window washers lessons in correct window washing technique.

I had to stop him from putting money in other people's parking meters to keep them from dipping into odd numbers of remaining minutes.

And I had to stop him from arresting an old lady who let her dog urinate against the fire hydrant that was in front of Burgerville headquarters.

"You'll blow our cover," I said.

"But what if there's a fire?"

"The fire department will come and put it out," I said.

"With what?"

"Water," I said.

"Not from that hydrant," Monk said. "It's inoperable."

"No, it's not," I said. "It can still be used."

"There is urine all over it," Monk said. "No fireman would dare touch it, nor would any other human being."

"Firefighters run into burning buildings," I said. "They aren't going to care about some dog pee on a fire hydrant."

"They would if they knew," Monk said. "We should call and warn them. Call Joe right now. He can get the word out faster than we can."

"Every fire hydrant in the city has dog pee on it, Mr. Monk. It's how dogs mark their territory. I can guarantee you that every male dog that has passed that hydrant has pissed on it."

He looked at me, wide-eyed. "No."

"It's what dogs do," I said. "The firefighters know this."

Monk swallowed hard. "And they still use the hydrants?"

"Of course they do."

"They are the bravest men on earth," Monk said somberly.

"You may be right," I said.

"But if my house is ever on fire, whatever you do don't call the fire department."

"Why not?"

"I would rather be cleansed by fire than be hosed down with dog urine."

It wasn't until a few minutes after eight p.m. that something finally happened. Andrew Cahill drove out of the garage in his black Maybach, a car that Mercedes made to make its other cars seem affordable.

I started my humble Jeep.

"What are you doing?" Monk said.

"Getting ready to follow Andrew Cahill," I said.

"Why would you want to do that?"

"Because he's going to lead us to the hit man," I said. "Isn't he?"

"He's not the one who hired the hit man," Monk said.

"Then why aren't we parked outside of Veronica Lorber's house?"

"Because she didn't hire him either," Monk said. "Archie Applebaum did."

CHAPTER TWENTY-NINE:
MR. MONK AND THE REVOLVING DOOR

I looked back at the Burgerville headquarters, where Archie sat at his desk, reading the *San Francisco Chronicle*.

"The security guard?" I said. "He's the guy who is supposed to protect Lorber, not kill him."

"That's why he was in the perfect position to get away with murder," Monk said. "He not only knew when Lorber came and went, he also had access to the security system. He didn't have to steal Lorber's card, he just made one for the assassin with the same encoding. The hit man didn't have to guess when Archie would be away from his desk, Archie told him. The hit man didn't have to figure out where the security cameras were, Archie gave him the specific locations."

"What pointed you to Archie?"

"I knew we were looking for an inside man. Archie is the one person with access to everything, from the security cards to the

351

shredded documents," Monk said. "And, being an ex-cop, he's also the person most likely to have the contacts who could put him in touch with a hit man."

"But why would Archie want to hire an assassin to kill his boss?"

"This isn't just Archie's job. It's his future. He was relying on his pension for his retirement," Monk said. "Somehow Archie found out that Lorber had pillaged the pension plan. Archie was so angry about it that he decided to get revenge."

It made sense. Then again, it also would have made just as much sense for Andrew Cahill or Veronica Lorber to have hired the hit man.

"What evidence do you have that it was Archie?"

"None at all," Monk said.

I gave him a look. "None?"

"Not even a candy wrapper," Monk said.

"Then how are you going to prove you're right?"

"I don't have to," Monk said. "Archie is going to prove it for me. That's why we're here."

"How can you be sure it's going to happen tonight?"

"I'm not," Monk said. "But eventually Archie and the hit man are going to meet."

"Eventually?" I said.

"What else do you have to do tonight?" Monk said.

"Eventually could be a very long time, Mr. Monk."

He shrugged. "It's okay. I don't have any other plans."

By ten p.m., I was crashing from my caffeine high and fighting to keep my eyes open. Monk's idea of passing the time by singing "A Thousand Bottles of Windex on the Wall" wasn't helping me stay awake either. Quite the opposite, in fact.

Slumber was winning the battle for my mind and body when Monk nudged me hard in the side.

"Archie is going on his rounds," Monk said.

I marshaled all the strength I had and bench-pressed one of my eyelids open. I saw Archie heading for the elevator.

"Good for him," I said and let my eyelid drop.

I was instantly at Lake Como in Italy, water-skiing with George Clooney in front of his villa. I was behind his boat, effortlessly skimming over its wake, and he was at the wheel, but I could see his sparkling eyes and hear him perfectly over the roar of the motor.

"You know what I love the most about you?" he asked with that confident, sexy grin of his.

"My body?"

"I adore that, of course," he said, "but what I cherish is your neediness. I find needy women irresistible. I like to be needed. Especially by you."

"I need you, George," I said. And then, through the magic of dreams, I was in his arms in the boat and he was leaning his face towards mine for a kiss that would change my life.

"Eventually is here," George said.

"Oh yes," I said.

But he didn't say it in that wonderful voice of his. He said it in Monk's voice.

I felt a stab of pain in my side. Someone was nudging me. Suddenly George's boat became my Jeep and George became Monk.

It was a major letdown.

In my head, I asked Monk what was going on, but I think it came out as "Humble-fliffendorf." Maybe it was Dratch.

Monk gestured to the Burgerville headquarters. There was a man standing at the employee entrance, running his key card through the scanner. He wore a long, tailored, black overcoat and a fedora that was pulled down low to shield his face from the security camera mounted over the door.

On most people that outfit would have looked almost as ridiculous as a Confederation uniform. On him, it looked cool and menacing. He could have been George Clooney.

Or maybe I was still half asleep.

Before I could say anything, Monk bolted from the car and headed across the street.

I tried to shake the grogginess from my head as I hurried after him.

"What are we doing?" I asked in an urgent whisper.

I don't know why I was whispering. It just felt like the right thing to do. The fresh air, the chill, and the realization that we were running *towards* a hit man instead of *away* from one were waking me up fast.

"Does your cell phone have a camera?"

"Yes," I said, "but the photos won't win any awards."

"I only want to win a conviction," he said.

The hit man slipped into the stairwell at about the same moment we reached the employee entrance. He didn't see us. Or at least I hoped he didn't.

"Shouldn't we call the captain?" I asked.

"We don't have anything yet," Monk said. "We're in luck. The hit man wedged the door open with a stone."

"How is that luck? You aren't actually intending to go in after him, are you?"

Monk answered my question by going in after him. I stupidly followed and, in doing so, accidentally knocked the stone away. The door clicked shut with the finality of a prison cell.

But Monk didn't notice. He was over at the security desk, examining the video consoles.

On the monitors, I could see Archie walking down the hallway on the fourth floor, checking the doors.

"Our lucky streak is continuing," Monk said. "These video feeds are being taped."

"I'm not seeing this streak," I said.

"We'll have tape of Archie and the hit man together," Monk said. "It's evidence."

The man in the overcoat was slowly ascending the stairs and managing to avoid showing his face to the camera as he did so.

"The hit man did a great job of hiding his face from the cameras the last time he was here," I said. "And he's obviously no less camera shy now."

"That's what your cell phone camera is for," Monk said. "You can get a picture of him when he emerges from the building and his guard is down."

"Won't he see me?"

"You'll be in hiding."

"Hiding where?" I asked, looking around the wide-open lobby. There was a potted palm in one corner, but it wasn't big enough to hide me.

"Outside," Monk said. "Behind one of those parked cars. He'll never know you're there."

"There's one little problem with that plan," I said. "We're locked in. I accidentally knocked away the stone that was propping open the door."

Monk glanced at the desk and spotted a set of keys. "No problem."

He sorted through the keys and singled one out among the twenty on the ring.

"This opens the revolving door," he said.

I studied the key. "How do you know?"

"I can tell," he said.

"How?"

"I recognize it," Monk said. "I saw it when Archie unlocked the door before."

"But they all look the same," I said.

"Every key is unique," Monk said. "That's why they are called keys. You go outside and I'll hide in the shredded-paper closet once I unlock it."

I took the key and looked at the monitors. The hit man was on the fourth-floor landing. He paused, reached into his jacket, and took out a gun.

"This can't be good," I said and gestured to the screen.

"We have to warn Archie." Monk quickly checked the console until he found the button for the speaker system. "Where's the microphone?"

I pointed to a telephone receiver that rested in the console. "I think that's it."

The hit man screwed a silencer onto the end of his gun. This definitely wasn't good.

Monk picked up the phone and flicked the speaker switch just as the hit man was about to step out of the stairwell into the hallway that Archie was patrolling.

"Archie, this is Adrian Monk."

Both Archie and the hit man looked up at the sound of Monk's voice. It's instinctive when you hear a voice on a public address system, but if you think about it, it makes no sense. What do we expect to see? God floating over our heads? Then again, if Archie didn't listen to Monk, that was exactly what he'd be seeing.

"You are in mortal danger," Monk said. "The hit man is in the stairwell and he has a gun."

What happened next happened amazingly fast. Archie turned towards the stairwell at the same instant that the hit man stepped out. Before Archie could react, the hit man shot him twice in the chest with the same cold efficiency he'd displayed when he killed Conrad Stipe.

The hit man looked up at the monitor and brazenly showed us his face.

I recognized him from one of the sketches Disher had showed us of the customers who bought Confederation uniforms.

He smiled at us, turned, and headed for the stairwell again.

I knew there could be only one reason he would risk showing us his face. He was going to kill us and take the tapes.

"We have to go, Mr. Monk," I said. "He's coming for us."

I grabbed the keys again, ran to the revolving door, and unlocked it. But when I looked back, Monk was still at the guard's desk. He hadn't moved.

"Mr. Monk, hurry up," I said. "He'll be here any minute."

Monk shook his head. "I can't go through that door."

"You've done it before," I said.

"There were people to fill the empty spaces and the timing was precise. We don't have those people tonight. Even if I tried, I'd never get through it before he gets here."

"If you don't go through this door, you're going to die," I said. "It's just a revolving door. You can survive this. You can't survive a bullet in the head."

"Go, Natalie," Monk said. "Call the police. I'll stall him as long as I can."

"I'm not going to leave you, Mr. Monk."

Monk glanced at the screen. I couldn't see the monitors from where I was, but I could imagine what he saw. The hit man was getting ever closer, moving slowly and methodically down the stairs.

"You have a daughter who needs you, Natalie," Monk said. "I have no one."

"You have me," I said. "I need you."

"Run," he said.

I didn't want to go, but he was right. I had to.

"Please, Mr. Monk," I said, my eyes filling with tears. "Come with me."

"I can't," he said. "It's who I am. You have to go now, Natalie. He's almost here."

I pushed through the revolving door and ran across the street to my car, dialing 911 as I went.

But I couldn't get a signal.

I tried again. Still no good. I looked back at the Burgerville lobby as I got into my car.

The hit man came out of the stairwell and

walked up to Monk, who said something to him. The hit man replied.

I couldn't sit there and watch Monk get killed. I had to do something. So I started my car and peeled out of my parking space.

As I was closing in on the lobby, the hit man raised his gun and pointed it at Monk's head.

That's when I jumped the curb and plowed through the plate-glass window. Monk and the hit man dove out of my way. I smashed into the security desk, decimating it in a shower of wood and sparks.

I looked out of my driver's-side window. Monk was on the floor, dazed but alive.

"Get in!" I yelled.

Monk hesitated and stared at all the shattered glass. "You broke the window. It's in a million pieces."

"Forget about that," I said and glanced out the passenger side of my car.

The hit man was dazed but okay, too. He stood up and started looking for his gun, which must have flown out of his hand when he fell.

The gun was a few feet away from him, not far from the potted palm. He walked over to get it.

"Get in the car!" I yelled to Monk.

"Who is going to clean this up? Who is

going to put all of this back together?"

I looked back at the hit man. He bent over and picked up his gun.

"For God's sake, Mr. Monk, please get in the car," I said. "Or we're both going to die."

Monk picked up a piece of paper from the floor and used it to start sweeping up the glass.

"This will only take a minute," he said.

I looked back at the hit man. He was standing beside my car now and aiming his gun at Monk.

First Monk was going to die and then me. I couldn't watch this happen. I closed my eyes and said good-bye to my daughter. She was too young to have lost both of her parents. But she was strong. She'd make it somehow. She was a Teeger.

There was a loud bang, which I found odd, considering that the hit man had a silencer on his gun.

When I opened my eyes, Monk was still alive, brushing up the glass, and the hit man was lying across the hood of my car, staring at me with dead eyes.

Who shot him?

I looked to my right and saw Archie Applebaum standing outside of the stairwell, his gun held in both hands. The two bullet holes in Archie's shirt were bloodless and I could see the blue of the Kevlar vest that he wore underneath.

Archie lowered his gun and staggered up to my car. "Are you okay?"

"It depends," I said. "Are you going to kill us?"

He shook his head. "I'm not a murderer. I just hired one once."

"Then I'm okay," I said.

Monk looked up at Archie. "Do you know where I can find a broom and a dustpan?"

Monk finished sweeping up the glass into the dustpan I was holding just as the guys from the morgue zipped up the hit man's body bag and wheeled it away. It was perfect timing.

He smiled, satisfied with himself. "Everything is cleaned up."

"Including three murders and one desecration," Stottlemeyer said, ambling over to us with Disher at his side. They'd spent the last hour or so interviewing Archie Applebaum. "You were right, Monk."

"Of course I was," Monk said. "You should know that by now."

Stottlemeyer shrugged. "I follow the evidence where it leads me. That's just how I've got to do things. I'm not big on blind faith."

"What did Archie tell you?" I asked.

"That he's never quite given up being a cop. Since he had the building to himself at night, he liked to snoop through the desks. One night he stumbled on the report that showed Lorber was fleecing the company and the employees out of their retirement," Stottlemeyer said. "Archie knew that rich guys like Lorber never really do hard time and that he would get away with some of his fortune intact. But the little guys, the innocent victims like Archie, were going to lose everything."

"So Archie decided to make sure Lorber got what he deserved," I said.

"Archie wanted justice," Disher said, "but he broke the law to do it."

"At least his heart was in the right place," I said, then turned to Monk. "Right before I drove through the window, I saw you talking to the hit man. What were you saying?"

"I asked him what he left behind in the taxi," Monk said.

"And he told you?" Disher said.

"He was granting me my second-to-last request," Monk said.

"What was your first?" I asked.

"That he would clean up the broken glass after he killed me," Monk said.

"Naturally," Stottlemeyer said.

"So what was the incriminating item he left in the taxi?" Disher said.

"His BlackBerry," Monk said. "It slipped off his belt while he was sitting in the backseat. It had all the e-mails between him and Archie, photos of Lorber, and a diagram of the building in it. When he realized he'd forgotten it, he called it from a pay phone at the airport and Stipe answered. That's how the hit man knew who'd found his PDA. He couldn't take the chance that the cabbie or Stipe would scroll through his messages. So he told the cabbie to hold on to the PDA and then killed him when the man delivered it to him."

Disher stepped up to Monk. "You did great work here today."

"Thank you, Randy," Monk said.

"How would you like to be a consultant to the Special Desecration Unit?" Disher asked. "We could use a man like you."

"I'd be honored," Monk said.

My bashed-up Jeep was evidence at a crime scene, so Stottlemeyer arranged for a patrol car to drop me off at home and to take Monk wherever he wanted to go. We got to my place first.

I was about to get out of the car when Monk touched my arm. It surprised me.

Monk rarely, if ever, touched me.

"Did you really mean what you said tonight?" he asked.

"I'm afraid so," I said. "Every fire hydrant in the city is covered in dog pee."

"Not that," he said. "Do you really need me?"

I looked at him and I thought about his question. But I realized it wasn't something I had to think about. It was something I had to feel.

"Yes, Mr. Monk, I do."

"Not just for a paycheck?" he asked.

I shook my head. "I'm a very needy person."

"Me too," he said. "Sometimes I think it's not such a bad thing."

"I think you're right," I said.

"I always am," he said.

ABOUT THE AUTHOR

Lee Goldberg has written episodes for the USA Network television series *Monk,* as well as many other programs. He is a two-time Edgar® Award nominee and the author of the acclaimed *Diagnosis Murder* novels, based on the TV series for which he was a writer and executive producer. His previous *Monk* novels, available in paperback, are *Mr. Monk Goes to the Firehouse, Mr. Monk Goes to Hawaii, Mr. Monk and the Blue Flu,* and *Mr. Monk and the Two Assistants.*